D0604946

WHERE I LIVE

WHERE I LIVE

BRENDA RUFENER

HARPER TEEN

An Imprint of HarperCollinsPublishers

HarperTeen is an imprint of HarperCollins Publishers.

Where I Live

Copyright © 2018 by Brenda Rufener

All rights reserved. Printed in the United States of America.

ISBN 978-0-06-257109-0

18 19 20 21 22   PC/LSCH   10 9 8 7 6 5 4 3 2 1

❖

First Edition

For my perfect triangle

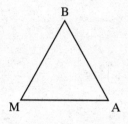

≈

*And in memory of my grandparents, who passed away
during the writing of this book*

You must be a lotus, unfolding its petals when the sun rises in the sky, unaffected by the slush where it is born or even the water which sustains it!

—Sai Baba

WHERE I LIVE

CHAPTER ONE

SOME SAY WE ARE ALL a single step away from homelessness. One bad choice. One wrong turn. One oversized setback.

I say, bullshit.

One step from taking a pregnancy test sophomore year? Possibly. Overdosing on energy drinks? Perhaps. Driving off a bluff? Conceivably. We're all footsteps from death's iced embrace. But homelessness? I'm one step ahead. Living by rules I designed will keep me there.

Rule #1: Prevent the in-class nap.

Because teachers sniff out sleepiness like a lit cigarette. And where smoke lingers, attention follows. It doesn't matter if my night's sleep is ninety minutes long, while I'm propped against the baseball dugout walls. It doesn't matter if my mattress is dirt. When in class, I dig my fingernails into the tender side of my wrist and produce enough pain to keep my eyes wide, mind sharp. If I make it indoors, away from the weather and wind, and sleep a full night, the bruises on my arm fade from indigo to violet. Wide awake, all eyes and ears. That's me. Linden Rose.

Rule #2: *Never carry too many belongings.*

Because as soon as my backpack tips and shit spills, like plastic bags of pink powdered soap and half-eaten dinner rolls, hawk eyes zoom in and accusations fly. Teachers might wonder why I lug around items in my backpack that belong in a dresser, refrigerator, or bathroom cabinet. I don't need publicity, good or bad, from anyone, not even my friends.

Rule #3: *Avoid looking the part.*

Because in theory people shouldn't figure out who I am by the way I dress, look, or smell. People know if I shower, wear the same shirt two days in a row, or drop another pound. There's so much emphasis on details. The least important thing becomes the most important topic, which means I must fight to shirk the eyes of Hinderwood High School. Eyes that scrutinize, search for clues, and analyze.

If I want my life to matter, these eyes can't see who I really am.

Who I'm striving hard not to be.

The homeless girl hiding in front of them.

I tap the door with my toe to crack it an inch, just enough to peek inside, make sure the toilet stalls are free of feet and showers are in the off position. The room is on mute, except for Coach Jenkins's occasional whistle blows penetrating the vents. I toss my backpack at the wall and beeline for the sink. I dab my finger in the water and scrape the morning gunk from my teeth, my eyes. Something I should have done when I woke, but my sunrise routine was interrupted by football practice and early-morning cleat stomps. Players like to piss before they kick and tackle and throw. The luxury.

I am on day four of week two in my second year at this school. I have slept eight hours in three days, and that ramen dunked in tap water for breakfast was a shitty decision. My stomach burns, so do my eyes, and as soon as I lean against the gritty gray cement wall, my eyelids drop and my body folds into a collapsed letter U. Five minutes of sleep is what I need, even more than a soak in a bubbly tub. But ninety seconds deep in my slumber, someone hollers outside the door and I jump.

"Coach needs three towels." I recognize the voice. Toby Patters. Barking orders. Probably pumping his muscles in some freshman's face for intimidation purposes. With the initials T.P., one can only imagine what an asswipe he is.

I scramble for the nearest stall, latch the handle, and tuck my knees to my chest with feet flat on the supposed-to-be-white-now-yellow toilet seat. A bang hits the wall and I suck in air like I'm plunging underwater, headfirst.

There's a grunt. Then a moan.

I shift to the side to see whose knuckles drag the floor but only catch a glimpse of his padded purple-and-gold jersey.

Number 22. BONNER. Definitely a freshman because I'm unfamiliar with his name. If PATTERS or CLEMMINGS were on the uniform, I might care. A little. But right now it doesn't matter who it is. What matters is my backpack, and where it sits matters more. Abandoned at the sink, unzipped, exposed. While my bag looks at home in a guys' locker room, all greasy and gray and dusty with dirt from the dugout, it's open, which means my shit's on exhibit. And by shit, I mean my threadbare underwear and bra.

Cleats scratch at the floor as Number 22 passes, punching the locker doors with his hand, elbow, forehead. I smirk at the visual, but my leg twinges because I've contorted myself into such a gargoyle crouch on the toilet. Not a full-fledged cramp, but it's headed that way. Water. A simple luxury. One I need more of in my life, my body. One I neglected when I couldn't find the water bottle I'd been using the past month. It turns out a few slurps from the fountain aren't enough to offset the fluid I lose when I sweat. At least not during warm end-of-summer days when I'm racing from security. Now's not the time to dwell on thirst, though. More important things flood my mind. Like staying out of sight.

I peek through the stall door crack and fight for balance while knuckling at my thigh muscle, smoothing out the cramp. Number 22 lingers at the bench, fumbling folded towels with his gloved hand. He yells, "How many towels?" and I jump. No one else is in the room, dude. But he looks like he's waiting, pausing for a response. So of course I take it upon myself

4

to communicate with him telepathically. *Three. Three towels, Boner. I mean Bonner.*

Number 22 mumbles, "Did he say two? No. No. Three." I'm surprised he can count that high, but more excited he will now scoot from my bathroom after finding what he came for.

His cleats scuff the cement. Then stop. I jiggle my leg and hold my breath, struggling for balance.

"What? The? Fuck?" he says.

I roll my eyes and stoop forward, confirming what I already know he found.

My bag.

None of these small-town football players are as clueless as I expect them to be. None as thickheaded as they act in groups.

I squint through the crack and watch Number 22 dig his hand deep into my bra, loop the strap around his wrist, swing it toward his flared nostrils, and sniff. *Ew.* He clomps toward the exit, shouting, "Who scored a piece of ass last night, and who forgot to share the wealth?"

Okay, forget that last statement regarding singular intelligence. Yeah, I retract it.

I drop my head back, stare at the ceiling, and fight against my next move. While I hold my breath, the cramp in my thigh stabs and jabs. My palms start to slide from sweat, and when I grapple at the toilet seat, my foot slips off, too soon. My leg reflexes forward and snaps against the stall door with a thud.

"Who's there?" Number 22 whisper-yells.

I hold my breath.

"I said who's there?"

I refuse to answer. That's not *me*. That's not Linden flying beneath the radar, hiding in plain sight. But when you own only two damn bras, and your favorite, least worn out one is wound around the fist of Edward Sausagehands, a decision must be made in the moment. No matter the cost.

I sigh extra loud, then flip the latch up like I'm flicking a tick off my arm and side-kick the door in true ninja form. It slams against the next stall and shakes the wall.

"Hey!" I shout with arm extended, fingers wiggling in the gimme position. "Hand it over. The bra. It belongs to me."

"Uh . . . you . . . uh . . . guys' . . . uh . . . locker room . . ."

I want to snap his dropped jaw back into place, but instead I snatch my bra from his wrist and fling it over my shoulder. Sure, I could stay and answer questions. I could even tell him the truth. Why I stash my belongings in the boys' locker room instead of the girls'. But what fun is that? Besides, it's all risk with little reward, other than selfish satisfaction. What would he do with the information, anyway? Share it? He's already planning who to tell. It's in his eyes, all blink, no bite. Maybe he won't go through with it. One can only hope. It's been a week filled with near misses and mess-ups. One more round of questioning in the principal's office could set off alarms I don't need.

I whip around and wiggle the cramp from my leg as I walk

toward my bag. I listen for the cleats to twist and grind. He'll leave once the shock wears off.

After five exaggerated seconds, the door bangs and Number 22 stomps out, shouting, "Coach? Co-oach?" Each vowel lifting higher in pitch.

I shove my bra into my bag and race for the door. I figure I have ten seconds before Coach arrives with the principal in tow. I glance both ways before darting across the hall. The last thing I need is Coach Jenkins catching me in the guys' locker room. He wouldn't listen, and as a result wouldn't understand. It's just easier, you know, using the guys' locker room. Boys take less time in the bathroom than girls. They zip in, zip out. Lines to the girls' restrooms are always longer than lines to the guys'. Shit's fact.

I slip into the main corridor and hear more voices than usual for this time of day. Near the front doors a group of students forms, pushing and shoving their way to the steps. When I head-check to make sure Coach Jenkins and Number 22 are nowhere near, two hands clamp down on my shoulders and squeeze. I whip around, fists clenched, and sink my elbow deep into flesh.

"Jesus, Linden." Ham coughs for effect.

"Jesus, Ham. You scared me."

"Excitable, are we?" Ham smiles and massages my neck.

I shake my shoulders and his question aside. "What's with the early release?" I motion toward the crowd, gathered fifteen minutes ahead of time.

"As usual, someone pranked Mr. Dique."

"And he kicked everyone out of class?"

"Dude went on a rampage," Ham says. "At least that's what I heard. Said he wasn't taking another year of our shit. Can you blame the poor bastard?"

Poor Mr. Dique. I mean his name is Dique, pronounced Dick, not something French or Spanish or anything extraordinary. Just plain old American-sounding Dick. And: he teaches high school biology.

"Watch it!" Ham shouts at a curly-haired guy shoving his way to the door.

The guy flips around, glares, and points at Ham. "You watch it, Pudge!"

Ham and I scrunch our noses, drop our jaws, and say, "Pudge?" in unison. Then we burst into laughter as best friends do. Ham loops his arm around mine and we walk out the front doors toward the steps to smell something other than inequality and BO.

"So what was this prank against Mr. Dique?" I ask.

"A drone," Ham says. "Remote-control operated, of course. Buzzed into class covered in condoms."

I shrug and smile. "Yeah. The usual."

"I'm sure Mr. George will want us to investigate," Ham says, emphasizing *investigate* with air quotes. "See if we can finally solve the mystery."

The buzzer blasts and students mash back to the front of the school. We slide to the side and linger behind the crowd.

8

We both know dealing with Mr. Dique is anything but exciting. Besides, breathing fresh mountain air in my best friend's presence nearly wipes away the locker-room scare. I'm almost relaxed.

We stroll behind the crowd, shuffling our feet, and pass a couple of students dressed like cowboys and a guy who looks like he could use time in the sun, or quite possibly an hour on an IV. Cowboy dudes are authentic, even smell like hay when they stroll by wearing wide-brimmed hats and silver-tipped boots. Cliques in this one-horse central Oregon town don't go beyond haves and have-nots. Cowboy dudes have each other. I have Ham.

I hold the door for my best friend and bow as he walks under the arched entryway sketched with wooden letters that read:

Hinderwood High—Where We Are Judged by Our Acts & Our Hearts

"Let's stop by the newsroom," Ham says. "I'll grab the camera."

"And take a picture of what, exactly? We're school journalists, Ham, not paparazzi. Besides, if Mr. Dique is mad, snapping photos during class will only aggravate him more."

Ham rolls his eyes and begins to protest. He's interrupted when we turn the corner near the administrative offices. Principal Falsetto's voice squawks, ear-ringing and mousy

9

high. Her soprano-pitched tone rubber-stamps the nickname given to her by students years before my arrival at Hinderwood High. Principal Falls, her actual name, just doesn't feel right to anyone anymore. Falsetto's calling shots into the air and her cell phone. I crane my neck to see who is on the receiving end of her yells, but all I see is the back of someone short-haired, seated in a padded purple chair. I keep glancing back until I catch a profile shot of the girl mopping her face with her shirtsleeve. As expected, Bea.

Ham shouts, "Hey! It's Bea!" I whack him on the back. *Thank you, Captain Obvious.*

Bea whips her head in our direction and shoots me with eye darts. The kind designed to shut organs down, starting with the heart. She blows them into every weak point of my body as I stare into her mesmerizing eyes, painted with pain and a topcoat of judgment.

I jerk my head in the opposite direction. Breaking Bea's spell and showing I couldn't care less if she's crying, hurting. I'm showing her I don't give a damn. At least that's what I try to convince myself of. But pain and misery boomerang, and when you dish out hurt, it whips around and slaps you in the face. I tell myself that Bea is immune to victimization because of the form-fitted jacket of judgment she wears. It makes dealing with her much easier. It lifts the burden from my back, at least for a brief moment.

"Hey. Hey. Hey. What are you kids doing out of class?"

Fuck, Coach Jenkins. I mean, Fuck Coach Jenkins.

"Should you be in class?" Coach Jenkins asks, his whistle aimed and ready, finger already cocked.

"Of course we should," Ham mumbles beneath his breath.

We scoot sideways toward the newsroom, and I crane my head back toward Bea for one last look. Despite what I tell myself, I care. How can I not? Her pain hits close to home. Too close. I watch as Principal Falsetto circles Bea like a mother hen, arms flapping and tail in full flutter. Bea rolls a tissue into a ball and stuffs it into one nostril.

"Bea was crying," Ham says an inch from my ear. "Did you see her? Did you see that? And did you see her new haircut? Not many girls pull off hair that short. I would venture to say Bea is the only—"

I cut Ham off with a snappy, "So."

"So?" Ham scrunches his face. "Her nose was bleeding," he says. "Did you catch that, Linden? Her lip, too."

I shake my head. "No. Ham. I didn't see shit."

It's been a while since I had to face someone else's blood, let alone care about it. Memories jab and poke like that leg cramp in the locker room every time I think about Bea, or her beat-up face. But tears won't get rid of the pain this time. All the waves in the ocean wouldn't wash those thoughts away.

"Well, I saw shit," Ham says, "and I might finally ask her about it. I mean, somebody should do something. Don't you think?"

I answer Ham in my head: *Yes.* And as I'm ready to quiz Ham on how Bea will respond when he asks her why she stands still while a guy pounds the gristle out of her, Coach Jenkins toots his whistle long and hard and shouts, "Onward! Onward! Get to class, idlers!"

"I really do detest that man," Ham says, loud enough for Coach to hear.

CHAPTER TWO

WHEN WE REACH THE NEWSROOM, Mr. George is absent. His briefcase is gone, his slippers are missing from beneath his desk, and the computer screen is black. Ham rummages through a closet for the camera, and I check the storyboard for messages. The cork is blank, except for two neon-orange Post-it notes scribbled with Mr. George's handwriting, instructing us to interview Mr. Dique because he's pissed after being pranked. Mr. George's words, not mine.

"You were right!" I shout at Ham.

"As always!" Ham shouts back. "About what?"

"Mr. George wants us to interview the Dique."

"Already on it, boss." Ham loops the camera strap around his neck.

I read Mr. George's note aloud. "'See Mr. Dique ASAP.

Drone covered in condoms buzzed into his classroom. No controller found. Driver is MIA. As always, he's pissed. Tread lightly—appease Old Man Dique.'"

Ham smiles. "The condoms really are an appropriate touch."

We walk the hall, which will fill in ten minutes. Long enough to interview Mr. Dique and for Ham to snap photos for the news blog. Then, if all goes as planned, we can kill time by hanging with Mr. George and learning journalism's best, or worst, practices. I half expect Mr. Dique to cooperate. I mean it's only the second week of school and he hasn't hit burnout status. He also reconciled with his wife over the summer, and they didn't lose their house despite the mountain of bills he's always complaining about in class. Let's just say Mr. Dique's mood should be as elevated as his . . . ahem . . . drone.

I stomp down on a piece of paper and slide it underfoot toward the trash can. No one picks up around here. No one throws trash into the can, where it belongs. No one cares what this place looks like, except me. Of course, no one calls school their home, either.

Ham lags behind, his tail wagging, tongue flapping, smile wrapping his face like holiday paper. He dawdles at a window and sneak peeks through the glass. When he reaches the limit his five-foot frame allows, he pushes onto his tiptoes.

"No time for peeping," I whisper-yell, tapping the nonexistent watch on my wrist.

Ham grins and fast walks the hall. When he reaches me,

he says, "Have you noticed everyone looks different this year? More, I don't know, grown up."

"Nope." I crimp my bangs between my fingers and stretch them over my eyebrows. That trim I gave myself a few weeks ago is finally taking shape. "Haven't noticed."

"Come on, Linden. Don't even tell me you haven't eye-balled Reed Clemmings, or his new ride." Ham smiles out of the side of his mouth he doesn't normally smile out of. "You can't ignore his sudden disregard for the jock jacket and affection for man scarves on shearling. And the man bun and beard? Nice touch."

I roll my eyes. "Jock jacket?"

"Letterman jacket, Linden. If they still call them that. Do they call them that?" Ham's arms wave like crab's legs. He's a hand talker, in the best way.

"You don't look different this year, Ham. Your dimples are still dimpling and your smile remains contagious. You might be a bit more squeezable than last year, but to me that's a good thing." I prop Ham's knit hat into a cone, and he whips it off and throws it at me. His hair shoots in all directions and changes the shape of his face. Less round, more texture. Let's face it: Ham's adorable.

"I don't know what you see in that guy," Ham says, slicing the air with his hand. "You can't change an asshole, with or without a trip to the city for a wardrobe upgrade."

I stop walking, grab Ham's shoulders, and look him straight in the eyes. "Listen when I say I see nothing in Reed

Clemmings, and believe me when I tell you he is incapable of seeing anything in me." I whip around and head down the hall, shouting, "What about his ex, though? You're the one suffering from the *Bea* sting. Better watch out for her boyfriend, Ham. Toby Patters has always had a problem with you. With everyone. Besides, Bea's much more an asshole than Reed."

I turn back around and watch Ham's face drop. "Bea can't be an asshole, Linden. She's a girl."

"Girls are assholes, too!" I shout. "Equal rights!"

Ham squishes his lips together and winks. "Point noted, Linden, as you are clearly the most adorable asshole I know."

I laugh, shaking my head, and sprint down the hall until I reach Mr. Dique's door. I wait for Ham to catch up. There's that fast walk again.

Ham. Maple sweet with a smoke flavor all his own.

Not his real name, though. I mean, who names their kid Ham, right? But it's the only name I've ever called him. A name that rose to fame after Reed Clemmings, and his buddy Toby Patters (a.k.a. T.P., a.a.k.a. Asswipe), pushed him off the monkey bars. The fall busted Ham's tailbone. Only in second grade the tailbone's called the butt bone. Any second grader knows that. And in second grade, Ham wore forty pounds of baby fat around his waist like an inner tube. Weight that dripped and spilled down his butt like two scoops of ice cream in mid-July. When Ham's seven-year-old ass hit the pavement, in theory, it should have bounced. Any theorist knows that. But theories aren't always as rational as they claim to be. Ham dropped like a bowling ball hitting turf. He squealed, classmates circled, and the teacher rushed in to help. "Franklin," the teacher said. "Are you okay?"

As Ham tells it, he answered his teacher like a *real* second-grade man. "Hell no, I'm not okay. My *ham* hurts." The class laughed, Ham's chest puffed, the teacher's cheeks pinked, and the name stuck through elementary and middle school, along with a grudge toward Reed and Toby. Ham's name made its way into the halls of Hinderwood High and became his pride and joy. It will be on his college application, résumé, and marriage license.

"Damn, Linden. What's the hurry?"

I slap his back. Hurriedness is as much a part of me as my friends. The rush, head checks, constant motion ensure I won't get caught. If I pause even for a moment to catch my breath, my secret's out—my charade over.

"Just protecting us from the assholes in this school."

Ham smiles. "Thanks, Mama."

I wince and tap my finger on Ham's chest. "Don't call me *mama*. Ever."

Ham shoos my hand away and points at the door. "The usual?"

I nod, thinking about Ham's word choice, remembering Bea and her beat-up face, nostril stuffed with tissue. The boomerang of hurt barrels my way. My eyes sting and I blink five million times to fan away any moisture. "Yeah, Ham," I whisper, drawing a deep breath. "The usual."

Mr. Dique catches us waiting at the door and waves. My prediction is correct. Mood up, interview on. One must avoid Mr. Dique when he's in a bad mood. Students with him last year during the breakup of his marriage paid the price with pop quizzes three days per week. Mr. Dique holds up a palm, signaling we remain in the back of the class, near the door.

"Hey, buddy!" Ham shouts with little regard for the quiet classroom.

Seung, sitting at the back table, quick-nods at Ham. I smile and Seung smiles back. My face warms—well, maybe just my cheeks. I lock my grin into place while Mr. Dique continues his one-sided discussion of meiosis. Seung teeters back in his chair, closes his eyes, and pretends to fall asleep. He snores and I giggle.

Papers rustle and a chair squeaks. Seung opens his eyes, smirks at me again, then drifts into pretend slumber. Mr. Dique is now speaking at the whiteboard, his back to the class. Toby stumbles out of his back-row seat, zigzags forward, and kicks the leg on Seung's chair. Before Mr. Dique can turn around and shoot questions, Seung's on his back, cradling his desk chair in his arms, and Toby's groaning about having to piss.

"Seung Rhee?" Mr. Dique asks. "What happened?"

Ham rushes the door, shouting, "T.P., you shitwipe—" but I grab his shoulder and shake my head.

"Seung can handle it," I whisper, not wanting Ham to

worsen the situation by drawing unwanted attention in any of our directions.

Seung untwists his limbs from his chair, slowly climbing to his feet. "Guess I slipped." Seung glances back at me and winks.

"I hate that guy," Ham mumbles, and shudders. "And hate's not a familiar emotion to me."

A throat clears behind us.

It's Bea, back from the office, waiting for best friend Beth and boyfriend Toby. He's had it in for Seung since Bea realized Seung's cute and charming and always there for his friends. Bea's had it in for me since I stumbled upon her secret.

Bea's famous at Hinderwood High. Famous for stirring up mixed feelings I don't want to feel. I lean in to Ham, ready to engage in make-believe conversation, but he's too busy smiling at Bea and mouthing, "Did you come to help?" and "Are you okay?" to notice. The buzzer rings and the class scrambles for the door.

I rush for the front of the room, passing Seung, who's now limping. "You okay?"

He shrugs. I know not to push. I don't want to embarrass him even more.

"Meet us at lunch," I say, grabbing his elbow.

Seung smiles. "Usual place?"

I glance back at Ham, then at Seung. We nod, in unison. Our equilateral triangle, Me-Ham-Seung, always in agreement.

Seung shoots a thumbs-up (*normal response*) and squeezes

a second wink (*abnormal response*). And just when I'm about to ask Ham if Seung started lifting weights, Bea shoves in front of me and says, "Tell Mr. George I won't be working in the newsroom today. Something came up."

Ham slides in front of me. "We saw you with Principal Falsetto. Are you okay?"

Bea narrows her eyes and snaps, "Why wouldn't I be?" She tosses something sticky and it hits my hair, then plops onto my foot.

I stare straight ahead and pretend the trash isn't meant for me. Bea doesn't have to say it, but of course she does, because she never shuts her mouth, even after an asshole slapped it. "Trash for Trash," she hisses with her eyes as much as her lips.

I fixate on the bubble smoldering on her lip while she aims spit at my shoe. As gorgeous as this girl is, every time she spits at me, her beauty chokes, shrivels, dies.

"Kids. Over here." Saved by Mr. Dique, waving his pointer in the air and signaling us to the front of the room like he's directing air traffic. "I suppose you want to discuss the drone?" he says when we reach the front of the room.

I refuse to glance back at Bea, but I feel her acid eyes sizzle my skin. More poison-dipped darts. I slide the pen from my ear, then proceed with a professional salutation reserved exclusively for Mr. Dique.

"Hey, Mr. D." Because I can't bring myself to speak his last name in his presence. "Sir, can you tell us what happened from the beginning?"

I scratch down Mr. Dique's recollection of events on paper. My notes splatter with complaints, few facts. Ham, always trigger-happy, snaps photos from all angles of the drone dripping with condoms—they dangle from the tail and landing skids. Ham flicks the tip of a rubber with his finger and I cringe. Mr. Dique doesn't seem to mind Ham taking photos; in fact, he looks pleased, so I don't stop him.

Mr. Dique rants more about the interruption than about what he actually saw. I detail *important* stuff. A buzz. A laugh. More buzzing. More laughing. Mr. Dique comes nose to face with the drone as it hovers into class, condoms swinging. It lands on a desk and Mr. Dique, as usual, charges the door, shouting, "I've got you! You're mine!"—only to find an empty hallway.

Same stuff, new month. If I pull up last year's blog, I could almost plagiarize this. Mr. Dique continues animating his tirade and I start checking to-do boxes in my head.

This morning was strategy hell.

I stashed my sleeping bag in the vacant music room behind the in-need-of-repair kettledrums. In walked a band kid with raised eyebrows and a grimacing side eye. I pointed and yelled, "You're late for practice and the teacher's downright pissed!" because I've learned to move fast on my feet. It worked. The guy tore into his trumpet case and flew through the gym toward the football field. I heard his warm-up routine go from allegro to presto on my way to the theater, where I stuffed my toiletries in a garbage bag in the back of the room. As I left, Drama Jarrell, who happens to be cool because he plays football, volunteers in the newsroom, and has balls enough to be in drama at this rural school where football reigns, walked in. I acted like I had business being in the theater room, but I don't think my explanation was necessary. Drama Jarrell said, "Hey," and because his pecs practically pushed the words **THERE WILL BE DRAMA** from his T-shirt into my face, I said, "Hey," back, and smiled. He asked something about Ham, but I was already out the door and marching to my locker to stuff it with a spare set of clothes.

With football practice in full swing, I juggle dressers and bathrooms to avoid locker-room traffic during the morning hours. Later in the year, I'll relocate my belongings to the library because stage equipment will be in use in the theater. With thousands of hours of practice living in my high school, I should be an expert by now, but hiding stuff never gets easy and always grows old. I anticipate the moves of everyone around me. Shit impacts my sleep.

We thank Mr. Dique for his time and assure him we will work hard to find who is behind the prank, although I don't believe a word we promise. Pranking Mr. Dique is legendary. It always happens twice a year, near the beginning and at the end. Freshman year, balloons in the shape of wiener dogs decorated a helicopter. Then a phallic hot dog rode into class atop a remote-control car. Mode of transportation varies between cars and helicopters and drones. The most theatrical hit was last year's pink animatronic dildo. Thankfully, I never saw it in person. I was crashing at Seung's, sick with a cold. His mother doting over me, like my own used to do. Though I missed the actual event, Ham later supplied me with eighty-five pictures, because he's thorough at his job.

My gut tells me the mystery pilot is one of Mr. Dique's colleagues trying to loosen up his tightly wound demeanor, but he refuses to believe that anyone other than a student is behind the prank.

On the way back to the newsroom, Ham and I reroute through the math corridor, just in case Coach Jenkins is still making rounds and whistle-blows and ordering every student, with or without a valid excuse, to class. We pass Mr. Ryckman, the janitor, unjamming his mop from a metal bucket. His lips dance, but his mouth makes no sound. We're hit with a horrific smell of lemon-zest-meets-beer.

"What the hell happened here?" Ham asks.

The janitor whips his head around and glares. "Somebody yacked, smart-ass."

Ham grumbles various names reserved exclusively for male anatomy as Mr. Ryckman shakes his mop handle at us. "Out!" he shouts.

And only because the guy creeps me out do I hike my shirt over my nose, grab Ham's arm, and pull him down the hall.

Outside the newsroom, Toby, Reed, and Coach Jenkins pow-wow. Ham tenses, so I slip my arm around his shoulder and squeeze. Coach Jenkins stands between the guys, hands pressed flat against their chests like he's pushing them apart.

T.P. grapples for a shirtsleeve but ends up tangling his hand up in Coach's whistle. Coach's neck jerks forward and he yells, "That's enough, you two!"

It's obvious the only sober one is pretzled in the arms of his two best players, getting choked out. "T.P. must have been drunk in class," I say. "When he kicked Seung's chair."

Ham scoffs. "Don't make excuses for him. He's been messing with Seung and me for a decade."

Coach Jenkins unwinds the noose from his neck, and one of Toby's brick feet steps on the other. He buckles and drops to his knees, sending Ham and me into a fit of laughter.

Coach whips his head around and shouts, "Scram! No business of yours."

Toby glares with eyes glazed and blurt-belches a deep and thought-provoking "Fuck you."

He points. So naturally, Ham and I point back.

"Did you hear me?" Coach Jenkins shouts. "Scram!"

Ham raises his fists and yells, "I really do detest all of you people!"

CHAPTER THREE

THREE FIFTEEN ON A WEEKDAY and I have a choice to make. Go to work or go to work.

Which job I choose matters most. I have three, but only two pay. My nonpaying job lets me stay unnoticed in the newsroom until 5:30, sometimes 5:45, or until Mr. George chases me out. One of my paying gigs, the one I'd quit if food and tampons didn't cost money, places me at Bea's house every other Saturday. I scrub Bea's toilet, dust her mom's collection of glass owls, and tidy up the basement. While my job is to clean Bea's home in four hours, I race to finish in three so I'm out the door before Bea and her boyfriend arrive. I can handle picking up after Bea, especially since I don't have to clean her room (mom's orders), but I can't stomach hearing Bea fight with her boyfriend.

My regular job, which only pays sometimes, sends me over the hill to read with the residents of Nowhere Near Like Home nursing facility. I renamed the place because Just Like Home was a lie and I don't like it when people lie to the elderly.

Employment choice is contingent on fatigue. The walk to the nursing home only works if I've slept the night before. Today I'm tired and my muscles ache.

Nowhere Near Like Home is a sweet gig on nights I'm not hanging with Seung and Ham, or when I need a couple of bucks for peanut butter crackers or peanut butter cups or peanut butter cookies from the school's vending machine. Peanut butter's packed with protein, and protein packs my stomach for more than eight hours.

The nursing home splits into two wings that house residents with faculties on one side and those without on the other. I used to spend a lot of time in the dementia units, but there's no reason to now.

I've grown to love my rounds at Nowhere Near Like Home. The old lady who only wants me to read the newspaper— obituary section—with highlighter in hand, those who want to know what the Kardashians are up to these days, and the few who drop a Bible on my lap. It's bizarre how every room in the nursing home houses a Bible, yet few can read the fine print. I'd much rather stick to the newspaper or grab the dinner menu from the nurse's desk, because the Bible instigates arguments. In order to keep the peace, I read stuff the old folks *really* want to hear. Call it hope. Call it prayer. Call it

26

reader protection. I try to tell my elders things that push smiles onto their shriveled faces. Things like their childhood dog is waiting for them with tail swinging. Just take a left at the gate of pearls. I tell them their loved ones who refuse to visit are on God's shit list. The smirks on the old women's faces are worth more than their quarters.

On a good night I leave Nowhere Near Like Home with a few extra bucks in my pocket. Old people tip well, and I've got that face, you know, the one any great-great-grandparent with smudged trifocals would love.

I vacate the school grounds near sundown when the janitor checks every room for warm bodies before locking doors. In the winter, when daylight shrinks or the weather's too frigid to walk to the nursing home, I juggle between Seung's house and Ham's. When I beat out Bea and a book-smart girl named Kristen for the lead reporter position of our school's blog, I gained widespread access to Mr. George's newsroom. I needed the nonpaying job more than they did. Kristen wanted it for her college transcript. Bea just wanted it to mess with me.

Even though I beat Bea and Kristen for the head job, they accepted secondary roles. I'm technically Bea's boss, but she never forgets she's the true queen. The reporter gig makes me marketable to the college I'm planning to attend with Ham and Seung. It's basically my ticket to a better life. If it weren't for the promise I made my mother, I'd have turned down the editor job for the sake of damage control. Bea makes my life miserable. But I can't break a promise. Especially one made to my mother. Besides, building a college résumé helps fill time slots and calendar holes. Let's face it, when you're homeless, free time sucks.

"Want to come over for dinner?" A finger pokes my side and I jump.

"Seung. Are you inside my head?" One. Two. Three seconds of silence. Awkward. Then, "Of course I want to come over for dinner. I mean, if it's okay with your parents."

I link my arm around Seung's and watch his cheeks go pink. So much for the wink of courage in Mr. Dique's room earlier today.

"What are we having?" I ask. "Asian or American?"

Seung hikes his backpack higher on his shoulders and clears his throat. "What day is it?"

"Tuesday, I think. Why?"

"On days starting with *T* we eat American food. All other nights, Korean."

"Why am I only hearing about this now, Seung?" I lift my hands, shake my fists. "You know how much I like schedules. You know how much I love your mom's food."

Seung half smiles and looks at his feet. "It's been that way my whole life, Linden."

"Tuesdays and Thursdays, American," I say tapping my temple. "I'll remember that now. And, for the record, I haven't known you your whole life. This is only our second year together."

Ham's right. Some people are changing this year. For the better. And it's impossible not to notice. If Seung weren't my second-best friend, I'd . . . No, I wouldn't. Seung is the guy I'd die for, not date. Just like my Ham.

"Two years of high school is the pinnacle of my life," Seung says all dramatic-like, and I wonder if he means because that's how long he's truly been alive, you know, since I came into the picture.

"Should we invite Ham?"

"Well . . . I was thinking . . . maybe just . . . " Seung leans in near my ear and the tickle makes my stomach flip, then flop, in the most superb way.

On cue, Ham turns the corner. "Guys!"

"Guy and girl," Seung says. I look at Seung. He doesn't look back. He referred to me as a girl? He referred to me as a girl. First the winks, now this.

"Correction." Ham points his finger at Seung and says, "Guy," then at me, "and asshole. What are we doing tonight?"

"Dinner at Seung's after I finish posting about Mr. Dique's drone." I can't wait to spend some time in the newsroom alone with the guys.

"I'll call my parents and meet you in the newsroom." Ham spins around and slow-jogs out the door.

The greatest thing about having best friends who are guys is that they never ask to hang at your house or demand a Saturday-night sleepover. When it comes right down to it, they are still members of the opposite sex, and when you live

29

at home, like Ham and Seung do, rules govern visitations. Sure, they ask to come over to my house, but they never press the issue when I refuse. With a secret like mine, the best thing to do is insert partial truths into the umbrella of lies. It helps when remembering details.

Seung knows how much I love his perfect parental units, so he doesn't push to meet mine. Plus, he has the basement we all adore. His parents always knock, rarely barge in. Ham, on the other hand, is highly persistent in a tolerable way. He invites himself to my *house* all the time. Says it's only proper to become acquainted with his best friend's *living space*. Claims he wants to see where I rest my head at night. He knows more than he thinks he does.

When Ham's father drops him off for school, he opens my front door and wipes his feet on my welcome mat. He walks the main corridor (my foyer) and turns the corner toward the lockers (my coat closet). After PE, Ham showers in the locker room (my master bath) and heads toward the cafeteria (my kitchen). As far as seeing where I sleep, well, it changes. There are nights when I huddle in a ball covered by theater curtains, other nights when I doze off in the library while studying. On unfortunate nights when I get locked out of my own *house*, I spend a cold five hours curled up in the baseball dugout, using plywood for a mattress and my arms as blankets. Those nights are shit.

With Seung and Ham, I won't censor myself. I don't have to. I leave out minor details and insert partial truths. When

Ham first asked about my family, I told him my mother was dead and that my truck-driver stepfather was on the road seven days a week. Partial truths. The only time I flat-out lie is when they interrogate me about my home. If I steer the conversation, I minimize the lies. I hate misleading my friends. In the short time I've known them, they've become family to me. They're all I have.

After thirty minutes in the newsroom, Seung asks, "Are you done yet?"

I tap the keyboard trying to get a response. Pictures of the drone upload onto the school computer.

I glance at the clock. "Five minutes. I promise." If I don't hurry, I'll spend the night in the dugout. Even though the weather is still warm, plywood makes a hard and horrible bed. I must get to my locker or get locked out. I'm always planning my next move or second-guessing my last one. My mind never rests.

Seung drops his head back against his chair and stares at the ceiling. I ignore his moan, even though it's adorable.

I proof the text one more time and hit publish, then spin around in my chair as Kristen walks in the door.

"Why are you still working?" Kristen asks, her breath huffing and puffing like she hurried to get here.

"Because I work here," I say.

"Not for much longer."

Seung whirls around in his chair. "What's that supposed to mean?" he asks, annoyance scribbled all over his face.

"Nothing." Kristen purses her lips together, and the sides of her mouth pucker.

Seung exhales irritation.

"Spill it," I say, pointing at Kristen. "You're about to combust."

Kristen picks a piece of fuzz from her sweater and sighs. But with minimal prodding, she overshares at a high rate of speed. "Principal Falls, I mean Falsetto, was talking about Linden with her sister."

"So?" Seung and I snap at the same time. We look at each other, then turn our heads and smile at our feet.

"You think it's funny?" Kristen says. She spins in a circle, one hand on her hip, the other pledging allegiance to an invisible flag. "Why are you smiling? You think *I'm* funny?"

"Settle down," Seung says. "We think you're great. You're Kristen the Great. Wisest of the wise. Royalest of royals."

Seung's slight sarcasm, misinterpreted by Kristen, relaxes her shoulders and stance. Her hand falls from her hip.

"I'm just saying, they were talking about you, Linden. Her sister is a reporter or journalist or something. She works at station K-O-something, something. She was asking questions. About you."

"What kind of questions?"

"For one, your name," she says. "For another, your address."

I nibble my lip. I don't like people asking questions. They might get answers.

"Probably acknowledging what a great job Linden does on

Hinderwood High's blog," Seung says. "Falsetto raves about you all the time, Linden. Probably bragging to her sister about that big piece you did last year." Seung leans forward and teeters on his elbow. His voice is breathy, his words slow. "That really was a sexy read on tardiness."

I wave away Seung's whispers, even though they summon swarms of butterflies, deep in my gut. "Yeah, maybe." I make a mental note to ask Mr. George what he knows about Falsetto's journalist sister. "What'd she look like, anyway?" If I see her, I'll talk to her myself.

"Blond. Bountiful highlights. Bouncy hair. A whole lot of lipstick."

I wonder what I'd say if I saw her. I hope Seung's right, because there is only one reason anyone ever asks for my address. They want to know where I live. "Maybe I'll Google the letters to the news station tonight. Check out her street cred, or something."

Seung stares. "Thought you didn't have internet?"

I gulp. "I don't. Didn't say I'd look at home. Did I?"

Ham bursts into the newsroom from his third bathroom break, holding his nose and giggling at something Drama Jarrell is whispering over his shoulder. He pats Jarrell's chest, and Jarrell catches Ham's hand and holds it for a second.

I glance at Seung to see if he's witnessing this peculiar yet lovable exchange, but his eyes are fixed on his phone.

"Do not go down the senior hall," Ham says, tugging his hand from Jarrell's shirt and stuffing it deep into his pocket.

"Get another ass kicking?" Seung asks without looking up from his phone.

Ham rolls his eyes and flatly says, "No, Seung. My ass is perfection." He turns to the side and squeezes a handful, skillfully showing us that his butt remains intact.

Jarrell coughs and Seung says, "C'mon," in full groan. "Nobody's interested in your ass."

"Agree to disagree." Ham grins. "And since nobody asked, Toby Patters and Reed Clemmings are fighting in front of the row C lockers. It's causing quite a scene."

"Again?" I ask.

"Who cares?" Seung flicks a chunk of paper off his desk chair and looks annoyed.

"I care," Ham says. "Especially when Bea is in the middle. I don't want her to get hurt again. Right, Linden?"

I scoff and drop my arms on Seung's desk. He jerks back against his seat. "Relax," I say.

Seung stares at my hands folded on his desk.

"I don't get why Bea dumped Reed for that buffoon we affectionately call Asswipe," Ham says.

Seung groans, then sighs. My signal to proceed without caution.

"Bea doesn't discriminate when it comes to guys," I snap. "Why else do you think she dumped Reed for his best friend, Asswipe? She refuses to cut the leash. Maybe she enjoys them both barking at her heels. But remind me again why we waste precious minutes of our lives discussing Bea?"

"Bea doesn't know what's good for her," Seung says.

Now it's my turn to stare. Ham perks up, too.

"I suppose Seung Rhee knows what's good for her," Ham says.

I watch Seung's face for sudden movement. A twitch. A smirk. Nothing. He's stoic.

"While I rarely entertain drama," Kristen says, sliding a pencil behind her ear and gazing at the ceiling, "I can't help but remember that time in class when Bea and Beth referred to Seung as *One of Two.*"

"One of who?" I ask, an eye fixed on Seung.

"I was there," Jarrell says. "I heard that, too."

Kristen takes a breath. "Apparently there are two guys Bea and Beth wouldn't mind hooking up with. Although I'm not sure they meant hooking up with at the same time. I mean, it is Bea and Beth we're talking about. They do everything together." Kristen smiles as if she's proud of her comment. "I didn't catch the other guy's name, though—only Seung's. Your name stood out." Kristen smiles at Seung and tucks her hair behind her penciled ear.

"Me," Jarrell says, tapping his chest. "I'm the other guy."

Ham's face scrunches like he's tasted lemon. He clears his throat and says, "And how do you feel about that, Jarrell?" in his best TV psychiatrist voice.

Jarrell shrugs and stretches his arms above his head. A one-inch band of stomach peeks between his T-shirt and jeans. Ham's jaw hits the floor, but he quickly looks away.

I glance at Seung as his eyebrows shoot up. There's that arch I was looking for. As hard as I try, I never get used to Seung's eyebrows. All fluffy and unkempt. Seung shakes his head, trying to act unflattered, but his cheeks blush, so his false humility is impossible to buy.

"Bea said you were hot," Kristen clears her throat. "I mean, I get why she said those things." Her face flushes and she twists the toe of her shoe on the tile.

"Ohmygod," I snap.

"Whatever," Seung says, brushing his hair back, then forward. "Bea's not my type. She's Ham's type. Right?"

I wish I believed him. And from Kristen's soured face, she's wishing on the same shooting star. "More like Ham's obsession," I mumble.

"Who's Ham's obsession?" Ham asks, unwinding his arm from the headlock he twisted Jarrell into.

"Bea, something-something a threesome, something-something Seung." Seung tap-kicks my shin. "Ouch."

I smile and he looks away.

Seung's always refused to look me directly in the eye, and as a result I always snag a really good look at him. Sometimes at night, when I wake from a nightmare brought on by my reality, I imagine Seung asleep in his cozy bed. He doesn't know it, but I've memorized every feature of his face. Full cheeks, boxy jaw, single freckle on the bridge of his nose.

It isn't until we all reach the main corridor (my foyer) that I remember my locker and the door I need to position for tonight's sneak-in ritual. I never really forget, but this afternoon I'm distracted.

"Guys," I say. "I forgot something in my locker. I'll meet you at Seung's car."

I run down the hall but turn and jog backward to see if anyone is protesting. Seung kicks the door open, and Kristen passes him as they walk outside. Wind whirls and orange leaves float inside the corridor. Ham squeezes Jarrell's arms and says, "Good-bye, friend." Jarrell ruffles Ham's hair. Those two are more chummy than usual. Ham, always a love-stuffed volcano, usually oozes his attention onto Seung or me. I guess with Seung's sudden annoyances when Ham's near, it's only natural for him to direct his affection elsewhere.

"Be right back!" I shout.

Here's me, waving and grinning while running backward. When I hit my turn I sprint, then skid to a stop at my locker.

I spin the lock and it opens first try. I lift two books on Shakespeare and a copy of *Smart Girl's Guide to Money Management* that I *borrowed* from the library last night because I'd hit my checkout limit. They are tonight's reading if my flashlight batteries don't die, and if I make it back into the school in time.

I feel beneath the books and find the wedge of wood I use to jam in the fire-escape door. I slip the wood into my pocket, lock my locker, and race the back way toward the gym.

Here's me, running. Always rushing. Sliding. Stopping. Peeking. Listening.

There's silence, so I sprint again.

At the sophomore hall, I creep around the corner by the computer lab. The darkness means Mr. Ryckman finished cleanup. Mr. Ryckman's on schedule tonight even with a pile of puke to clean. The janitor complicates my life yet makes it cleaner, brighter. Ridiculous joke, I know, but the little things I think about at night help when I'm alone in the dark, and they're better than thinking about why I'm alone.

I squeeze the gym doors shut and race for the stairs behind the locker rooms. Tonight is shower night. I can already feel the sandpaper concrete massaging the cracks on the bottoms of my feet. The ones screaming for lotion that hasn't been watered down to make it stretch for another week.

Living homeless teaches me to lengthen and stretch all my possessions. Stretch my bra one more wear. Stretch my sweat-shirt over my hair. Stretch the theater curtains to cover my feet, keeping my body full of heat. Stretch the canned chili two more bites. Stretch my hope one more night. My life now a doleful poem. But I have no time to lose hope.

I jump the stairs two at a time. Turn. Listen. Crack the door and wedge the wood into the gap.

I wait.

One. Two. Three. Four seconds.

The door holds and I exhale. Big and loud.

I backtrack toward the front of the school and slip into the theater to unlatch the back door. Double protection against sleeping outside tonight. I'm nose down, tapping the cracked screen on my pay-as-you-go phone, when I round the last turn toward the main corridor. Reed Clemmings jumps in front of me and blocks my exit.

"Where do you think you're going?" he says, arms spread against the doorframe.

"Home," I snap, and stare straight into his eyes. Reed doesn't look away. Instead, he repeats my word.

"Home," he says, and I nod, breaking the spell.

"If you could please . . ." I flick my fingers and motion for him to step aside. He won't budge. He's staring, but looking through me.

My heart pounds. Cheeks heat. Not from Reed, but the race I just won. The clock I beat.

I lift my eyebrows and he answers back by raising his.

We stare at each other for a few awkward seconds, until he says, "You work in the newsroom with Bea, right? Have you seen her?" His chin drops, and when he looks up with only his eyes, they're filled with tears, or maybe they're glassy. Either way, awkward.

"Nope. I haven't."

"You sure?" He squeezes one eye shut.

"Absolutely sure."

"Well, then."

"Well, then."

Reed shifts to the side and extends his arm as if giving me permission to pass. I'd rather have permission to wipe the tear from his cheek, but that could be misconstrued as overdoing it. I mean, Reed is incredibly beautiful, especially close up, but it takes more than good looks, good hair, good body. *Shit.*

I will my hands not to move toward his face, then half smile, half nod, and head for the front doors. I feel his stares, but I'm not worried he saw me hide the wedge of wood in the door. He obviously has more on his mind than me. If he and Asswipe were fighting, Reed triumphed. He didn't look beat up. If anything, he seemed beaten down, hurt. I almost feel sorry for him.

I pause at the door and glance behind me. He's gone.

If I were Bea, and I most certainly am not, I would run from Toby and beeline back to Reed. Actually, I'd sprint toward Seung and tackle him. But let's hope Bea won't ever do that.

I push the doors and breathe in fresh mountain air, side-scoop my hair, and wait for Seung to park his car beneath the awning. He's driving extra slow due to weather conditions. A slight breeze, light drizzle. That's Seung. King of Safety.

The delay gives me thirty seconds to catch my breath. I shut my eyes right there in the doorway. All this waiting, listening, hiding. In such a short time, it's become a part of me, who I am.

Linden. Stay in the closet. Nobody hurts you when they don't know you exist.

Yes, Mama.

I snap open my eyes. The drop-drop-splat of rain taps the

tin roof. I squeeze my eyes shut again and force a fresh image, with less hurt, more victory. I muster up a picture of Seung pulling up in a decade-old limo, picking me up for a dance. He reaches for the door, but I bump him out of the way and open it myself. He tells me I look beautiful, and of course, I agree. My hair's blown out and my lips are lined in pink. My body's wrapped in a snug-fit dress and I'm moving, comfortably, like water, not struggling to breathe.

These thoughts nourish me, push me forward on shitty days. Hope stops my arms from tossing in the towel and giving up. Hope keeps the smile on my face even after a cold night's sleep. Hope refuses to let me surrender.

"Hey, asshole. What'd you forget?" Ham's affectionate greeting jolts me back where I belong. Right here, in reality.

CHAPTER FOUR

"I AM LOVING THIS MEAT, Mrs. Rhee," Ham says at dinner. "Will you pass me the potatoes?"

Seung slides a bowl of mashed potatoes to Ham and waves away the plate of roast his mother pushes at him. "I'm vegetarian, Mom. Remember?"

Seung's mom smiles and says, "Please. Please. Eat all you want, kids."

Mrs. Rhee is as warm as melted butter and not in a margarine sort of way. Her kindness is genuine. Nothing fake. Not even her blond hair or sunshine-kissed skin. She looks like I imagine a southern belle should look, minus the accent and the fact that she's from somewhere deep in the south of California. Huntington Beach, I think.

Mr. Rhee stands and excuses himself to the kitchen. On

his way he says, "More tea, hon?" Mrs. Rhee smiles and nods and holds her cup in the air. When she twists around in her chair, her hair falls in her face and Mr. Rhee sweeps it back over her shoulder. He grabs the cup from her hand and mouths a kiss. Mr. Rhee has mad doting skills. I soak up so much when I observe their relationship. It's the kind I want in my own life.

Whenever I talk to Seung about his parents, he groans or rolls his eyes. "Why do you care how my mom and dad met?" he asks. He's told me a half dozen times and I never tire hearing their story. High school sweethearts who loved at first sight. Is that even possible? But they seem to really know each other, without gaps and holes in history. They have a past that links back to when they were kids. They know each other without doubts.

Mr. Rhee returns from the kitchen and puts the teacup back on the table. He leans in and kisses his wife's cheek, which almost makes me blush.

"Get a room, you two." Ham giggles. Nobody else laughs.

Instead, Seung aims a balled-up napkin at Ham's head. It lands in a puddle of gravy on his plate. Ham flicks the paper from his potatoes and dives in for a scoop.

I'm the only one watching Seung's parents. The only one who sees Mr. Rhee wink at Mrs. Rhee, then motion with his head toward the kitchen. Now I'm sure I blush.

"Want to watch *Donnie Brasco*?" Seung says. I fork two bites of potatoes before I realize he's talking to me.

"Oh, uh, what time is it?"

"I don't know. You have somewhere else to be?"

"Home by ten if possible. Ten thirty and I risk being beaten." Again, the partial-truth insert. Seung is thinking beaten by a stick; I am thinking beaten by the clock.

Seung bites his lip and points his fork at my face. "Are you serious, Linden?" His forehead wrinkles with worry.

"As heart disease," I say, forcing a chuckle. Sometimes I'm all margarine, and I hate the taste.

Seung sets his silverware on the table. "I'll drop you off at nine fifty-five. You won't be late. I promise."

The first half of the summer Seung didn't drive, but now he drives everywhere. Pre-license and carless, our trio walked all over this four-mile-wide town. One of the reasons I chose to stay here was because of the small size. Ham's house sits at one end of town, Seung's at the other. Our high school is planted in the middle, which makes our dwellings equidistant and my map optimally designed. But now that Seung insists on driving those four miles, I have to be quick on my feet.

"It's okay," I say. "I love walking at night." I am on a roll tonight with my half truths. "If I leave at nine thirty, I'll be home in plenty of time. And after your mom's meat and potatoes, I could really use the exercise."

Ham erupts with laughter. "Please, Linden. You're as thin as paper. If you turn sideways . . ."

I snatch my plate and start for the kitchen. Seung yells,

"No!" and I turn around.

"What's wrong?" I ask.

"Do not go in there," Ham says, pointing at the kitchen door. "When a late-eighties indie band's a-playin', Seung's parents' hips start swayin', and when the hips begin to rock, Mr. Rhee whips out his—"

"Now's a good time to shut the hell up," Seung says, cutting off Ham in midrap. Seung's cheeks are red, but I can't tell if the annoyance is directed at his parents or Ham's feeble attempt at spitting rhyme. I push my plate on the table and decide to find out what's bothering Seung.

"You okay?" I ask, turning toward him. "Is something or someone bugging you?"

Seung pushes his back into the chair, bending his arms behind his head and rolling his eyes.

"That," I say, air jabbing my finger at Seung. "Right there. The eye roll. You're doing it more than usual."

Seung purses his lips together and stuffs his hands into his armpits. Clearly he's not talking. But Ham will. He always does.

"Nothing's wrong with me," Ham says. "But everything's wrong with Seung. The whole world is crashing upon his shoulders. Boo-hoo. Life's so unfair."

"Shut up!" Seung snaps.

"Careful," Ham whispers. "Your stress is oozing all over me."

Seung stands and points at Ham. "I am not stressed."

Ham stands and points back at Seung. "Buddy, I'm afraid you are. For those reasons you told me."

Seung scoffs and snatches his plate. He hits the kitchen door so hard, it swings back and bangs against the wall. Mr. Rhee stumbles on his words, "Oh, hey, kid, uh, we can clean that up," and Seung shouts, "Get a freaking room!"

I turn to Ham, now back at his plate about to tackle Mount Mashed Potatoes. "Stressed, huh?"

Ham reaches for another dinner roll, and I'm reminded to sneak two into my pocket before I leave. I hate stealing food from friends, but I also hate when my stomach growls attract attention. I figure if I ask Seung, or his parents, for two dinner rolls, fresh carrots, or extra cookies for the road, they will say yes. They always do. So I don't ask, but I don't steal, either. I borrow from friends and always pay back my debt. I keep track of what I take in a notebook stashed inside my backpack. Tonight I will log two dinner rolls and tomorrow I will help Seung with two trigonometry questions, or maybe yell at Toby twice. Once for pushing Seung in the hall, once for calling him a racial slur. Maybe I'll yell once at Toby and help Seung with one math problem. Either way, debt paid. I believe in owing no one anything. It's one of the reasons I live on my own. I owe the state zilch, and as a result, they have no control over where I live. It's all about freedom. And what my mother wanted for me.

"Seung's wigged out over the SAT," Ham says. "Too much pressure on getting into his dad's alma mater."

"Duke?" I drop into the chair and rub my forehead with my knuckle. My head shakes madly, "No. No way. Seung's

46

going to Willamette with me. With us."

"Linden, you're high," Ham says. "You might be going to Willamette, but I'll be shit-kicking it with cowboys at some state school. Duke's Mr. Rhee's alma mater, so it's technically Seung's destiny."

I grab handfuls of my hair and tug. "This is the first time I'm hearing about Duke. Why am I hearing this now? Why didn't someone mention this last month, last year?" I hit my hand on the table and the dishes clank. "What will become of our triangle, Ham? We stay together or the Triangle—me, you, Seung—falls apart."

Ham stares; his brow lifts.

I continue to rant. "So I'll help you study, Ham. You *will* get into Willamette. I *will* talk to Seung or Mr. Rhee or the goddamn president if I have to. We stay together. You don't just eliminate one side from our triangle because a parent says you're going to college a million miles away. You don't do that, Ham. You don't take away sides. Our triangle stays intact. There are no two-sided shapes!"

Ham tilts his head, eyes wide and mouth gaping, but only to breathe. He finally shakes off my words and says, "How am I going to get into Willamette without smart-kid classes, Linden? I'm not like you or Seung or Kristen or Jarrell."

"No. You're better!" I shout. "You're Ham, dammit. You do things. Tons of things. We just need to get creative and fluff up your application, like I'm doing with mine. Besides, your parents are rich. That's got to account for something."

"Mob-movie buffs and overstuffed C students don't exactly hook colleges, Linden. Your expectations are out of whack."

"What about the school newspaper? Who got you and Seung jobs at the paper? Thank you very much." I curtsy and push a smile.

"It's the school blog, Linden. And job is a bit of a stretch. It's not a job unless you're paid."

I pat Ham's back. "When I'm through with your college application, Ham, you will look like the lead photographer for the the *Times* of London. Seriously, the school blog is our ticket to a better life. It's the fast train to success. And it's all I fucking have."

Ham rubs his eye with his knuckle and half smiles. I can tell he's trying, hard, to believe me. He stuffs his hands in his pockets and teeters in his chair. "Well, I *was* thinking of joining drama."

I snap my fingers. "Now you're thinking. It's all about extracurriculars."

Ham drops his head to the side and moans. "There's just so much more to Ham than we can put on paper. So much about Ham nobody knows."

"The royal we, Ham. Really?"

Ham winks and reaches for my hand. "While you're working all kinds of magic, Linden, how about finding me my one true love?"

My eyes widen and Ham grins, all teeth.

"You're my best friend, Linden," he says. "Well, one of.

But Seung's stressed, and stress turns him into an asshole."

On cue Seung swings the kitchen door open and announces that we will reconvene in the *underbuilding*. He means basement. Ham declared we rename the basement like we did Seung's car, but his muse failed to create anything beyond *man cave*. I, of course, vetoed Ham's suggestion. I am not a man, and as far as chest hair goes, neither are Seung and Ham.

Seung stomps toward the stairs, and Ham and I follow like the obedient children we are on occasion.

"Donnie Brasco?" Ham asks, and hits the button on the television. No sense in arguing we watch something else. All films must pass a three-theme litmus test before they're shown on the screen in Seung's underbuilding: friendship, devotion, and heavy-cream tomato sauces. The television remote has been missing for weeks, so we take turns getting up and manually operating the channels and volume.

I nod, Seung grunts. "I have a hard time watching Johnny Depp in any role now that he's been openly accused of hitting a girl."

"Agreed," I say. "He repulses me."

Ham opens the movie cupboard and runs his fingers up and down the shelves, humming an unrecognizable tune. "Got it," he says and slides another mob movie into the archaic DVD player.

I kick my shoes off and nestle into my usual corner of the sectional couch. We have reserved seating and never cross each other's boundaries. I snuggle in one corner while Seung sprawls across the center section. Once in a while our heads meet on the same pillow, but tonight is different. Nobody's talking. College and SAT pressures must be tormenting Seung, because two cushions divide us.

Ham relaxes in his usual manner. On his back, legs draped up and over the couch. Most nights he watches the entire movie upside down with his hair stick straight and his shirt riding up his chest. "Perspective" is what Ham says his movie-watching position offers.

Normally Seung sets his phone alarm. And normally Seung remembers without my asking. But tonight I'm distracted by the thought of leaving this town without my friends-slash-family. Seung, going off to college across country. Ham, not sticking to our plan. I'm also preoccupied by Seung's breathing. Within thirty minutes he's asleep and I watch more of Seung than the movie.

The last thing I remember is Bugsy saying, "You thought you could steal from me?" Then I'm asleep, too. So asleep that I don't hear Ham stomp upstairs when the movie ends or realize Seung's head has joined mine on the pillow. What wakes me is his hand on my forearm and fingertips grazing my side.

I jump to my feet, rubbing one eye into focus. I know it's late because the basement assumes a familiar gray hue from the streetlight. It's the lighting that tells me, *Linden, you are so screwed.*

Here's me, losing my shit. Quite literally.

I pat the floor for my jacket. If I don't get back to school by the ten-thirty security check, I am cold Linden, aching Linden, royally fucked Linden.

Seung rolls over and sighs. His partially open lips puff when he exhales and make me stop and stare for two seconds longer than I should. Every moment counts. In a perfect world, I wouldn't have to react and rush and run. I could give in to wants once in a while, rather than needs. Maybe even respond to Seung and his arm grazing.

I find my jacket behind the couch, sling it over my shoulder, slip into my shoes, and run upstairs. I think about the rolls I planned to not-steal when I pass the dining room, but I can't risk waking Mr. and Mrs. Rhee. I'll have to risk the stomach growls during class. I tiptoe to the front door, twist the lock to make sure it's secure, and squeeze it shut without a sound. Of course I remember my phone as soon as the screen closes, which means I have no idea what time it actually is. All I know for sure is it's late and I better move ass, quick.

I sprint down Seung's street, looking for time cues. If Mr. O'Leary's car is parked in his driveway, I will know it's after 11:30. Mr. O'Leary closes the drugstore he manages at 11:15, drives straight home, flips the TV on, and kicks back in a cat-hair-covered recliner with a can of beer and a bag of pork rinds promptly at 11:35. He never misses *The Tonight Show*. He never skips his beer. And I never overlook the details behind that large open window.

When I near the third block north of Seung's house, I notice that Mr. O'Leary's Buick isn't there. Victory Number One.

I keep running, ignoring the side ache pinching my ribs. A car slows at the stop sign, so I dodge into a clump of tumbleweeds piled against a retaining wall—and immediately regret my decision. Thorns poke my pants, but I force myself to freeze. The car creeps slower than it should, and I hope to the gods my jacket blends in with the cinder blocks. If I'm caught after curfew, I will be forced to call my parents . . . which is fine if you have parents.

After my third city-curfew infraction, the deputy grew wise to my lame excuses. The first time, I told the police my stepdad was at a casino one state over. The second time, I informed them he was passed out drunk and wouldn't answer the phone. The third time, I insisted he was away on a long-haul truck drive, somewhere in remote Nevada where cell phone service was nonexistent. A fourth time will push the limit. Deputy Boggs is really not as gullible as he looks.

The car passes by, turns, and drives out of sight. I draw a deep breath and dig my foot into the dirt for takeoff. It hits something hard, sharp. A broken railroad tie. Perfect for wedging into doorways, stronger than wood. I slip it into my pocket and sprint across the street. Another mile and a half and I'm home. I turn the corner at the last intersection and face the highway. Only eight hundred feet of pavement and heavy traffic (three to four cars) and then I'm on back roads.

It sounds safe, the whole three to four cars, but if one is a patrol car, which is usually the case, I'm screwed.

I look across the street and my stomach drops. The Dairy Queen is dark. It closes at 10:00 and the assistant manager turns the lights off by 10:25. So much for Victory Number Two.

But I have to take a chance. As Ham always says, with reference to his mob movie obsession, Joseph Pistone (a.k.a. Donnie Brasco) lived to take chances. I can't run a five-minute mile, but if I sprint the highway at full speed, I'll at least avoid police attention. On the positive side, it's not Saturday night. That's when high school seniors cruise the main drag in search of directions to keg parties bunkered in the hills. I breathe through my nose and wait for the start-pistol to fire in my head.

And I'm off.

My rhythm is fast. My stride loosens with each step. It's amazing how adrenaline transforms you into a bona fide runner. But within fifty feet of my finish line, a loud horn wails, and I hear, "Hey, Linden! Linden!" *Shit*. It's Seung and Ham and failed Victory Number Three.

Seung's hand-me-down, decade-old gold Volvo, which goes by the name of Gold Nugget, inches beside me. Ham rolls the window down and says, "What the hell, Linden? A little early for school."

I stare at the track, then the baseball field. I'll be sleeping in the dugout tonight.

What do I say? Why am I at the back of the school at this hour of night? My friends think I live on the other side of the building, over a mile away.

"I can't find my phone," I snap, ready to insert the partial truth. "Thought I left it in the newsroom. Hoping security hasn't locked the doors yet."

The guys, eager to hear my explanations, make the partial truths sting what's most tender. My heart.

"At this hour?" Seung says and extends his arm out the window. "Your phone, milady." He leans across Ham. "Get in. We'll take you home."

But Seung, I'm already here.

I climb into Gold Nugget's backseat and rub my hand against the worn leather. I could use a little luck right now. The heater blasts and stirs smells from the bacon-infused air freshener dangling from the rearview mirror. According to Seung's dad, boys love bacon, but Seung quit eating meat months ago.

As we circle the high school parking lot and pull toward the second exit, Deputy Boggs arrives for the first watch of the night. There are always two. One at ten thirty, the other at three in the morning.

Finally I exhale and whisper, "I don't want to go home." If I'm sleeping outside tonight, then at least I want to stretch out the time and have fun with my two favorite people.

Seung taps the brake before reaching the highway. He switches off the turn signal and whips around in his seat, eyes smiling. "Where do you want to go, Linden Rose?"

Cue the stomach cartwheels. "I don't know," I say, locking eyes with Seung. "Drive around, maybe. I'll give you gas money." I reach into my bag, but Seung swats my hand.

"No way. My car. My gas money."

"You two do what you want," Ham blurts, "but I need to get home before eleven."

Seung laughs. "And if you aren't home by eleven? What happens? Hammy goes to bed without a story time?"

I smile and my shoulders start to relax. These guys make me feel good on every side. Like I'm part of something. They're the reason I get up in the morning. Well, them, and the fact that if I don't get up I will go to jail for breaking and entering.

"I *could* get in trouble," Ham says. "I just don't like to risk it. My parents believe I'm a certain way, you know. And I'd like to keep it that way."

"Ham, I've known you since second grade," Seung says. "You have never been in trouble. And it's not that you don't do anything trouble-worthy. I mean, your mouth never stops."

I sigh. "Please don't argue. Let's make this a fun night. A night to remember."

"Turn right," Ham snaps. "I'm going home. Expecting a phone call and need to be alone when I get it."

"With pleasure." Seung cranks the wheel and the tires squeal.

"Who's calling?" I ask Ham, a little hurt by his lackluster acknowledgment of making it a memorable night.

He shrugs and mumbles something I can't make out, so I ask again. "Hammy? Who's calling?"

"A friend," he snaps.

Seung chuckles. "All your friends are in this car."

Ham scoffs. "This might surprise you, Seung, but I'm making new friends."

We pull into Ham's picture-perfect Tudor. Amber lights circle the drive. Seung stops in front of the stone steps that lead to the arched entryway.

Ham climbs out of the car. Before shutting the door, he says, "I'll see you assholes in the morning. No offense, Linden."

"None taken." I climb out of the backseat and move to the front. "See you tomorrow, Ham Hock?"

He smiles. "Definitely."

"Hey, Hammy!" I call after him. "I think it's great you're making new friends. Just promise you won't forget about the old."

Ham skips up the steps. "Never!" he shouts, and fumbles in his pockets for his house key.

Even though Seung's irritated with Ham, he waits in the driveway until Ham is safely inside the well-lit foyer. Ham turns and bids us adieu with both middle fingers lifted high above his head.

I laugh while Seung eases out of the circular driveway, navigating the fountain that sits in the middle of a spread of weather-wilted pink petunias and stubby green shrubs.

"You tired?" Seung asks, eyes fixed on the road.

"Not even close." And although I push my head against the

seat and exhale, my exhaustion is mental, not physical.

"Slushies and Triangle Park?" Seung asks.

"You are always inside my head."

"I am?" Seung's face performs a contortionist act and I smile to myself.

We drive to the only twenty-four-hour convenience store within a two-hundred-mile radius. It's smack-dab in the middle of town, a mile from the high school. We mix every flavor of slush into twenty-two-ounce cups, sneak a few bonus gulps before filling up again, and make small talk with Mr. Q, the owner.

"Staying out of trouble tonight?" Mr. Q asks, ringing up our slushies and Seung's oversized bag of M&M's, which I'm expecting him to share.

"Us?" Seung answers. "Always." He pulls out his wallet and swats my hand away. I make a mental note of what I owe him. Gas money. Slushies. I don't care what Seung says—I repay my debts.

"Say hello to your mother and father for me, Seung."

Seung nods at Mr. Q and holds the door open for me when we leave. I crinkle my nose at him, but he either doesn't see me or pretends not to.

I punch the numbers on the car stereo but can't find a station powerful enough to seep into the walls of a town filled with fifteen hundred villagers. So we sit in silence, the occasional melody of unified slurps filling the air.

Triangle Park is at the end of Main Street, at the bottom

of a hill, before the road splits into highway. It's a plot of land in the shape of a triangle. Nothing fancy like most places in this town, but it's our park, our place. It was called a park before parklike structures were built, such as picnic tables and grills perched on top of pipes. We pull into the entrance, and Seung's headlights reveal a truck and motorcycle in the gravel lot lined with railroad ties. I recognize the jet-blue bike right away. Reed Clemmings's new ride. He won't be alone like he was at school, blocking my exit, flashing his too-perfect teeth and watery puppy-dog eyes. Where Reed is, Toby typically lurks. And where T.P. is, Bea is bound to be. My stomach flip-flops. A tiny part excited to see Reed, a giant part dreading to see Bea. What if another fight breaks out?

Seung squints to see who is sitting on the picnic tables. "You sure you want to stay?"

Well, I guess so. I mean, didn't you see Reed Clemmings? Sexiest man alive. Sitting right there.

I wish I could think this way about Seung. But we're close. Not strangers like Reed and me. I want to tell Seung it's time to take our friendship in a new direction, drive straight through the fence, break all the limits. But I've built a protective barrier to hide who I truly am.

"I don't care," I mumble, and climb out of the car, marching toward the playground. "We could swing until Deputy Boggs, or his posse member, stops by to enforce curfew."

Seung jogs up behind me and beep-beeps his car alarm. We pass a picnic table, and Reed says, "Hello, Linden Rose," but his voice is surreal and the words don't resonate. Reed Clemmings saying my name? Out loud. In front of people. Maybe we're on a first-name basis since I saw the tear in his eye. I nod, trying to push down the smile spreading all stupid-like across my face.

But my smile retreats as fast as it arrived when I look toward Reed and see Bea's friend Beth piggyback him. Where Beth is, Bea is. I glance over, and as expected, Bea is sprawled across a table on her stomach. Toby sits on her butt like he's just conquered prey.

"There's your girlfriend," I whisper to Seung, nudging his rib cage with my elbow. "One of Two, remember?" I wink.

On cue, Bea shouts, "Hi, Seung!" And Seung actually lifts his hand and waves back, then jogs toward the swing, his shoulders bigger and broader. I roll my eyes and trot along behind Seung and his newfound confidence. I blame vegetarianism. Weight lifting. The universe.

We swing until our butt cheeks are numb from squeezing them into child-sized seats. We won't admit it, but our eyes are still focused on the picnic tables—well, at least the corners of our eyes.

Sometimes I think my friends are all I need. The two I have now, anyway. It wasn't like I was a friend magnet at my old school. Sure, there were girls I sat with at lunch and talked television with, but they didn't know me like Ham and Seung do, or at least who I'm pretending hard to be. Of course, I've never attended a single school for longer than a year. My mother always moved us when the knocks on the door grew too loud to ignore.

The guys came along when I needed friends the most. Ham and Seung took me in when I knocked. Never asked questions, never judged. Fifteen hundred people in this town and I had the privilege of meeting the perfect two. Now I'm falling hard for the perfect one.

Seung shifts in his swing and I smile, my heart woolly and warm.

Toby stands and reaches for Bea's hand to help her to her feet. He growls something at Reed and pushes Bea behind his back. She stands poised with a hand on her hip, while the boys raise their fists at each other. It's hard to tell who wants to jab first. Everyone in their group is punch-drunk. All four look confused.

I force my eyes on Seung, refusing to see Bea's abuse or abuser, right there in my face.

I know Bea is someone else's problem. Not mine. Besides, it's not like I can help her, even if she'd let me. I'm not exactly good at saving other people, even the ones I love.

"Get out of my face!" Bea shouts, and I drop my eyes and kick at the dirt. I can't look at her. I refuse to feel what she makes me feel.

Principal Falsetto should do more than make a few phone calls, shout a couple of warnings. When Bea showed up in her office at the end of last year with bruises on her wrists, arms, face, the principal didn't do shit. At least not that I could see from my trajectory. Now it's a new school year and Bea's already paid Falsetto a visit. I wonder how bad it's going to get before someone does something.

"Quit acting like a little bitch!" Toby shouts.

Seung digs his heel in the dirt, cranes his neck, and says, "That guy's a real little bitch."

A screwed-up batch of friends, if that's what you want to call them. Bea and her shadow, Beth. Toby Patters and his football-shaped head. I wonder why Reed insists on hanging around after Bea dumped him. Hasn't he stomached enough?

Sometimes Bea and Toby look like the perfect couple. Bea seems happy, part of the time. But she's also great with masks. Probably why Principal Falsetto doesn't make more of a move. Bea's mask fits her face snug with no gaps, like a tight, white glove on a hand, preventing her skin from showing through. Maybe Bea keeps Reed around for protection. Maybe she's afraid of being alone with her own boyfriend. Maybe I should just make an anonymous phone call and get her help.

Reed shouts something about sloppy seconds, and I cringe.

"Shut the hell up!" Toby shouts, his shadow monstrous.

Bea cackles and my brain buzzes with images I frantically shove into dark corners covered with year-old dust. Eyes swollen shut. Neck wrapped in thumbprints. On the floor, an earring post that looks like it's been dipped in blood.

Bea laughs again. Beth parrots Bea.

Finally Reed tells them to hush as he spews lines from

Mr. George's assigned reading. "It all ends in tears anyway," Reed wails with his face toward the sky. Somebody's just discovered Jack Kerouac.

A beer bottle clanks against a metal can, then another, and another. One misses and rolls in front of our swings.

The night is basically a comedy of errors designed to ping-pong my mind from the pain of my past to the fact that tonight I'll be sleeping outdoors. But my stomach is full of food, thanks to Seung's mom, and I'm in the company of the guy I adore, so shit could always be worse.

"I don't know why everyone worships that guy," Seung says after our swings slow. We rock back and forth with our feet grounded.

"Because he's perfection personified," I joke. But I don't think Reed is perfect. He's just being what everyone believes he should be. A football-throwing, motorcycle-riding cliché in a small town obsessed with football and motorcycles. And this year he thought he'd expand on Mr. George's reading list, suck down some Jack Kerouac, and grow his hair out.

"I know you have a thing for Reed Clemmings," Seung says.

"Excuse me?"

"You'd be weird if you didn't."

"Well, then consider me weird." I blow a kiss at Seung.

He smiles and kicks the gravel with his heel. "I already do."

Reed announces their departure by spreading his arms and shouting, "The park is yours, beautiful people!" He then bellows, "The only people for me are the mad ones," and his voice trails off because he's too drunk to remember more lines from *On the Road*.

The foursome walk toward the steroidal truck, and the girls hop into the cab. Reed zigzags behind. When he reaches the truck, he leans against the grill until Toby arrives for a tête-à-tête in front of the headlights. Toby jabs his finger eye-level with Reed. There's a long pause before their shadows pat each other's backs, making room for their drunkenness to fix what needs mending. When they split apart, Reed slides onto his bike and Toby swings into his truck. They synchronize the revving of engines. Low bass meets high rocket whirl.

"Good-bye, Seung!" Bea shouts, leaning the shitty half of her body, the half with no heart, outside the truck window.

There's that wave again. Damnitall, Seung.

"A complete bunch of asswads who should not be driving drunk," Seung says, but I know he's not referring to Bea. He hates Toby, and Reed by default. If I had a dollar bill for every time Toby told Seung he should move back to his motherland, I wouldn't be homeless, or worried about scholarship money to pay for school. I could also afford to hire someone to kick T.P.'s ass and rescue Bea anonymously.

Reed backs his bike out of the parking space and turns parallel with the road. He waits for Toby, who sits in his truck fumbling for the right song, revving the engine. Reed must get tired of the wait, because he spins his back tire and heads toward the hill.

"What's Toby doing?" I ask, squinting at the headlights.

63

"What asswads do best."

And before I can clarify what it is exactly that asswads do, Toby pounds the accelerator and drives straight for us.

I fall out of my swing, landing on all fours in the dirt. Headlights blind my vision.

"Run!" I scream, as much at myself as at Seung. I scramble to my feet and lunge in the direction of the picnic tables.

The engine revs. Guitar riffs roar. Tires squeal.

I reach for a bench, grab on, and flip around. Seung rocks back and forth on the swing, calm and composed. His body shines like chiseled onyx in the headlights. *What the hell is he doing?*

"Seung! Move ass! RUN! RUN! RUN!"

But Seung's like a mountain. He digs his heels into the dirt and grips the chains of his swing. He refuses to budge.

The truck plows toward the swings, bouncing up and down as it hits lawn divots. The bumper shoots a plastic garbage can through the air that lands inches from a picnic table.

"Seung!" I shout, climbing on top of the table and waving my arms. "Move!"

The girls scream, "Stop!" and Toby yells what sounds like a *Yee-haw.* Drums on the stereo beat their chorus, and I slap my hands against my face, peeking through my fingers. "Ohmygod. Ohmygod. Ohmygod!"

Do I charge at Seung? Grab him by the shirt? Drag him to safety?

Before I have time to react, Seung stands, lifts his arm in

the air, and flattens his palm like he's trying to do what? Signal a stop? Holy shit. He's signaling a stop.

And it works. Toby twists the wheel and sends up a cloud of dirt over Seung. The truck hits a railroad tie but doesn't stop. Toby leans out of the window and shouts, "Go back to China and stay away from my girl!" and then cranks the wheel and drives toward the road.

When the dust storm clears, I see Seung back on the swing, coughing and sweeping off his face.

I race toward him and grab the chains on his swing. "Are you okay?" His hair is gray under the yellow of the streetlight. I reach toward his head to brush off the dirt, and he grabs my wrist.

"Of course I'm okay, Linden."

I wiggle my arm out of his grip. "Then why the hell didn't you run?"

Seung stands and pats dirt off his jeans, then his shirt. "I'm done running," he says. "Time to stand up and fight for the shit *I* want."

And before I can clarify if the shit he wants includes Bea or me or something totally unrelated, he stomps off toward Gold Nugget.

CHAPTER FIVE

SEUNG IS SILENT WHILE WE drive, except when he tears open the bag of M&M's. And when he asks if I'd like to replace my slushie, since I dropped mine on my shoe, scrambling to avoid becoming Toby Patters's hood ornament.

I shake my head, still in shock. "Have to get home. You can drop me behind the school."

The boys believe I live in a trailer park on the other side of the high school. Why do they believe this? Because I'm Linden. Liar and Friend.

"No way," Seung says. "It's a mile from your house. Unsafe."

"Oh, now you're suddenly concerned with safety?"

"I'm concerned with *your* safety."

My stomach jumps. What was Seung doing back there?

Trying to get my attention? Or was it Bea's?

"Were you peacocking back there?"

Seung shakes his head. "I don't even know what that means." He cracks the window. "That asshole tried to run us over. I'm not dropping you off at the school. I'm making sure you get home safely."

"That racist asshole doesn't know the difference between Chinese and Korean. I think I'll be okay."

"Nope. Not happening." Seung taps the turn signal.

"Well, I need fresh air. I want to walk."

Seung argues, "We sat in the park for over an hour. Lots of fresh air, Linden. Open your window."

"I need time alone to think after your escapade." I take a deep breath and try to slow my words, my lies. "If my stepdad hears a car pull up, I'm dead for sure." Untrue. No stepdad. Not even a dad. Just a dead mom and dead grandmother.

Ever since Seung aced the driving test—on the first try, by the way—he acts like he's my personal chauffeur. As much as I'd love Seung to pick me up every time I metaphorically hail a cab, my life doesn't operate like that, you know, on want and desire. Besides, Seung's acting suspicious. First questioning my internet usage, then begging to get himself killed. Now, insisting on driving me home.

"I'll drop you off at the trailer-park entrance, then. Watch you walk to your door. Make sure you get in safe."

"No, Seung!" I slap the seat, harder than I should. "You're not hearing me. I said behind the school." *Read the memo,*

Seung. Chivalry's dead.

Seung bites his lip. "Fine," he mumbles.

More silence, except for the engine purr as we turn onto the gravel road behind the high school. He stops near the red-cinder track and I zip my jacket, slide my phone into my pocket, and open the door. The crisp high-desert breeze blows my hair into my face, and suddenly I'm colder than I was at the park. I whip around to tell Seung I'm sorry, that I wish he'd refused to stand up to Toby, that I hope he wasn't showing off for Bea, and that I wish he'd run when his ass was almost pancaked. But I clamp my lips shut, because he's staring straight ahead. Probably wondering why I'm refusing a doorstep delivery.

"I'll see you tomorrow?" I ask, and wait.

After a long pause, Seung nods and rubs his forehead, still staring at the road in front of him. I push the door closed with my hip and walk toward the track, pretending to march to my fictitious trailer park.

Gold Nugget crawls to the first cross street and stops. Seung taps the brakes, and the taillights fill up the road. I stop, too, and wait, longing for Seung to put the car in reverse, back up, and shout, "Get in, Linden! Drive around with me again." I imagine us falling asleep beneath the black sky. Snuggling to keep warm.

After several seconds, the car crunches gravel and the turn signal flashes. I stand in the middle of the road and wait for Seung's car to hit the highway, and then I backtrack toward the chain-link school gate.

My stomach rumbles and my temples pound. It's not so

much the idea of the night ahead that bothers me as it is the hours behind me. Seung standing up for himself. Seung begging to drop me at my doorstep. Seung, in general.

I hate lying to my best friends. Spending the night huddled on a wood bench in the dugout is easy compared to camouflaging the truth.

And there's also first period tomorrow morning. My ass-sucking class with Bea & Associates. Reed probably won't notice me, but Bea and Beth and Toby won't forget tonight. Especially after trying to scare-kill us.

When I reach the baseball dugout, I push the button on my phone to check the time. Two hours before the next security check. I pull my notebook from my backpack and light it up with my phone.

I write:

Seung = 1 dinner. 1 slushie. 1 car ride home.

I tuck my knees to my chest and cover them with my jacket. I wrap my arms around my legs, lean against the plywood, and close my eyes.

Visions motorcade through my brain.

Because I'm exhausted. Because I'm huddled in a corner. Because I often remember, even—and especially—when I want to forget.

There's Mama with her feral curls and lipstick I want to smudge like finger paint.

There's five-year-old me.

Hush, Linden. Time for sleep.

Yes, Mama. (I'm whispering to her. My head bobs up, then down.)

No talking, remember? He'll hear you. You have to keep silent.

Yes, Mama.

When you close your eyes, you disappear. You can't see anyone. No one can see you.

Yes, Mama.

I haven't yet learned to question anything she says. Haven't learned that Mama's right only sometimes.

Something rattles behind the dugout and I jump off the bench, ready to grab my bag and run. A cat shoots across the field.

I exhale relief and scan the track for moving shadows. I tuck myself back into the corner of my wood shelter, yearning for a restful night, but every few minutes the wind blows and my eyes pop open.

I've trained myself to hear every sound, even while I'm asleep. This year has heightened my senses—made me smell more, feel more, see more. I smell the dash of vanilla Mrs. Rhee used in her cookies, the hint of lemon left on Seung's skin after he's showered. I feel the weather shift from autumn to winter with one breeze, the warmth of velvet when the theater curtains cloak my legs. And tonight, when I shut my eyes, I see headlights. Toby's headlights, Seung's headlights, a patrol car's headlights. I snap open my eyes.

Shit.

I crouch on all fours and crawl along the bench toward my bag. The patrol car flips a U-turn on the back road. Twenty seconds to do what I need to do. Run.

I stuff my notebook into my bag and race toward the fire escape on the other side of the school. I turn once for a status check. The cop car stops; the door opens. Headlights illuminate the track and make it look like day.

I sprint toward the dark side of the moon. If I avoid light, he won't see me.

At the fire escape I flatten my body against the brick. I'm not sure there's enough time to run up the stairs and check the door. Something I should have done when Seung dropped me off.

I grab the railing and speed-walk the stairs on tiptoes, so the metal doesn't clank. At the top, I hear the patrol car's engine idle, then hum. He's back in the car, heading my way.

I jerk the door handle, and as expected, it's locked. I drop to my knees and pat the metal grate until I find the wedge of wood I normally use to prop the door open. I stuff it into my pocket to avoid leaving clues, then hop to my feet and haul ass down the stairs, jumping two at a time.

I stick the landing with both heels digging deep into the dirt. I crouch in the dark spot beneath the fire escape and hold my breath while the police car creeps alongside the building. I drop to my knees and elbows and slink beneath the stairs, pausing until the car stops, the door shuts.

According to schedule, the officer will check the gym and fire escape first. I listen for boots on metal. Sometimes, depending on who the officer is, I won't hear footsteps. Deputy Boggs, despite his 350-pound frame, insists on checking the fire-escape door, but his partner, only tipping the scales at 120 after a plate of spaghetti, won't risk becoming breathless.

Pound-clank-pound-clank. Officer Boggs. *Nice.* I can outrun him if necessary.

I wait until Boggs reaches the top of the stairs and count.

One one thousand, *two* one thousand, *three* one thousand, *four* one thousand, FIVE.

I sprint to the far side of the building, slipping into my backpack as I pump my arms. It feels good to run, with the cold breeze blowing sweat beads from my forehead, clearing my clouded mind. My adrenaline surges. The run makes me reckless, my moves less calculated.

This is our nightly cat-and-mouse game of tag, except Deputy Boggs is always *it* and doesn't know we're playing. I move, he moves, I move, he moves. Every night that I don't make it indoors, the game is on. I dart toward the building one last time and huddle under the fire escape until the patrol car pulls away. I wait an extra twenty seconds just in case Deputy Boggs makes a sudden stop.

And so commences my night of hiding in plain sight.

I trudge to the wood shelter, kicking rocks along the way. Not long until I'm forced to wake wide-eyed, ready for class.

I cover my knees with my coat, wishing for the theater

curtains as I fall against the dugout wall, and anticipate another nightmare.

When I wake, the morning sun wraps me in a blanket of warmth and softens my stiff back. I shake my limbs to loosen the last drops of adrenaline in my blood, then press out the wrinkles in my pants. The seams push at the hips, ever since my body decided it wanted to become a woman. As soon as I collect another ten bucks from my cleaning gig at Bea's, I'll snag heavier jeans from a yard sale before winter. Maybe something denim, corduroy. Another scarf, too. I run my fingers through my hair to work out the webs of tangles and pinch my cheeks for color.

In thirty minutes the buses will back from the barn. If I'd chosen to live in a larger town, even a city, I could sleep in like normal kids, maybe hit the snooze two or three times. But in the wide-open spaces of central Oregon, some students live on ranches in the middle of nowhere and the bus drivers begin routes at the crack of dawn. It takes time to drive from Bumfuck, Oregon, to Bumfuck, Oregon.

My summer schedule was less complicated than the school year. Last summer, I'd slink out in the mornings and return late afternoon without notice. Most teachers vacate or work from home in late June through August. It's only the overly dedicated ones like Mr. George who cause problems. They work hard, and by hard, I mean they show up unannounced at all hours of the day. After careful observation, though, you learn their schedules and predictabilities. Even teachers are creatures of habit, and I've become a master of other people's itineraries.

I kick my leg onto the wood bench and stretch my hamstrings. I need circulation, more heat, so I jog in place for several seconds before realizing how ridiculous I look. I smooth over the dirt footsteps as I traipse backward to the grass. If I take my time and walk the long block encircling the school, I will blend in, looking like I was dropped off early for class. I might even be able to convince an early-arriving teacher to let me inside to use the restroom before the bell rings. I hate using the dugout "bathroom." Even animals don't shit where they sleep.

I climb onto one of the cement platforms at the front of the school. It's where cool kids sit when they arrive, but cool kids wouldn't be caught here this early in the morning. Instead they're at home enjoying a steamy shower, eating a balanced breakfast. That's how I define the word *cool*.

I lean against the wood beam and tap my phone, pretending to check something, anything, when Principal Falls, I mean Falsetto, marches up the front steps.

"Early morning, Linden," she asks more than says.

"Yes, ma'am. My stepdad needed to get on the road."

She tilts her head and looks at me sideways. I make eye contact with my phone. I won't bother asking if I can use the bathroom. Her answer never varies. Now is probably not the best time to ask about her sister, either, or why the two were discussing my home address. I'm not sure there *is*

74

a good time for that talk.

Cars pull into the parking lot. Coach Jenkins and Mr. George exchange good-mornings, and Coach jogs to the front of the building. Shouldn't he be using the gym door? The portal to his kingdom. He bobs up the steps, and by bob, I mean full-body-belly bounce, in classic coach form. Chicken-bone legs, bell-shaped belly. Coach looks my way, but since I don't play football, his glance is abbreviated. I won't ask him to use the bathroom. He'd just grunt and bang his knuckles on the steps.

Mr. George is my best possibility. My boss, English teacher, mentor. Plus, he wears T-shirts that say *Love Is Love* and doesn't care what small-town parents whisper behind his back. To me, Mr. George is like Seung, a work of art in a humdrum school.

"Good morning, Linden," Mr. George says, jogging up the steps. He flashes his teeth and I'm all over it.

I leap from the platform and tag behind him.

"Mr. George? May I use the restroom? I've been here awhile and my bladder's about to burst." Not to mention my bowels.

Mr. George glances at his watch, nods, and winks. Normally I use the restroom before anyone arrives. Make sure my hair's in place and my face is fresh. But this morning's schedule is out of whack. Sleeping outside wrecks my day if I let it. Mr. George motions for me to move fast, make it quick, and just as I'm slipping inside, Principal Falsetto opens the door, heading back to her car.

"Oh, Linden," she says, each word increasing in octave. "You know the rule."

I spin around on my heel and sigh. "No students indoors before the buzzer," we sing in unison.

I shuffle back to the platform, watching the principal return with her briefcase. She nods in my direction and I shoot her a scowl. She's not really looking at me anyway.

Thirty minutes until everyone arrives. I wish Seung and Ham would show up earlier, but it's not their habit. Since Seung started driving, they kill time at the convenience store or zigzag side streets until first period. Last year their parents dropped them off at school on their way to work, so I never sat alone for long.

Bea drives up in her convertible. It's tan and white and never topless. Her hair might tousle and that would blow. Her convertible doesn't fool anyone. She's not rich. No one in this blue-collar town has money, or a lot of it, except Ham's white-collar parents. Bea always pretends to be something she's not. I mean, her mom pays me twenty bucks to clean their entire house. The rates suck, but they pay for cans of refried beans, peanut butter, and minutes on my phone. Bea's convertible is fifteen years old and the paint's overwaxed.

Kristen arrives in her mom's minivan. She slips into her backpack, scoops a stack of books from the backseat. I watch as Beth climbs out of Bea's car. They exchange hi's and fake smiles with Kristen, then beeline toward me with Bea leading the march. I shoot my chin down, poking around the cracked screen on my phone.

"You're unfortunately alive," Bea barks, walking up the steps.

"I am," I say, still staring at my phone. "Thanks for noticing."

Beth stops behind Bea, awaiting her next move, and Kristen waves and nods in my direction before walking into the school like she owns the place.

Someone yells, "Hey! Where are *you* going?" and Kristen snaps, "I don't just go to school. I work here, too."

Bea's not budging. She's busy scanning me and my slushie-stained shoe. I kick one leg over the other and smile. She shakes her head, laughs, and says, "Nice hair." She clutches her nose and keeps the compliments flying. "I can smell you from here." She squeezes her nostrils. "Used tampons and campfire."

Beth gut laughs and Bea squints her eyes at me, then hikes her backpack onto her shoulder and stomps off, with Beth walking like a cadet behind her.

Sometimes I piss myself off. I'm slow with comebacks, especially in the morning. They fully form in my brain but refuse the ride to my mouth. I'd like to tell Bea her lip is healing nicely, her boyfriend is a douche, and we all know her bullshit secret. But my own secret's more important. Besides, Bea's pain surfaces, with or without my comeback. Slinging sarcasm would only make me feel better for a moment. But sometimes, I live for that moment.

I brush my hand over the top of my hair and feel a crunch. When I shake my head, a leaf falls onto my thigh. There's the campfire Bea was talking about, ready to ignite. I twist my hair into a knotted bun, lick my fingers, and smooth my eyebrows.

Just as I'm completing my makeover, Reed drives front and center into an unmarked parking spot. The one with his name written in invisible ink. The one no one else dares park in, ever. It's not like he'd hurt them or anything, but at this school it's all about respect. Some argue the qualifications for admiration are predetermined. One flaw, one false perception, and you're swept from the top shelf. Except that some students at the top don't seem to want to be there, and those at the bottom aren't fully aware of the ceiling they're up against. Well, except for Bea and Beth. They seem to savor their bird's-eye view of Hinderwood High. But like everyone else, they, too, strive for departure. I'm just here to learn and get the hell out before anyone finds out I live here.

Reed waits on his bike for what seems an eternity. Bea's friends glance over at him two thousand times while tugging their shirts and skirts into even tighter form fits. I don't know why Bea dumped Reed and fell face-first into Toby's brutish arms. She always has one eye on Reed, that's for sure. She won't stop watching him. Maybe she's bent on making him jealous. But at what cost?

Bea catches me staring and shoots another eye dart. I force a smile. The sting hurts no matter how hard I pretend it doesn't.

Tires squeak and my knights in shiny gold armor finally appear. Seung and Ham sail through the parking lot, gliding Gold Nugget over speed bumps at moderate velocity. Seung drives like he's seventy, centering the Volvo in the middle of two spaces to protect the paint job in the unlikely event someone slams a door into his prized possession.

I jump from the cement platform as the bell rings. Everyone stampedes for the front doors. My belly pinches and cramps and reminds me I need a bathroom in the worst way. But I push the pain aside and wait outside for the guys.

"Linden," Ham says. "You're looking boyish as always."

I squeeze a smile out of the side of my mouth. God, am I happy to see them. So happy, in fact, that I grab Ham's neck and he grabs Seung's and we squish together while Ham recites his morning epigram: "Time for a Ham sandwich."

Seung pushes Ham back, clearly not ready for our morning mash, and I stumble into the back of Reed Clemmings.

"Hey," he says. "Watch it."

I whip around and try to act aloof. "Whoops. Didn't mean to, you know, do that." And then I smile because Reed has that effect on people, on girls, and I guess that's what I am, contrary to what Ham says. But who the hell cares? Can't a girl smile at a hot guy if she wants to without it meaning something? It means nothing. I mean, does it?

Reed smiles with his eyes. "No problem here." He licks his bottom lip and I feel sort of squeamish. He looks different than he did when he blocked my exit, more relaxed, composed, and he smells like the inside of a department store—espresso beans stacked on scented soap. Now I smell the same. Clean. Caffeinated. And—I'm not going to lie—damn good.

The crowd pushes and shoves, and Reed steps to my side. He reaches into my hair and picks out a piece of bark. I repeat, Reed Clemmings reaches into my hair and picks out a piece of bark. He rubs it between his fingers, smiles, and flicks it over my head.

I give him the guy nod that says I'm cool with him reaching into my hair uninvited. I think?

Then someone bangs into my back and I turn sideways, bashing into Seung's chest. His hand is in the air, fist clenched, as he shouts, "Tell your buddy he better not try that move again!"

I stare at Seung, my jaw drops. Didn't he see Reed touch me? Why is he interrupting this moment? I turn to Reed and he's staring at Seung, shocked. Reed asks Seung what he's talking about, and Seung channels his inner old man again and says in slow motion, "Tell Toby to stay away from me— and my friends. That's what I'm talking about."

Ham squeezes next to me and grabs my wrist. We wiggle our eyebrows at each other and stare in disbelief. It's one thing for Seung to stand up to Reed, right here, in his kingdom, but quite another for me to be sandwiched between the two hottest guys in school. I want to pump my fist and shout, "Look at me!" but then Seung opens his mouth and chases away my courage.

"Did you hear me? Are you going to tell him?"

Reed locks eyes with Seung. Neither says a word. I'm breathing for both of them. Seung looks surprisingly stiff, yet calm at the same time.

"You should tell him yourself," Reed says flatly.

Yeah, Seung. You should. Tell Toby yourself. Another day. Another year. But please remember Toby's built like a mountain, and you're, well, like an anthill.

"Maybe I will," Seung says.

"Maybe you should," Reed says.

Jarrell slides through the crowd and pats Reed's back. Just in time. "All good here?" he asks, and Ham squeezes my hand so tight my knuckles pop.

"All good," Seung says.

Jarrell smiles. "Wouldn't want you to miss the next game because of fighting. Right, Reed?"

Reed is the first to walk away with Jarrell's hands still planted on his shoulder blades, steering him through the mob. Reed nods his head in what seems like agreement or obedience, and disappears into the open arms of his people.

"Dude!" Ham slaps Seung's chest with both hands. "What the hell?"

Seung shrugs his shoulders, glances at me, and smiles. "Good morning, Linden Rose," he says with a hell of a lot of poise.

I'm shaking my head, arms flapping at my sides, in total disbelief. "What is wrong with you? Do you have a death wish?"

Seung won't stop smiling. He's oozing pride. Standing up for himself, his friends. And although I won't tell him how sexy this is, I'm happy for him.

"Linden?" Seung says, and points at his chest.

Yeah, Seung. I'm aware of your recent muscle expansion. . . .

"Linden?" He taps at his chest again.

"Yeah?"

"You've got a little something." He points at my boobs.

I roll my eyes. "Really? Thanks." *For finally noticing.*

"No. I mean, right there," he says, and taps my sweater.

I gasp, just a little.

"I could get it," he says, "but I should probably let you."

I roll my eyes again and glance down at my chest, and sure enough, right there, perfectly positioned and shooting out of my shirt, is a bark nipple. My cheeks go instantly hot.

Ham and Seung jog into the crowd, and I choke out, "I'll see you at lunch," then fast-walk to the bathroom.

CHAPTER SIX

THE LINE IS SIX DEEP for the restroom. If the hall were empty, I'd dodge into the guys' bathroom, but instead I race down the corridor and slip through the gym doors to use the public restroom designated for visitors—the one nobody visits. Immediately, I hear voices, loud and familiar.

"This is so fucked up!"

"Obviously."

I'm reminded of one of my first Saturdays at Bea's house, when I was scrubbing spots of toothpaste off a bathroom mirror and heard shouts in the hallway. I rushed to shut and lock the door, and within seconds Bea was screaming, "Get out!" I never saw who she was yelling at, but my money's on her boyfriend, Toby. Later, when I was leaving, Bea stopped me at the door and asked what I heard. "Nothing," I said, my eyes darting everywhere but her red cheek. "Are you sure?" Bea asked. And again, I answered, "I heard nothing." She didn't believe me.

This morning's different, though. My bladder and bowels refuse to care what I'm about to witness again, so I whip around the corner with my finger raised, eyes on the ceiling. "This restroom is not for you. Get out!"

Toby shouts, "Piss off!"

That's when I catch a glimpse of Bea hunched over the garbage can, crying. Twenty minutes ago she was *complimenting* my clothes. Now she's wiping her nose and darting into a stall to avoid eye contact.

Toby slaps her stall door and shouts, "You're going to have to deal with this, Bea! Once and for all! As much as I want to help, some shit you have to do yourself."

"Go away," Bea says, her voice muffled behind the door.

"Yeah," I say, pointing behind me. "Leave. . . . Just scram."
Scram?

Toby faces me and flexes his chest. I yawn and point toward the exit.

He shouts, "Time to choose, Bea! Time to fucking choose!"

Bea sniffs from the stall.

I barely manage to lock the door before tearing down my pants. I've reached the stage where I have to pee so bad, I can't anymore, so I draw deep breaths. Relaxation is impossible with Bea and Toby near. I don't have time for their drama, and I really don't want to see it up close and personal, so I close my eyes and force myself to unwind.

When I finish, I linger at the sink, soaping my hands two hundred times. I turn the water off and on, trying to rinse off the curiosity that keeps rearing its hideous head. I hate that I want to ask Bea if she's okay. She's not the kindest person I've ever met. Her sniffs from the stall tell me she's not fine, though. I can't just leave her in here, with him out there.

I stomp toward the exit, kick the door open, but remain inside. Within seconds, Bea swings the stall open, heads for the sink, and dampens a wad of paper towels to smudge snakes of mascara from her cheeks. I step from behind the wall and Bea jumps. "What do *you* want? Haven't you seen enough?"

My eyes widen and my sarcasm from earlier slinks out the cracked window. The only thing left on my tongue is sympathy splashed with shock.

Bea stares at me, one eye turning the shade of a stormy sky. The bubble on her lip from yesterday is busted open and her mouth is oozing a mixture of saliva and blood.

"Are you okay?" I ask, offering more paper towels.

She swats my hand away. "Of course I'm okay."

"You don't look okay." My voice is soft, almost a whisper.

Bea glances at herself in the mirror and after a long pause mumbles, "And you do?"

I sigh and drop the paper towels on the sink. "Look. I'm just trying to help."

"I didn't ask for help. Did I?"

She never does. Maybe she never will.

But I can't ignore the similarities Bea and I share. I never ask for help, either. And sometimes I wish I could. I can't even jump in her boyfriend's face and shake my fist, for fear I'll end up in the principal's office. I hate that Bea makes me want to care for her, even when she treats me like crap.

Bea and her friends never used to bother me. I'm not chubby or Asian, in a predominantly lean and whitewashed school tainted with an occasional racist and misogynistic asshole. I try to keep to myself, always covered in an I-don't-care-if-you-like-me sheen, but when it comes to Bea, I'd be lying if I said I don't care a little. Seeing her pain is hard. You don't even have to search for it—it's written all over her face. Swollen lip. Sad eyes. She stirs hard-to-face feelings.

"Why are you still standing here?" Bea asks. "Didn't I tell you to get out?"

I snatch the paper towels I tried to offer Bea like a white flag and wad them into a ball in my fist. I can't leave without asking her a question. "What did Toby mean when he said you'd have to choose?"

She dabs her lip with her tongue. "Why do you care?"

I shake my head and stuff the paper-towel ball into the garbage can. "Why don't you?"

We stare at each other until the moment grows awkward. My insecurities bubbling and stirring, hers masked with anger and pride. Words push at her lips but no sound escapes. I arch an eyebrow to encourage her, show her it's safe to open up, but she glares and returns a middle finger.

"You suck," she says, and spits blood into the sink.

I shake my head. "You're impossible." And I swing the door shut.

Why even try? Bea doesn't want my help. Pride is more important to her than happiness. At least that's how it seems.

I round the back hall on the way to my locker and see a handful of students gathering. Reed has Toby pushed up against the wall. I dart beside them and pretend not to hear Reed shout Bea's name like a drunken poet. He's punching the locker like a boxing bag. Dude's unhinged.

Nobody wants to see this shit. Especially here. Technically, they are in *my* house, yet I'm plowing through the middle of someone else's domestic disturbance.

Bea resurrects herself from the restroom and shouts. "Stop or I'm going to Principal Falls!" The boys break apart.

"But I love you, Bea!" Reed shouts, prompting me to rev up my speed. Basically, I'm sprinting my ass to class, now.

I walk into class and hear mouths buzzing about the altercation between Seung and Reed. Only Seung's referred to as *That Asian Guy*, and gossip has it that Reed threw the first punch. The story lacks facts, which really pisses me off.

Mr. Dique launches into a lecture out of the starting gate, and I'm willing my stomach to shut the hell up because it sounds like a monster dying for a kill . . . or perhaps a cheddar-stuffed corn dog from Cheese Country. I'm stuck in the middle row, jabbing at my arm with a pencil to keep my eyes open, when Kristen flits into class and says, "Sorry I'm late," then hands Mr. Dique a pink slip of paper.

She spins on her heel and marches toward her seat, staring at me and smiling. Her eyes say, "I'm sorry," for what, I don't know. Then she slips a folded piece of paper onto my desk and sits in her chair. I slap my hand over the top of the square and shift in my seat to catch Kristen's eye.

Drama Jarrell blocks my view. He smiles and says, "Good morning, Linden."

My eyes land on his shirt, which reads: **Save the Drama for Me and Your Llama**. I smile and slide back around to listen to Mr. Dique ramble on about a complicated form of replication. Usually I'd be hurriedly scribbling notes with a cramped hand, but I'm tired and cranky and craving lunch. Kristen clears her throat, and I swear I hear her cough out the words, "Open it." Jarrell jabs my back with a pen.

I half turn in my seat. "What?"

"Open it," he whispers.

"Later."

"She said to do it now." Jarrell leans forward on his desk chair and cradles his chin on his hands. "She keeps saying to open it. It's Kristen. Remember? She's infused with the inability to relent."

I grunt and unfold the paper just as Bea walks into the room.

She makes no excuses for being late, and when she passes my desk, she snatches Kristen's note and waves it like a flag.

"Excuse me, Mr. Dique," Bea says, interrupting the class.

"Questions at closing." Mr. Dique swats his hand without looking. "Answers, too, because you're late."

"But, Mr. Dique," Bea says, all grin, "Linden is disrupting class with a note."

Are you joking right now? I mean, where is Bea's confidence coming from? She's wearing a second face made of concealer and powder that's doing a fine job of hiding the damage, but why welcome the spotlight?

Mr. Dique whips around from the white board and says, "A note? Who cares? Pass notes all you want. Please, somebody, resurrect the lost art of letter writing. It's the phones I'll confiscate." Mr. Dique smiles and turns his back to the class.

I smile at Bea, and she scowls and throws the note at my head. It sticks in my hair.

"But," Mr. Dique says, twisting back around and tapping his pointer on the front desk, "no disrupting class. Understood, Linden?"

I nod. "Understood, Mr. D."

I pat the note and try to make sense of Kristen's words. It reads:

She talked to me again. Asked questions about you.

Who? That journalist lady? As if I don't have enough to think about.

I fold the paper into a tight square and stuff it into my

pocket as Jarrell pokes my back again.

"You've got to stop doing that," I whisper.

"More mail." He grins and shrugs and slips me another note.

Jarrell's right. Kristen is relentless, and I do need to find out more about this journalist lady, so I unfold the paper and read.

Mind your own damn business, T.T.B.
Stay out of mine. Consider this a threat!

Clearly the note is from Bea, not Kristen. Bea and Toby are the only people who refer to me with those initials, but Bea's the one with reason to threaten me.

I read the note again. Each letter pops in my head, over and over, until something inside me stirs. Anger, hurt, Seung's confidence rubbing off on me. Whatever it is, it's causing a reaction. My knee hits the desk and I'm up, wadding the paper into a ball and launching it overhead.

"Aren't you tired of living a lie?" I snap.

Somewhere, deep in the pit of my gut, I feel sorry for this girl. Call it hunger. Call it rage. But I'm too busy spitting questions at Bea to realize that the note bounces off her desk and lands at Reed's feet. He clears his throat and says, "That's enough, Linden."

Then Mr. Dique repeats, "Yes, Linden. That's enough."

Here's me, standing in the middle of class, staring at Bea, who's staring at Reed, caring little about the twenty other sets of eyes looking at me like I'm a monster. I glance at Reed and he stares at me for what seems like an hour, maybe longer, but enough time to sizzle the I-don't-give-two-shits sheen off my skin. He looks at the note, then back at me. He bends over and snatches the paper, knuckles his brow, and wipes away droplets of sweat. His eyes are glazed over. He might even be crying, because he has that same look he had when he blocked my exit and asked me about Bea.

"Is there an issue, Linden?" Mr. Dique asks.

I shake my head and plop down sideways in my chair, tucking one leg under my ass and locking eyes on the note. Reed flattens the paper ball, pushing the wrinkles out with his long fingers. He squints when he reads. Then cocks his head in my direction and smiles. I don't know if he's sympathetic, but his eyes dance over me, starting at the top of my head and ending at the slushie stain on my shoe. I shove my foot beneath my desk, but it's too late. Reed sees me. My clothes, my stains, my bark-filled hair.

I guess I do give a shit.

I'm T.T.B. Trailer Trash Bitch.

To Bea and her friends.

The irony? I nicknamed myself.

I'm the one who told the world I live in a trailer, as if living in a trailer is better than living nowhere at all.

The bell rings and I sprint for the door.

I refuse to face Bea or Beth or Reed and his perfect complexion. As hard as I try to blend in, Bea fights to make me stand out. Every time I turn the corner, there she is, in my face, scrambling for more ammunition to treat me like shit. I didn't want to overhear her fights with her boyfriend. I didn't willingly get involved. Now she assumes I see her as weak. If Bea only knew that I'm strong because I have to be, because I know what it's like to feel broken. I know what it's like to lose everything, in an instant, and have to fight and claw my way back from nothing. It's the fighting, clawing, and clinging to hope that make me strong. Unfortunately, right now, I'm the weakest I've felt in a while.

I want to help this girl. I want her to know she's not alone. But how can you help someone who hates you simply because you know they need help?

I wonder if Bea thinks she's beyond hope. Like nobody can save her.

And then she waves at Seung. And Seung waves back.

Maybe she's searching for a rescuer. Who better to run to than the King of Safety? Isn't that what I did?

Sure, Seung's more chiseled this year since he quit eating meat, but he'll need to shove a hamburger in his mouth if he's going to battle Toby.

I speed-walk the hall, a headache jamming the backs of my eyes. My brain aches from Bea's drama. When I round the corner, Ham's slumped against my locker.

"Skip second period," he hisses. "Meet me in the newsroom."

"Can't."

"But this is important," Ham whines. "I think Bea's in trouble."

I roll my eyes as I dig for my bag. I prop my books to hide my shampoo and deodorant from peeking out of my locker, slipping my hand behind a book and sliding my toothpaste into an unzipped pocket on my bag. Ham's too busy nodding at Jarrell as he passes to notice what I'm doing.

"Hello? Ham?" I say when I'm done reorganizing my *cabinet*.

"Huh? What?"

"Bea's in trouble?"

"Well, yeah," Ham says. "I think Bea's cheating on Toby Patters."

"Well, good," I say. "Maybe she's on her way to victory."

"Is that sarcasm, Linden?" Ham says flatly. "Because if it is, it's ugly. Hideous, in fact."

"Sorry, Ham. It's just that Bea hates me. How am I supposed to care about someone who hates me?"

Ham exhales. "She needs us, Linden. I'm pretty sure she's cheating on T.P. with Reed." Ham throws his hands in the air. "And we all know how I feel about Reed Clemmings."

On cue, Reed passes my locker and winks.

"Did he wink at you or me?" Ham asks. And before I clarify, Ham blurts, "Such a miserable person stuffed inside such a beautiful body."

My eyes widen, but when I follow Ham's gaze, Bea appears. I inhale all aggressive-like, ready to scold Ham about his infatuation with Bea, when Seung walks up and leans against my neighbor's locker.

"Mr. George wants to meet with us after school," Seung says. He's bright-eyed midmorning. Fresh and sparkly and smelling like a mix of cloves and evergreen. Basically, Seung's the holidays personified. I smile, and Seung holds my stare. "Did you sleep well last night, Linden?" he asks, a bit breathy, and for a minute I worry that he knows something he couldn't possibly know. Could he?

I shrug and wonder if he'll look me up and down like Reed did, or ask me if I know I'm wearing yesterday's clothes. But Seung just fixes on my face forever. "Lunch?" he finally asks.

"I'm not eating in that germ-infested cafeteria," Ham shouts, walking backward and pointing down the hall. "Let's meet at Cheese Country." He raises two index fingers in the air. "I need fucking cheese!"

Seung shakes his head. "Can't," he says. "I'm broke. Let's eat fucking cheese at my house."

Ham salutes us before walking away. Then he turns and shouts from the end of the hallway. "Linden, that journalist lady talked to me about you. I think you're winning a scholarship or something."

I slam my locker door. "Why didn't you mention this before?" But Ham disappears down the hall. My foot slips and I reach down to pick up a rolled ten-dollar bill. When I come up smiling, bragging to Seung about how my day escalated from suck to nonsuck, he's gone, too.

94

CHAPTER SEVEN

WHEN SCHOOL'S OUT, I RACE to the locker room to wash the gym shorts I've worn all week. The scramble during mass exits creates the best time to blend in among the mob. I unzip my bag and toss my shorts in the sink. I head-check behind me, then decide to wash my bra and a pair of socks, too. I wait for the water to gain heat and kill bacteria swimming in the ceramic bowl. Then I plug the hole with a wine cork and pump powdered soap into the water. I swirl and splash and soak.

A girl walks in and goes straight to a stall. I rush my process, but the soap takes forever to rinse out. When she walks over to a sink to wash her hands, she shoots me a side eye.

"Damn period," I say. "Always irregular. Always a mess." I smile, and she nods as I wring water out of the shorts and cram my bra and socks into a Ziploc bag.

I race to the newsroom for our meeting with Mr. George. Upon my arrival, the chairs are pushed together and desks clothed with oversized squares of construction paper. Beth scribbles wildly with a green marker while Bea hovers over her shoulder, shaking her head. She looks up when we barge in the door and glares at Ham when he steps on a sign, leaving a footprint and a hole.

"Watch where you walk," Bea snaps.

"And hello to you, too, lovely," Ham says. "Just the person I want to see."

Bea ignores Ham's remark and eyes Beth's kindergarten-level artwork. "Homecoming is one word, not two," she says drily, and Beth rips the poster in half.

I ignore B&B's art-slash-spelling lesson and park my bag at the computer. As soon as my back turns, Bea says, "Are you going to homecoming, Seung?"

There's a long pause, and I start jabbing a computer key one hundred thousand times. Each tap growing with intensity.

"Might go," Seung says.

"With who?" Ham snaps, and I flip around, stone-faced.

Seung glances over at me. "Someone," he says. "Forget about it."

Lately Seung's moves are effortless. It's like he cares nothing of what others think. He messes his hair and leaves it that way. He drives two miles *above* the speed limit. And he's still not eating meat, yet his shoulders continue to spread east and west. He's like me from Christmas past, not giving two shits what anyone thinks. But now I've become the old Seung, nervous, sketched out, and questioning everyone's stares.

Ever since Seung stood up to Toby's truck and Reed's chest, he's calm and casual and shuffling the school's hierarchy in his mind. It's Seung's world now, and everyone else inhabits it. I wonder if he even knows what he's doing.

Ham picks up on Seung 2.0, too. "What's with you?" he asks.

Seung brushes his hair back with his fingers. "If you only knew," he says, and his cheekbones surface when he flashes a smile.

Reed pokes his head in the door and says, "Hello, beautiful people," and he's staring right at me, which makes Seung snap his head in my direction and scowl.

"What are you doing here?" Bea mumbles, and checks her phone. "Toby's not here yet."

Ham stretches his neck like a giraffe and quick-nods in my direction as if to say, "I told you. She's cheating. Remember?"

I roll my eyes. I couldn't care less about Bea and her boyfriends, as long as she stays away from mine. Well, my friend, that is.

"Not looking for Toby," Reed says. "You and me. We need to talk."

"No way. Not here," Bea says, "unless we need witnesses."

Reed tucks his lips inside his mouth and tilts his head to one side. "My witness is the empty sky," he says, all breathy, and my stomach drops. I feel a jab in my gut. Quite possibly the slab of cheddar from lunch, or perhaps the sexiness that is Reed Clemmings.

I decide to roll my eyes, though, in case Seung's watching. In case Bea looks.

Bea grabs her bag and marches toward the door.

Beth says, "Should I come?"

"No," they both snap, and Beth slumps into her chair.

Mr. George whips around the corner. "Those who've been called to a meeting, stay, and those who haven't, please stray."

Beth collects her belongings and tidies up the posters, stacking them on a counter near the wall, and leaves the room.

Mr. George sets an oversized coffee cup and a dozen long-stemmed roses on his desk. "Hey, kids," he says. "I'm only here for a minute. Then I'm outie five thousand."

We smile at Mr. George's failed attempt to remain relevant in this decade. He doesn't need to try so hard, because if kindness were a style, Mr. George would be on a runway in Milan.

He slides a stool up to my computer. "So, Linden," he says, "what's hot off the presses?"

"Bea's not here," Ham interrupts. "Why is Bea not here?"

Mr. George shrugs his shoulders. "Is she ever here? Does she even still work here?"

"She was just here," I say flatly. "Maybe you should go find her, Ham." Ham welcomes the opportunity and stands.

Mr. George shakes his head. "No. Not now. Bea's not needed."

I couldn't agree more.

I punch the keys on my computer, and Mr. George says, "Linden, are you interested in covering a powerful piece for the paper? I need us to write something with meaning, value."

"Like that sexy tardiness piece," Seung says, and chuckles.

"Not exactly what I had in mind," Mr. George says. "But that was a nice piece, Linden. Not sure I'd call it sexy, though."

Seung winks at me, and my face heats up. I tap the keyboard and fight to regain some sort of focus. My mind is still preoccupied with that Seung Goes to Homecoming comment and how to ask Mr. George what he knows about the journalist lady.

"Something bigger, better, impactful," Mr. George says. "Something with a punch, a kick. Something, say, scholarship-worthy. Like a piece on underage drinking."

We all burst out laughing and Mr. George frowns. "What? What'd I say?"

"With all due respect, Mr. George," I say, "nobody wants to read about the dangers of underage drinking. Everyone drinks, especially in this town. The young, the old. There aren't many other options. Nobody at Hinderwood High cares what drinking does to the underaged body except us, of course."

Mr. George's eyes dart around the room and land on the clock, then his desk. "Well, I'm open to input," he says, standing up. "Always open to new ideas." He walks to his desk and grabs a stack of paper. "But I need you to come up with something

99

good, because I'll be submitting it." He hands me a folder.

"What's this?"

"Read and get back to me," he says. "Ideas, concepts. Something that'll leave an impression. Something you can bullet. You know how I love bullet points."

I flip open the packet and scan the paper: *Willamette University—National Scholarship for Journalism*.

Mr. George scurries to the closet behind his desk and wraps himself in his coat and scarf.

"So is this related to that journalist lady?" I ask.

Mr. George tilts his head. "Who?"

Ham reaches over my desk. "What is that?"

I fan the folder at him. "Principal Falsetto's, I mean, Principal Falls's sister was apparently asking some questions about me. Right, Ham?" I smile, basking in relief and possibility.

"Yeah," Ham says. "She was interested in what you write. I told her to talk to Mr. George."

Mr. George shakes his head. "Can't say anyone's spoken to me about you, Linden. But I'll let you know if they do."

I nod and snap the scholarship folder. "Okay, Mr. George. I'll do this. And I'll do it well. But I have one condition. If I may ask, of course?"

"Go on."

"We collaborate. Work as a team. Me, Ham, and Seung. The Triangle."

Mr. George shrugs. "That might work. Let me know what

ideas develop." He heads out the door and waves without looking.

I twist in my chair and create a new folder on the computer. I name it OH! Short for Operation Ham, or more accurately, The Triangle Goes to College Together.

Ham groans. "More work, Linden? You're signing us up for more work? You're already making me waste precious moments of my childhood studying for the SAT. Now we have to research an actual story?"

Ham's not seeing the potential benefits. He doesn't see how good I can make him look. London *Times* good.

Mr. George returns within ten seconds. "The flowers. The flowers." He frantically dashes to his desk. "My husband is going to love these."

I smile. "Thanks, Mr. George."

"Thank me by writing a good story," he says. "And for God's sake, lock the door when you leave. Someone left it open last night. If you want to be left unsupervised, then act like supervisors."

He winks and we wave good-bye. Seung slides his chair behind me. His knee bumps my butt and I shift on my seat. "Sorry," we say at the same time.

Ham breaks the clumsy silence by saying, "I have an idea for a story."

"I'm sure you do," Seung deadpans.

"Well, if you're not interested," Ham says. "Because really I'd rather not work unless paid."

"We are," I snap. "We're so interested. What's your idea?"

Seung's head falls back against the chair, and he sighs.

I close my eyes as my stomach drops. The new Seung is somewhat irresistible. He sighs more than usual, and his breath smells less like breakfast, more like toothpaste. But then, when Ham opens his mouth, my peppermint buzz dies.

"Let's write about Bea," Ham says with enthusiasm.

Seung sits up in his chair.

"Well, not Bea, exactly, but Bea's *little* problem," Ham says.

"Not the cheating crap again," I say.

"What cheating?" Seung asks.

I lift an eyebrow.

"She's cheating on Toby with Reed," Ham says.

"You're guessing," I say.

"How do you know?" Seung asks.

I drop my pen. "And why do *you* care?"

Seung squirms in his seat. "I don't care. Just curious."

"You sure about that?" I ask.

Now it's Seung's turn to lift an eyebrow. "I'm sure about a lot of things, Linden. Are you?"

Ham groans. "Why don't you two just bang and get it over with?" I swear I see Seung's eyebrows fast-dance on his forehead.

Seung pushes a button on his phone and moves his finger like his life depends on the speed of his swipe.

"We all know Bea has a little problem with boys," Ham says. "I suspect, much like the rest of you, that Toby is a girl beater, or shall I say Bea beater. Clearly it's why Bea is cheating on him with her ex. He's getting what he deserves."

"And this has to do with our story how?" I ask.

"Isn't it obvious, Linden?" Ham says. "We do a major spread on violence against women and the men behind the violence. You win scholarship money. I gain fame and fortune and status as Hinderwood High's Male Feminist of the Year. Then we all run away to college together. Boom. Mic drop."

Seung teeters back in his chair, still staring at his phone. "How could a guy ever hurt a girl?" he mumbles. He sounds so innocent and honest. "A guy hurt a girl, or a guy hurt a guy? When you're in love, you don't intentionally hurt each other. Right?"

Ham shifts in his chair, crossing and uncrossing his legs.

"Clearly it's not love," I say.

"Most definitely *not* love," Ham says.

The air's heavy with long pauses. Then Seung shakes his head and says, "I don't get it. The physical hurt. I mean, heartbreak happens. But a girl has two fists, two legs, a mouth. Why keep going back to take more shit she doesn't deserve?"

My mind wanders back to a past when *I* took more shit. Seung doesn't know anything about me or my haunted past. The history I fight to forget and rewrite. Every time my past calls, I answer. And it never says anything new. It repeats itself, over and over, until I create a new picture, paint a new scene. Seung doesn't know my mother was beaten bloody by the hands of a man. Seung doesn't understand the choices some women are forced to make. His eyes see only doting dads who kiss cheeks and rinse dishes. His ears hear only music and laughter and whispers filled with love. My eyes see blood. My ears hear screams. My nose smells death.

Seung scoots his chair next to mine. "Not to get off subject."

"Please, yes," I blurt before tears sting my eyes. "We should forget about Bea. She can help herself. She's not our job." Of course, I only believe half my words.

Seung nudges closer and whispers, "About homecoming, Linden? You going?"

My eyes fix back on the computer screen. Homecoming?

Seung taps my thigh with his knee. "Did you hear me?"

I fight the urge to rub the spot he bumped on my leg, while pictures of the limo parade through my mind.

"It might be fun," Seung says. "You know, homecoming, together."

I shift in my seat. "Together?" Like together, together?

"Yeah. We could all go together. Double-date, or something."

Screw double-date, it's the *something* I want to know more about.

"Double-date?" I ask, fighting to balance my wobbly voice.

"Something like that."

There's that *something* again. The something I want with Seung. And yet there are all the somethings I can't forget about, too.

I shake my head. "I don't think so." Immediately I'm filled with regret.

Seung's face drops. He leans back in his chair and scratches his ear.

"It's just, like, homecoming at this school is a ceremony to glorify football gods like Toby Patters and Reed Clemmings. Hard to care about. Impossible to support."

Ham plops onto a desk and kicks his feet over the seat. "Don't forget Jarrell. I mean, you are talking about football gods, yes?"

"Linden. The dance has nothing to do with football," Seung says, ignoring Ham.

"Well, I don't dance," I say, running out of excuses. Besides, I don't even know if Seung meant he wanted to take me. Double date doesn't exactly mean date.

Ham laughs. "Well, I dance."

Seung chuckles. "Yep. You sure do. We've all seen your moves." Ham jumps off the desk and spins around. "All wiggle and shake," Seung says, and twists back toward me. He whispers, "I don't dance, either, Linden," and his breath tickles my ear and inches along my collarbone.

I grab the scholarship folder Mr. George gave me and fan my face. Would it kill someone to open a window? "So," I say, "who is Seung taking to homecoming, on this double date?"

Seung smiles in slow motion and says, "Well, you're making this incredibly difficult, but I'd like to take you."

My jaw drops, even though I don't want it to. In fact, I'm

desperately trying to push out a smile, a grin, or even a smirk.
"Whatever," I say. Why am I even talking right now?

"I'm serious." Seung leans forward. His chest is practically on my forearm. "I want to take you, Linden, or you take me, or we just take each other."

I turn and stare at his chin. He lifts it up with two fingers and smiles. "Take each other?" I say, thankful for the grin that fought for my face and won.

"Yeah. That sounds bad, huh?"

Not that bad, Seung.

I swipe my tongue across my lips nervously. Then I turn back to the computer and stare at the screen. Saying yes should be easy. It's what I want.

"Come on, Linden." Seung 2.0 won't relent. "It might be fun."

He taps my thigh with his knee, once, twice. I'm losing count.

"Let's go." He slides his hand along my forearm. "Me. You. Ham. The Triangle."

I make the mistake of looking at Seung's hand, and he slips it back onto the table. There's a pink hue in his cheeks.

Ham sighs, damn loud, busting up my moment with Seung, who turns around in his chair and throws a pencil at Ham's chest. "What do you say, Hammy? Want to go to homecoming with Linden and me?"

"Uh, excuse me," I say. "I haven't exactly agreed to go."

"And *I* don't have a date," Ham says.

"Ask someone," Seung says.

"Not likely." Ham taps his fingers on his chest as if it's a piano. "I don't ask—they come to me."

"Well, I don't exactly see a line forming," Seung says. "You have to go, Ham. If you don't go, you might miss your opportunity."

"Opportunity for what?" Ham asks.

Seung smiles and reclines in his chair. He takes a deep breath and says, "Opportunity for love."

When I glance over at Seung, he catches my gaze and holds it for a million years.

It is in that moment that I agree to join the boys for homecoming.

Ham says, "I'll do anything for love," and Seung whispers, "So will I." I mean, who can resist this shit?

My two tugboats passing in the night.

With an arm twist, a bend, and one mighty yank, I concede. Our triangle is going to homecoming as an equilateral shape.

But for some reason, I can't help but feel the punch of a big mistake, deep in the pit of my gut. Can I still fly under the radar when the Friday-night lights beam?

CHAPTER EIGHT

COMMITMENT TO HOMECOMING WAS EASY. Harder for me were the fine print and footnotes tangling my life. Details demanding my attention include hair, makeup, shoes. Don't even get me started on a dress I can't afford. All things I discounted because I was busy imagining what it'd be like to dance with Seung, sink my fingers into his hair, graze my lips against his. *I'll go! I'll go!* my imagination shouted. *Pick me! Take me! Let me be someone I can't afford to be, someone I don't have time to be.*

"What's the magazine?" Seung asks, clamping his teeth around a Cheese Country cheddar-and-cucumber hoagie.

I push my back into the cushioned booth. *"Total Style!"* I flip the page, not at all embarrassed by the reading material I swiped from the library. "Apparently this homecoming thing means girls wear dresses and boys wear pants. Somebody scream sexism." I snap the glossy page.

Seung wipes mustard from his lip and says, "Homecoming is not sexist, Linden. It's all perception."

"Well, I don't see girls on football fields in jerseys and helmets. Not at Hinderwood, anyway. We are so behind the times."

"The dance?" Seung squints. "How is it sexist?"

I sigh, ready to step up to my proverbial podium. "Homecoming is a quintessential American tradition, where boys are kings in tuxes and girls are queens in satin sashes and tiaras. How is that *not* sexist?"

Seung shrugs and says, "Some girls like tiaras and satin sashes." He bites another chunk out of his sandwich and smiles.

"Well, what if a guy wants to wear a dress or a girl wants to wear a tux? At other schools, this happens. But not here. Not at Hinderwood High."

"Because *here* is the size of this." Seung makes a pinhole by pinching his fingers together. "Everywhere else"—he stretches his arms out—"is this size."

The doorbells jingle and three students walk inside, followed by a lady in a plaid pencil skirt and heels. The chilly air smacks me in the face and I zip my jacket to my neck. The lady leans against the counter and asks, "What's your special?" The guy at the register gives her a cold, flat answer. "Cheese."

I toss another cheddar-smothered fry into my mouth, happy to be sitting with Seung at Cheese Country. While I usually suggest Seung's house for lunch, today I insisted on scoops of cheese on something fried because I found another ten-dollar bill beneath my locker. I love buying Seung lunch, even though he kicks and screams like a baby boy when I push away his money. The debt I owe Seung and his family is snowballing. I need to pay them back, even if it means spending money for lunch that could be used for a homecoming dress. But Seung's worth every cent.

"If you're trying to back out of homecoming by playing a faulty sexist card," Seung says, "it won't work."

I smile and tear a chunk of bread from my grilled-cheese sandwich and throw it at Seung's face. He catches it in his mouth and quickly eyeballs his drink while his cheeks blush.

The lady from the counter passes our table, carrying her tray, and says hello to Seung, speaking to his forehead. He won't unlock his eyes from his drink. Her heels clomp and her blond curls bounce as she trots to the booth behind us. She wipes the table with napkins before sitting down, then leans in for a bite of what appears to be the chicken four-cheese wrap.

"Can I be honest about something?" I say.

Seung stirs his soda with his straw. "I'd rather you be honest than lie."

Ouch. I think about what to say, how to say it. Lying to Seung hurts my heart. The worst part about lying to those you love is that you question if they are worth the truth. If I told Seung who I am, where I'm from, where I live, would he wonder why I held the truth from him for so long? Would he think I believed he wasn't worth the truth? I've dug a hole I can't climb out of. Coming clean, telling Seung I'm homeless, rips apart everything I've worked hard to achieve. A place to live, friends to love, hope to hold on to.

When you're an orphaned teen, hope becomes stronger than fear. Hope makes you travel hundreds of miles in the back of an unlocked camper trailer with $3,000 stuffed in your backpack. Hope makes you remember the money your mother hid for you.

"In case of an emergency," she said. "In case I'm not around to take care of you," she said. "In case you need to take care of yourself."

Hope makes you work odd jobs at your grandmother's nursing home, accepting food over money. Hope strengthens you when your grandmother dies and the only shelter you find is a tin-roofed, weedy baseball dugout.

My mother told me if anything happened to her I should run, hide, fight for my life. Giving up meant giving in. For just over a year I've played this game of hiding in plain sight. If I fold now, I become a ward of the state and lose control of my life and everyone in it. When I turn eighteen, I'm home free.

The lady in the booth behind us sneezes, and Seung turns and says, "Gesundheit."

"Thank you." She smiles, her teeth shining behind matte

lips, and slips her arms into her blazer. Right away I notice the silver and blue letters.

KOIN 6. Principal Falsetto's sister, the TV journalist.

She lifts her tray from the table and sets it on a receptacle, then trots out the door, darting across the street to the parking lot and climbing into a compact white car.

"That's the news lady." I tap on the pane. "The one Kristen said was asking about me. The one who spoke to Ham."

Seung glances out the window. "Wonder why she didn't talk to you, then."

I shrug, thinking the same thing. Maybe she didn't recognize me. Maybe she doesn't know who I am.

Seung clears his throat. "You were going to be honest about something?"

My throat tightens. "Oh, yeah. I was."

Seung rubs his chin on his shoulder. "Well?"

I gulp air, several times, and begin my partial truths. "Number one. I can't afford a new dress." *True.* "Number two. I can't find a real job." *Almost true. The nursing home offers little income and there aren't enough Saturdays between now and homecoming to make money cleaning Bea's house. Real employers, unwilling to pay in cash, want a home address.* "Number three. My stepdad won't pay for shit." *False. I don't have a stepdad, but I imagine if I had one, he wouldn't pay for shit.*

Seung wiggles his straw up and down and chews the inside of his cheek like it's a steak. I mean, veggie burger. "I'm pretty sure I can help," he says, and we finally make eye contact.

During last period I fight to keep my eyes open, but the combination of a sleepless night and layers of cheddar on my Cheese Country grilled-cheese sandwich summons the sandman with open arms and closed eyes. I do the bob-and-jerk until someone pounds on the door, causing me to slam straight up in my chair, boot-camp ready. I hit my book with my arm and send it flying off my desk. It slaps the tile with a whole lot of power.

Mr. George rushes to the door. It's Principal Falsetto. She bursts into the room and says, "Please stay seated when the bell rings."

Someone shouts, "Lockdown!"

"No. No." Principal Falsetto says, palms in the air. "No lockdown."

I crane my neck but can't see through the guy's thick one in front of me. Principal Falsetto and Mr. George whisper with mouths aimed at the chalkboard, and then she walks toward the door on her tiptoes. The bell rings and Mr. George shouts a quick reminder to sit still, wait for clearance. I do the opposite.

"As head reporter of Hinderwood High, I need to know what's going on," I say when I reach Mr. George.

"Seriously, Linden? Does anything ever go on in this school, in this town?"

I shrug. "Well, what's going on?"

"Fight in the hall. Coach Jenkins is handling it."

I side-eye Mr. George, but he's telling the truth.

"Who's fighting?" I glance out the window of the door. Reed walks by with Coach Jenkins.

"Have anything you need proofed?" Mr. George says, interrupting my peeping. *Proofed* is Mr. George's code word for reviewing my stuff before it's posted to the school blog.

"Nope," I say. "Still in research mode." *Research mode* is code for I haven't done anything but plan to get right on it before Mr. George inquires again.

"Let's talk soon about the scholarship project," Mr. George says. "I'm anxious to hear your ideas."

I smile and shoot Mr. George a thumbs-up. He offers concerned father's eyes, so I barrel back to my desk before he decides to talk research.

A couple of minutes pass and Mr. George tells the class we can leave. I look around for Principal Falsetto in the hall. Now is as good a time as any to find out why her sister is speaking with my friends about me. It's probably nothing, maybe even coincidental, but when you have shit to hide like I do, loose ends must be tied up. I glance around the hall. No principal, and I don't have time to look for her.

I shoot by Seung, and he smiles and nods and stares at me for an un-Seung-like amount of time. I reciprocate the nod and grin, then beeline to my locker. It's time to go to work. Make money. Pad Linden's homecoming-dress fund.

At the front steps of the Nowhere Near Like Home nursing home, the bleach smell punches my nose, then burns my eyes. Callie, the newest nursing assistant, the one who changes bedpans and wipes asses and should earn a six-figure salary, opens the door and ushers me in. The door combination changes every couple of weeks, which is why Callie answered my knock. I ask if she will write down the new code, and she does without question. It's all about confidence when you want, or need, something. My mother taught me that.

"Hello, Ethel," I say to a wheelchaired lady wrapped in a pink jumpsuit.

Ethel waves, but I'm not convinced she remembers me.

I pass the nurses' station and tap the bell three times to wake them up.

"Linden Rose!" Eva, the head nurse, shouts. "Where have you been, little lady?"

"Here and there," I say, grinning. "Well, mainly school."

"You study hard, little girl," Eva says. "Make your grandmother proud."

Eva, my grandmother's nurse until she died, has known me since I stumbled into town last year, drenched in sweat and desperate to find the grandmother I'd piecemealed details about. I knew little about her. She and my mother weren't exactly close. She never joined us on holidays, sent birthday cards filled with cash, or popped in unannounced with an armload of homemade fudge. I didn't even know what my grandmother looked like, sounded like, when I arrived on the nursing-home steps. She could have been any puckered-lip lady perched on a paisley couch. But, for some reason, I wasn't worried about finding her. An address and a broken heart pulled me toward her. I imagined love pushing me, steering me, guiding me, toward the one person on earth who could fill the void I felt from losing my mom. I didn't need to know my grandmother to love her. She'd given birth to the woman I adored. She was the only family I had left. Now she's gone, too.

"Thought I'd see if anyone would like me to read to them," I say to Eva as I round the corner of the nursing desk. She signals my clearance with a wave.

The first room I hit is Mr. Wallace's. He's a fighter. Well, he and Mr. James, another resident. Mr. Wallace and Mr. James like to argue over saltshakers at lunch, couch cushions near the piano, and nurses who give the best back rubs. Mr. Wallace thinks one of the nurses is his reincarnated wife. I'll never judge.

I peek around the corner to make sure Mr. Wallace is alone, and clothed. He's sitting on the edge of his bed, rocking and humming.

"Hello, Mr. Wallace!" I shout. "Remember me? Linden Rose?"

"Honey, come in. Hand me that channel changer." I do as I'm told.

Mr. Wallace hits mute and I ask him if he wants me to read to him tonight. He shouts, "No!" Not mean, but in a hard-to-hear-you-and-I-refuse-to-wear-my-hearing-aids way. "I don't listen, I watch!"

"No problem, Mr. Wallace." I pat his shoulder and shout, "I'll catch you next time!"

The next room belongs to Peggy. She's a talker.

"Hello?" I knock on the doorjamb. "Miss Peggy? It's me, Linden Rose."

"Linden, dear, come in. Hurry, now—you'll let in a draft."

I shut the door behind me and ask Miss Peggy if she would like a magazine story read. She chuckles but agrees to let me read a new book she said one of the aides left behind last week. She's whispering and I'm whispering back, and I don't know exactly why she's shushing me until I see the cover of the book. *Fifty Shades of Grey*. Nice work, Miss Peggy. But I will *not* be reading it to my elders.

"You have to be eighteen to read this book," I lie, "so you'll have to find someone else."

Miss Peggy huffs, but she slips me two dollars on my way out and says it's prepayment for next week. Then she winks, twice. I remind her that I won't be eighteen next week, either, and shudder after I close the door. Again, no judgment toward Miss Peggy, but I don't think I can stomach reading that book to someone's great-grandmother.

The last room on the right is oversized compared to the single units. The room belongs to Margaret. Maggie is what her husband called her. He died a few months ago. Cancer. He lived in here, too, but they've since removed his bed.

"Miss Margaret," I say, and she turns around from the window. She clutches a photo in her hand.

"Linden. Sweetie. Come in."

"How are you doing?"

"Today's been tough."

She places the framed wedding picture on the bed and reaches for my hands. "You miss him, huh?" I say.

"You have no idea how much."

I walk to the portable CD player perched on a stand. "Do you mind?" She smiles and nods. I pick up another picture of her husband. He's twenty and hot in a wiry-rock-star sort of way. I push play. The music is cued where I stopped it last time. I slide the picture frame into Margaret's wrinkled hands, and she eases into her chair.

I kneel beside her chair and rock her back and forth with my hand since she is too weak to push her feet against the carpet and too focused on hearing her husband sing on the rerecorded CD. He was in a band when they met. She says she was a groupie. But they fell in love and it worked, and the magic lasted decades.

I hate thinking about her loss.

I fight the tears. Margaret's eyes and cheeks are damp. She sings along with gentle breaths and quick blinks. She knows every word, every note, every pause.

Three songs are her limit.

When she nods, I hit the player and cue it up for next time, then wait a minute before saying good-bye. Her eyes are closed tight and she's pinching the bridge of her nose.

I bend over her rocking chair and whisper, "Good-bye,

Maggie," beside her ear. A smile spreads across her face.

I tiptoe to the door to leave Margaret with memories of her husband, and she says, "Linden, dear. Go fetch my purse."

I wave my hands. "Oh, no, Miss Margaret. You don't need to."

She swats the air. "Of course I don't need to, dear. But there's a difference between need and want."

I shake my head. That's not why I'm here, in her room, helping her hear her husband's voice.

"Linden, please."

"But . . ."

"But nothing. I need my purse before you leave."

I hand her the bag and she holds up twenty bucks. I promise myself not to spend it on anything un-love-worthy.

CHAPTER NINE

"DO YOU FIND THE THEME for homecoming—how shall I say this?—racist?" Ham slams his notebook shut and falls back on the couch. He flicks a piece of popcorn onto the coffee table, pinches it between his fingers, and tosses it into his mouth.

I side-eye Seung. He's running his finger over a list of vocabulary words, pausing at each one, and whispering to himself. For the last seven days we've been prepping for the SAT. It's one of my better ideas lately, because (1) we need good scores if the Triangle wants to attend college together, (2) our study sessions keep me occupied after school, so I can (a) procrastinate on the story Mr. George insists I write, and (b) spend time with the guys, with Seung.

Added bonus includes hanging in a heated house five to six

nights a week. The schedule is well ironed now because I've made it back into the school every night this week to sleep in the theater room covered in velvet curtains. If it weren't for the occasional knocking of pipes in the night, I'd say I'm living in luxury.

"Racist?" Seung asks, glancing up from the word list.

Ham drops his voice a couple of octaves and says, "'Whispers of the Orient.' You're the one who said, 'Oriental is for rugs, not people, Ham, you fucking douchebag.'"

Seung Frisbee-throws a couch pillow at Ham's face. It's standard SAT-prep. Same bickering, same pillow tosses—different night.

"So, Linden," Seung says. "Did you get your homecoming dress or tux?"

I rattle off reasons for my lack of formal wear, and that I'm planning to refuse said dress because of my opposition to sexist conformance. Basically, I'm rambling about the right to choose between dresses and pants, when someone knocks on the basement door.

"What?" Seung shouts. Ham and I jump.

Mrs. Rhee peeks around the wall. "Sorry to interrupt, but you'll be glad I did."

The smell of fresh baked goods filters through the basement, which knows Mrs. Rhee's baking all too well. I'm hit by the goodness that is Toll House chocolate-chip cookies. Homemade by the hands of a mother.

Ham hops to his feet and snatches the plate from Seung's

mom. "Mrs. Rhee. If you weren't a married woman, or if Mr. Rhee couldn't kick my ass, or if I were of legal age, or if I were into older—"

Seung whacks the back of Ham's head with another pillow.

Mrs. Rhee glances over at me, ignoring the boys. "Linden? Seung tells me you might not have a dress for homecoming."

My cheeks turn to fire. I force myself not to look at Seung, but of course I do. He's licking chocolate off his thumb, avoiding eye contact. "No, ma'am," I say. "Not yet."

Mrs. Rhee smiles. "I have one that might fit you. It belongs to Seung's cousin and is only a year old. She wore it to spring formal, I think."

"Oh no, Mrs. Rhee. I plan to buy an outfit as soon as I scrape up more cash."

Mrs. Rhee studies my face. She smiles and the edges of her eyes scrunch together like Seung's do when he laughs. Her head tilts to one side. "Sure, honey. I understand. Why would you want to wear last year's fashion?"

She's wrong. I don't give two shits about last year's style. I would wear last decade's fashion if it weren't for the fortress I insist on building around me. The wall I would smash apart if it promised me a mother like Mrs. Rhee, a family like Seung's.

"You could check it out," Seung says, still sucking chocolate off his thumb. "You might like it. Then you could use your money for something else. Something you need."

Seung smiles, and there's that tickle in my stomach I've tried to push aside all week. Ever since Seung said he'd rather

I be honest than lie. Ever since he asked me to homecoming.

I glance over my shoulder at Mrs. Rhee. She's collecting our used glasses and soda cans, still wearing her scrubs from the hospital. "Thanks, Mrs. Rhee. I'd love to see the dress. Maybe even try it on." And the smiles between Mrs. Rhee and Seung are worth caving to my make-believe sexism, at least for one night.

When we finish studying, I've already consumed six chocolate chip cookies and pocketed three more for breakfast. Seung suggests we watch *The Sopranos*, Season One.

"Hell, no," Ham says. "Seen it four times four."

"You have better ideas?" Seung asks.

"Something with action. *Scarface*-ish," Ham says. "'Say hello to my little—'"

"No. No." I wave my arms. "Enough. I don't want to hear you or your terrible Tony Montana accent."

Ham winces and shows signs that he's a wee bit hurt. "Geez, Linden," he says. "What's up your ass?"

Between Seung and me, Ham is taking a beating. Lately I find myself wishing Ham weren't here with us. Wishing Seung and I could study alone.

Ham's fake accents, bad jokes, and movie requests, stuff that used to be the most adorable things on earth, only annoy me when Seung is near. Ham's getting the hint, too, because he's left early the last two nights. Even walked home once, and we all know Ham doesn't walk when there's a perfectly operational Volvo in the drive.

"Sorry, Ham." And I am. Guilt yanks at my heart for my aggravation and annoyance. Ham deserves better from his friend, from me.

"Whatever." Ham kicks the couch. "I guess I won't tell you what I'm planning for homecoming, then."

I force myself to look eager and interested. Seung yawns.

Ham continues. "Aside from the fact that I could quite possibly have a date, I'm planning something big, huge, un-fucking-real."

"A date?" Seung and I snap in unison.

Ham groans. "Yeah, yeah. I said *possibly*."

"Who?" we snap. Seung and I are in literal jinx mode.

"Nope," Ham says, finger in the air. "Not going to jinx it."

We groan.

"Didn't you hear me say I was planning something big?" Ham says. "Linden, you'll appreciate it. A way to finally get revenge on Toby Patters."

"Who cares?" Seung says. "Who are you going to ask to homecoming?"

"Ask?" Ham says. "I told you. I don't ask. They come to me."

Seung throws a pillow at the ceiling. "You're full of shit."

Ham chuckles. "I need to get home." He snaps his finger twice. "Get your asses off the couch and take me."

Seung and I spring to our feet, ready to break free of our tricycle's squeaky third wheel. Ham stuffs handfuls of cookies into his pocket for the mile ride home, and as I slide my notebooks into my bag, a can of Beanie Weenees rolls out, and I quickly kick it back into my backpack and zip.

"You're not coming back?" Seung asks, eyes wide.

"Oh. No. I mean, I thought you would just drop me at the trailer-park entrance after you drop Ham off." I glance out the window trying to gauge what time it is. "It's getting late, isn't it?"

I refuse to click my phone to check the clock. I don't want Seung to answer me. I'm tired of being bound by hours, minutes. Tonight I want to tend to wants, not needs.

I lead us up the basement stairs, and Seung leans over my shoulder and whispers, "Maybe we could drive around, or something. Slushies and Triangle Park?" I smell the sugar and chocolate on his breath and shut my eyes as my stomach executes cartwheels.

We drop Ham off in his driveway and he sprints up the stairs to his house, grabs onto a column, and hooks his leg. He spins like a larger-than-life pole dancer. It's adorable, really, until he shouts, "Shape the fuck up or my friendship's moving elsewhere!"

Seung chokes out a contagious laugh. "He's such a jack-ass."

"Yeah," I say. *And I do really love that jackass. But point taken. We need to be nicer to Ham.*

We drive in silence until we hit the two-lane highway taking us toward town. "Slushies?" Seung asks.

I worry about the lack of money in my pocket and the

debt I'm about to incur from the dress. "Just the park," I say. "Slushies another night."

The drive to Triangle Park takes longer than it should. No matter how hard I try, my words won't build coherent sentences or budge beyond my lips. Maybe I'm tired, hungry, preoccupied with the scholarship article and SAT. My future, our future, supposedly hinging on pieces of paper. Maybe I've hit the stage when you feel awkward around your best friend because you want him to be more than a best friend.

The car crunches gravel in the parking lot, and with two of the three streetlights burned out, the park looks abandoned. The engine idles and Seung stares at the steering wheel, until he finally says, "Sorry about the dress, Linden."

"You don't need to be."

"My mom."

"Yeah." I smile. "Your mom."

"I mentioned you might need a dress and she jumped at the chance to find you one. I wanted to tell you earlier, but—" Seung rubs the back of his neck. "If you hate it, you don't have to wear it. We could find a nice pantsuit or tux."

I laugh. "Thanks. But I'm sure I'll love the dress."

"We're still going to homecoming, together, right?" And the way he enunciates *to-geth-er* makes my legs prickle.

"One big, happy Ham sandwich," I say.

I open the car door and climb out. We walk toward the swings. I don't know what it is about tonight, but everything feels lighter, less cramped. The clouds making room for the stars, the stars performing the streetlights' job. I hold my feet into the air and let the swing move how it wants, without force.

We swing for five minutes, maybe longer, in silence, before I ruin the moment.

"So who do you think Ham's taking to homecoming?"

"Himself."

"Seriously. I think he's for real."

"Hope so," Seung says. "Then maybe he'll leave us alone for two minutes."

Seung pumps his legs, inching higher and higher with each swing.

He wants to be alone with me. Here, and on homecoming night.

I want to be with him, too, but without limits and lies. Without worries that I won't make it back to school in time to sleep inside, without looking over my shoulder every time a can of beans or Baggie of bread spills from my backpack. Seung drags his feet in the dirt to slow his swing. I imagine him jumping off, grabbing me, and lifting me out of the seat. I'm not sure I can wait until homecoming to kiss him. I'm not sure I can wait another minute.

Seung's swing jerks to the side. "There's something I need to tell you," he says.

I swallow hard. Maybe Seung can't wait another minute, either.

He exhales and I freeze. Should I close my eyes? Wait for the kiss? "My dad wants me to go to college on the other side of the country," he says.

"Oh." I sigh, trying to prevent my voice from sounding disappointed. I clear my throat. "Yeah. Ham told me."

Seung bites his lip. "Linden, I don't want to go. I want to be with you. I mean, I want us to go to college together." He digs his heel into the dirt and rocks back and forth.

"So tell your dad."

Seung scoffs. "I'm not independent like you."

I laugh. "I wouldn't exactly say I'm independent." I depend on more than Seung realizes.

"You rely on yourself," he says. "I rely on my parents. You're the lucky one."

I drag my heel across the dirt and stop swinging. "Me? Lucky?" My words tumble out more harshly than planned.

Seung senses something's wrong and backtracks. "Not what I meant."

My cheeks go hot as I stand and grab the chains, twisting Seung's swing directly in front of me.

"What do you mean, then, exactly?" I ask. "Because the last time I checked, luck is made. Earned. It's not something you get by wishing on a star or blowing out a candle."

Seung chews on his lip, all jittery, jumpy, and stressed.

"I'm sorry, Linden." His voice is soft, practically a whisper. "I mean, you choose what's best for *you*. You always do."

I draw deep breaths and shake my head. I want to tell Seung the truth. That he's wrong. Every choice I make in my life depends on the one I made before. I want to tell him my choices aren't always my own, even when they seem to be.

"You have a stepdad who's practically absent from your life," he says. "No one forces your decisions or makes sure you're on the right track. Their track."

No, Seung. I'm driven by a past I never want visiting my future. A past that made me who I am today, at this moment. A past I fight and claw to prevent from swallowing my future in one big gulp of slush.

Seung's the lucky one. Two parents who look at each other with love in their eyes. Two parents who can't keep their hands to themselves when they're close to each other. Two parents who conceived him in love, not power or control.

Seung squeezes his legs around me and pulls me forward. He reaches for my hand and I reluctantly let him take it.

"I'm sorry," he says, and his face relaxes except for a residual twitch in his lip. For a second I think he's going to kiss me, but instead he closes his eyes and sighs. "I really am sorry, Linden. I should have told you a while ago. About my dad, about college. I guess I kind of lied to you. I hope you're not mad."

Seung reaches for my other hand, and I realize he never let the first one go. He pulls me toward him and I slip my legs over the swing and sit on his lap. I want to stay like this all night. My legs wrapped around him, holding hands, and staring at each other's faces without looking away. Seung's voice is soft, and the way he breathes when he talks is like commas taking their rightful places in the spaces between our words.

But as soon as I start to soften, my hard fortress walls shoot up and surround me with my lies. They buzz inside my head, bounce from ear to ear. I'm the one withholding truth. I'm the one afraid to let my best friend in.

I'm blocked by lies, preventing access. To me.

I slip out of Seung's arms and slide off the swing, then march toward Gold Nugget without a word. I can't deal with Seung right now. I want him close, and I know he wants to be there, too. But how close can anyone ever be to me?

When I reach for the door handle to signal it's time to leave, take me home, the car beep-beeps. "Unlock it!" I yell.

Seung sits on the swing in the same place I left him, mouth open, one hand on the chain, the other in the what-the-hell-Linden position. "Not until you explain what just happened!" he shouts. "Would really love an explanation!"

I fold my arms and lean against the car.

Seung is whistling now, looking at me, then looking away. If only I could do what I want. Jog back over to him, climb on the swing, grab his face, and say I'm sorry, too. Tell him all the things I've kept hidden, show him who I really am. All I want is to kiss him and let him kiss me back. Instead, I stand here, pouting, aching inside to let my guard down.

"Please open the door!" I shout.

"Not a chance!" Seung shouts back. "Not until you explain yourself."

An engine roars on the highway and I whip my head toward the road. Oversized headlights illuminate Gold Nugget. I focus on the gleam and pray the truck will pass, but it corners the entrance and skids in the rocks.

My night careens out of control.

The truck pulls up beside me, and Toby kills the engine. His electric-guitar-infused country-rock whines as I shift to my side and cling to Gold Nugget's locked door handle. I wiggle and jerk, fighting to break in.

Seung surfaces beneath the spotlight of high beams, and I shoot telepathic messages insisting he open the damn door, but he's now a statue.

Toby swings the driver's-side door open and jumps off the running board. A girl yells, "Hey! Isn't that—" from inside the cab.

He flips around and snaps, "What the hell are *you* looking at, Trailer Trash Bitch?" My eyes are fixed on the car door, not him. His breath tainted with beer, all sour, overripe.

I wish that my mother had been right when she told me to shut my eyes so no one could see me, because now is a perfect time to be invisible.

I glance at Seung. He's standing now, staring in my direction, shining bright in the headlights that Toby, I mean Asswipe, forgot to shut off.

"What's wrong, T.T.B.? Didn't hear me?"

I take a step, Toby's chest inches from my face. "I heard you. Just can't quite put a finger on what I'm looking at."

Toby scowls and puffs his pecs in my face. He thinks that because he requires more space than the rest of us, he can wreck his way around. He's a human demolition-derby car, pushing and smashing and crashing his way through a crowd. He hates Ham for no reason, Seung because he's Seung, and me and Bea because . . . he sees us as weak?

I squint as anger washes over me, and I jab my finger into Toby's meaty chest. "If I focus my eyes like this, it would appear that I'm staring at an oversized Asswipe." I tap my finger to the rhythm of my words. "Yeah. Definitely. An. Ass. Wipe."

Toby narrows his eyes and meets me toe to toe. The truck door swings wide and Bea and Beth spill out, followed by another whiff of barley.

Bea says something about That Asian Guy, and the wrench twists in my gut, walls crumble. Words leap from my tongue before I can cage them.

"Seung," I snap. "His name is Seung. Not *that* guy. Not *that Asian* guy. Just Seung. The hottest fucking guy in school."

I'm spitting on Toby's face because he refuses to move from my space. I flip around in haste, and my hip drives deep into the only soft spot on his body. I shudder times a thousand.

"Oh, that's what you want, Trailer Trash Bitch. That figures. That's what every girl wants." Toby raises his chin and laughs at the sky. I cringe.

I don't see Seung standing next to me or feel his hand on my shoulder. All I see is the blurred image of my fingers lifting in the air, forming a half-cocked fist, and slap-punching Toby's cheek, jaw, nose, and tobacco-packed lips. "That's for trying to kill my friend," I shout. "Nobody tries to kill my friends!"

I whirl and slam into Seung. He mumbles, "For God's sake, Linden," and pushes me behind him all protective-like, stepping up for his time at the plate.

"Oh, no," Toby says. "I'm not fighting you. I want your girl-friend."

I flip back around. "Oh, yes," I say. "You're not fighting him. You're fighting his girlfriend."

Seung lifts his fists, ready to defend me and get his ass handed to him, when Bea and Beth circle around, begging Toby not to fight. "He didn't do anything," Bea says, tugging on Asswipe's arm.

"She did." Toby points at my face.

"That's right," I say, my head bobbing as I stomp forward. "I did."

Seung whips around and shoots me a look that says, *Now wouldn't exactly be the best time to open your mouth.*

I glare at Toby, who is now pretzled in Bea's arms. She rubs his face, causing my stomach to ache, and I swear I see my knuckle-printed iron-on festooning his cheek.

A whine comes from the road, single light shining. I know immediately who it is, and apparently so does Bea. "Shit," she hisses. "Reed. We need to go." And the way she insists is so sad and desperate. I want to shout, *Bea! Stop! Quit rubbing his face and stand up for yourself.*

Seung signals to Gold Nugget with his thumb. "Linden. Please. Get in the car."

I kick at the ground and shuffle to the other side of the Volvo and climb in. I don't need Seung rescuing me from Toby. My handprint on his cheek attests to my strength, or maybe my weakness.

"Get your girlfriend out of here!" Toby shouts.

Seung's face twists. He says, "She's not really, exactly, totally my girl—" He stops talking when Bea's smile meets his eyes.

Reed climbs off his bike, looks over at me in the car, and mouths, "Hi." Then Seung says something to Reed. The two shake hands, bump fists.

Toby moves toward me, still sitting in the car like the distressed damsel I'm not, and points. He holds his finger in the air for an exaggerated length of time and the blood sizzles in my face. I'm breathing through my nostrils, reaching my boiling point. My hand is on the handle, ready to jump, although I'm not exactly sure what I'd do if and when I exit the car, but this anger bubbles in my stomach, ready to burst. Reed reaches for Toby's arm and Toby pushes his hand away. They exchange words and Toby snarls.

Bea and Beth jump into the cab of the truck and slam the door. I tighten my fingers on the handle in case I need to hop out and save Seung's life, but Toby turns and walks toward Gold Nugget. He grabs his crotch and says, "Maybe you can enjoy this some other time."

My heart races. Unable to sit still any longer. Not when Toby *propositions* me. Not when he assumes every female wants him. Not when he's hurting Bea. How can I do nothing? So I don't. I attack.

Not Toby, but the ground. I launch from the car and reach into the dirt. I pick up a pile of earth. Gravel, dirt, dog shit. I don't care, as long as it's a handful. I sling it at Toby's face, right there in front of Seung and Reed. Then I fly back into the car and lock the doors.

Toby slaps both palms against the window, and I push the button twice to make sure the door's locked. He pounds the glass once with his fist and pierces me with his eyes. I can't help but notice the handprint outlined in red on his cheek.

The sight of his face makes me laugh, almost hysterically. His eyes squint and he pounds the glass like a monkey beating plexiglass at the zoo. I can't resist laughing. I mean, I try. I really do. Until Bea climbs out of the truck and stands next to Seung. She reaches for his arm and squeezes and suddenly looks the most relaxed I've seen her.

I glare at Toby, then slap the glass and shout, "How does it feel to get hit by a girl?"

Bea whips around and stares. Her relaxed look replaced with fear.

Reed strolls over to my window and shouts, "What did you just say?" His face is like stone, solid and firm.

I shake my head and shrug my shoulders, my palm still spread against the glass. Reed flattens his hand against the window to shadow mine, and I feel the heat. His eyes stare deep, focusing, centering me in his cross hairs. My hand slips

135

and falls onto my lap. Reed grins and begins another Jack Kerouacian rant, "A pain stabbed my heart, as it did every time I saw a girl I loved who was going the opposite direction in this too-big world."

Toby pounds Gold Nugget's hood, interrupting Reed, and shouts at Bea. "Get in the truck!" She obeys him. She always fucking does.

Toby climbs into the cab of his truck and points in my direction. I want to say something about eating dirt and dying, but instead I slither my hand toward the door handle and triple-check the lock.

Reed marches to a picnic table and climbs on top. He starts regurgitating *The Dharma Bums* and Seung stands still, waiting for Toby to put the truck into reverse. Bea stares at Seung through the window while Toby flaps his lips, yapping something at Bea, but she's not listening. She's busy looking at Seung and he's smiling at the truck and kicking at the dirt.

I pound the windshield three times to remind Seung I'm here, waiting, ready to go, and he glares for three-point-forever seconds before stomping toward the car. He jerks the driver's-side handle and it snaps back. Oops. I hit the button to unlock the door.

Seung climbs into the car without a word. He turns the key and checks his mirrors three times before backing out. I glance at him twice but he doesn't look back, so I accentuate a sigh. Clearly he's ignoring me. It takes three head slams against the seat to finally trigger a scoff.

"What? What'd I do?"

Seung shakes his head. I tap my fingers on my knee and try again. "Aren't you sick of him always pushing you around? Pushing everyone around?"

"I can take care of myself, Linden."

"He tried to run you over. Kill you. Remember?"

"You threw dirt in his face. What are you, five?"

"I think he beats Bea."

"So this has nothing to do with me?"

"I'm sending him a message."

"What message?"

"Don't mess with my friends."

"And Bea's your friend?"

"Yeah . . . no. . . . Well, I was mainly talking about you."

"You should have walked away, Linden." He pauses. "But I guess the best way to destroy your enemy is to make them a friend."

"That's original," I say, folding my arms and slamming my back against the seat.

"Not really," Seung says. "Abe Lincoln said that, or maybe it was Al Pacino in *The Godfather*."

I roll my eyes. "So now you're friends with Toby Patters? Or maybe just Bea. She looked real cozy standing next to you."

"I don't need you to fight for me, Linden."

"And I don't need *you* to fight for me."

Seung punches the brake at the stop sign and I jerk forward.

He turns sideways, his face wrapped in concern. "What are you fighting for, Linden?"

If he only knew. Some days I fight for dignity; other times, self-respect. I shrug my shoulders and lean my head against the glass. I'm tired of this fight. Unwanted attention is wearing me down.

Seung stares straight ahead. I swear I see a tear in his eye, but it could be the one I'm looking through. I bat it away before more show up.

The blinker clicks and Seung turns onto his street.

"I can't come over," I say. "I'm already late."

"I'm not taking you home," he mumbles. "I'm taking me home. Sorry, Linden, but I've had enough of you tonight. You'll survive."

I fight back the tears. *Yeah, Seung, I'll survive. I always do.*

I climb out of the car and march down the road. I shouldn't expect him to drive me to my fake home entrance, but I do. I shouldn't expect him to say he'll see me tomorrow or thank me for looking out for him, but I do. Don't friends do those things for each other?

My stomp becomes a jog as I try to remember what exactly I am fighting for. My friends. My future. Friends who are my future. Friends who've become family.

When I first arrived in this town, I had a clear mission. Do whatever it takes to survive. This meant making friends with people I thought could help me. Of course, they didn't know they were helping me. It wasn't like I could shout out my

138

circumstances. Hey, my mother was murdered by a guy who came knocking on our door once a month for money, or sex, or possibly both. A guy I should have protected her from, but I was too busy hiding in the closet with buds in my ears, doing what I was told and pretending to be invisible.

In the distance, headlights bounce off the sidewalk and tree trunks. I turn around and wrap my forearm around my eyes. The gold shimmer refracts off a porch light. I smile on the inside, purse my lips, and march like I'm still pissed off, not done fighting. In other words, like a big damn baby.

Seung pulls up beside me and the window lowers halfway. "I need to ask you one question before I go home," he says.

I stomp to the tempo of my own stubbornness, occasionally glancing over when Seung calls my name.

"Linden," Seung says on repeat as the car creeps beside me. "Linden. One question. No. Make that two."

More stomping. More *Linden, please stop.*

I finally slap both hands on the window and snap, "What?"

Seung's face softens. "You referred to yourself as my girl-friend? And I'm the hottest fucking guy in school?"

CHAPTER TEN

"ONE MORE QUESTION AND I could quite possibly die," Ham says, doubled over with one hand on his heart, the other on his brow.

"You need stamina, Ham," I say. "Keep studying. We're going to miss three days of SAT prep thanks to homecoming."

"If it takes you three days to get ready for a dance, Linden, you're not the girl I thought you were." Ham sinks his teeth into a popcorn ball stuffed with candy corn and chocolate chips. Mrs. Rhee's newest creation of food art.

I pick at the sticky mass of popcorn and pretend to ignore Seung's eyes, all over me. He's been staring so much, so often, since the girlfriend comment, since I declared him the hottest guy in school. Seung's organizing puzzle pieces in his mind, determining the fit, wondering why they don't quite link together the way they should. I mean, friends becoming more than friends. Does that actually work? Seung's organizing a puzzle, struggling to fit a piece of the sky into the ocean because they're both blue and look like they belong together. He wants them to fit, but he's unsure I feel the same. I haven't exactly been clear with my feelings. One minute I want to let Seung wrap his arms around me, the next I'm stomping down the street, baffled and scared. How does a homeless girl date a guy who doesn't know she's homeless? And if I come clean now, will he hate me forever?

I look up, trying to meet his eyes, but he whips his head toward the wall. We continue this cat-and-mouse game most of the night.

Seung's not the only confused person in this relationship. My identity crisis caused me to spend five dollars buying lotion and lip gloss at the Four-Quarter Store. I chose makeup over food. I repeat, makeup over food. I'm uncertain who I am anymore.

"My parents want pictures of us dressed to the nines," Ham says, a piece of popcorn dangling from his upper lip.

"My mom wants us to meet here," Seung says. "She wants pictures, too."

"Yeah, yeah, well, I have a date," Ham says, all matter-of-factly. "So you'll need to meet at my house."

Seung and I lock eyes. Finally.

"Who?" we snap.

"Did I say date?" Ham backpedals, shaking his head. "Not what I meant. I meant Jarrell. He's meeting us for dinner, then heading back to school for the game."

Seung chuckles. "So your date plans never formed, huh?"

"No, Seung," Ham snaps, and falls over on the side of the couch, groaning and covering his head with a pillow.

"Well, I was thinking," I say nervously, "couldn't we get ready here? Your parents take pictures before we go to Ham's house for the same song and dance."

"Sounds like a huge hassle to me," Ham says, his voice muffled beneath the pillow.

Seung bounces his foot on his knee. "Linden?" he asks. "Are you worried about your stepdad?"

I immediately see the open window and leap. "Yes!" I slap my lap with both hands. "Totally worried. He blocks all my plans. He's always in my way, complicating everything." Which is not entirely false, if my stepdad were a metaphor for my life.

Primping in a mildew-infested locker room surrounded by gray light is not how I imagined homecoming night. Although I never thought I'd care about a dance as much as I care about this one. Details drop into my mind like bombs. How do I curl my hair when I don't own a curling iron? How do I make my eyes pop with liquid liner when I can't afford eye makeup? How do I shave my legs when my razor blade's over a year old? I have to solve these mammoth problems just to feel normal, just to fit in.

"We should ask Kristen to join us."

Seung's face scrunches and Ham lifts the pillow from his face and shouts, "Kristen? Why?"

"I think it'd be nice to have another girl around. Maybe you'll end up with a date after all, Hammy." Plus, I need help with my makeup, my hair.

Ham laughs. "Date Kristen? No way. No thanks."

Mrs. Rhee taps the door and pokes her head around the corner.

"What?" Seung snaps, and we all jump.

"You've got to stop doing that," I say.

Seung leans back and tucks his arms sexily behind his head. He pauses, whispers, "Sorry," then winks. "Bad habit."

I toss a pillow at his face and he catches it, wraps it in his arms, and squeezes it to his chest. He smiles and I smile back. Puzzle piece securely locked in place. We're fitting together.

Mrs. Rhee trots over to the ottoman and sits. "How's the studying going?" she asks as she yanks her front bangs from her ponytail and masters another work of art—the side braid. Her fingers flicker like butterfly wings.

"Good, Mom," Seung says. "But homecoming's taking precedence."

Mrs. Rhee smiles at me. I smile, then zoom in on the popcorn casing stuck on Ham's lip.

Seung shifts in his chair and clears his throat like he's ready to say something, but Mrs. Rhee interrupts. "Anything new happening at school?"

"Same shit," Ham says, "I mean, same crap, different day. Sorry, Mrs. Rhee."

Mrs. Rhee nods like a mother who's okay with her kid swearing once in a while.

"Linden's working on a big story for Mr. George and the school blog," Seung says.

Mrs. Rhee perks up. "Seung's shown me your pieces, Linden, and they are wonderful. You're a good writer."

Now it's my turn to shift in my chair and clear my throat. "Well, I'm not exactly working on a big story, yet. Still in research mode."

"What's the topic?" she asks.

"Oh. Well. I'm still unsure if I've actually committed to the project. What were we talking about, Ham?"

Ham stares at me blank-faced. Two pieces of popcorn remain fixed to his bottom lip. "I have no idea what you're talking about, Linden."

I huff. "*We* were thinking of doing an article on gender-based violence. Ham's helping me." I wink at Ham. "It's a scholarship piece."

Ham snaps his fingers. "Oh, yeah! That's what we're doing. Research on gender violence."

"Heavy stuff," Mrs. Rhee says.

"Seung's helping, too," I say. "It's a group project."

Seung shrugs, and Mrs. Rhee walks beside him and drapes her arms over his shoulders. "That's my boy." She kisses his cheek.

Seung flings himself back against the chair and groans, but his rosy cheekbones display nothing but love for his mom.

I don't remember shying from my mother's kisses. Ever. When she tucked my hair behind my ear and pecked at my cheek with her beaky nose. She'd nuzzle a path from my cheekbone to the bump above my nostrils, then drop a kiss on the tip and swaddle me with both arms. She'd say, "You're going to do something, be someone, make something of your life." When I was younger, I'd just stare at her with owl eyes, but when I got older, I'd squeeze her back and say, "We are, Mama. Both of us."

Mrs. Rhee continues chatting about the paper I'm supposed to create for Mr. George, like I'm writing it, doing it, making strides and pages come alive. But I'm stuck on inspiration. Where it's supposed to come from? Ham thinks it's Bea. And maybe it should be. But if this were true, and it's not, my mind wouldn't go blank every time I tried to craft the words.

"So homecoming plans are brewing?" Mrs. Rhee asks, and I snap back into the middle of the change in conversation.

Seung clears his throat again. "Can Linden get ready over here?"

Cue the flushed face.

"Of course," Mrs. Rhee says. "Why don't all of you get ready here?"

Ham kicks at the carpet. "Can't. My parents invited relatives to dinner and expect me to be home. Besides, Jarrell's

145

coming over, too, so you guys can pick me up. I'll be the white guy stuffed in a tux looking like pre-diet Jonah Hill."

The week crawls toward Friday. Classes move in slow motion.

My sleep is broken with dreams of Seung, followed by nightmares starring Bea and my mother. All this talk of violence churns up my past. Every night I shut my eyes and watch Bea run while I chase her—or am I running away, too? Once in a while my mom joins us, but she's always behind me calling for me to slow down. I never do. Then Seung shows up to rescue Bea. But never me . . .

Today the only thing keeping me awake in class is Toby Patters. Ever since I smacked his cheek at the park, I'm fixed in his crosshairs. He seems to be watching me in the halls, tracking my whereabouts. Every time he passes my locker, he scratches his crotch—and I make the mistake of looking down, then wish for a scalding shower. I'm not proud of the slap, but I'm not sorry, either. If he's hitting a girl, then maybe his antidote is to be clobbered by one.

The buzzer rings and I run to the newsroom to steal a nap in my safe place, away from anyone with eyes. With homecoming, work in the newsroom has mushroomed, but since I've slammed the brakes on the scholarship story due to lack of inspiration, I have nothing but time.

I open the homecoming folder and add captions to photos that need to be uploaded. Hinderwood High is ravenous for homecoming buzz.

Tuesday was Pajama Day, which I refused to participate in because pajamas do not exist in my wardrobe. When you sleep in the same clothes you wear to school, every day is Pajama Day.

I click through thirty pictures Ham snapped of Bea and Beth wearing matching silk cotton-candy-colored robes. I stop on a photo of Reed looking like he borrowed a robe from either King Arthur or Hugh Hefner. I zoom and stare at the frown on his face. Apparently Reed chose Pajama Day as his moment to suffer from an existential crisis. He should be the happiest guy on earth with Bea and Beth hooked to either arm. He's picture-perfect for his arrival at the Playboy Mansion, but a closer view of his face makes it look more like the gates of hell.

I push delete. Homecoming's supposed to be happy.

Wednesday was Eighties Day. Halls filled with students in hair-sprayed bangs and rubber jewelry in neon colors. Everyone in school took part except me. I barely have money for everyday clothes, let alone things I'd only wear once.

On Eighties Day, Ham wore gold, rust, and purple pants that fit tight at the ankles and wide at the hips. He claimed they accentuated his hourglass figure, but in actuality it was the breakdance attempt outside Mr. Dique's room that accentuated his everything. He gathered quite a clapping crowd. Typical Ham.

Thursday was Thursday U, where everyone wore college favorites. This was the day I showed school spirit and wore my prized possession. A Willamette University hoodie. The sweatshirt that wraps me in my goals, warmth, and possibility. I also wore the hoodie on Pajama Day and Eighties Day, but on Thursday I finally blended in with everyone else.

Today is Friday. Homecoming. School Spirit Day.

The halls burst with purple and gold, which is royal and regal and shitty on the eyes. No one matches, yet everyone fits in. Well, everyone except me. I'm still wrapped in my college hoodie.

I select more pictures for today's blog and watch the second hand on the clock bounce. My mind skips through the rabbit trail of items to bring to Seung's. Deodorant, free perfume samples, and sandwich bags. I bought Ziploc bags with another ten-dollar bill I found beneath my locker. Someone's lack of responsibility has become a passive income. I plan to stash leftovers from dinner in the plastic bags and stuff my backpack with refreshments from the dance. If I don't, the weekend will be long and hungry.

Seung and I haven't spoken since yesterday. If we weren't best friends, I might think he was avoiding me. I spotted him this morning at his locker. He didn't notice me, though. He was all ears and smiles, talking to Bea as she pointed at a page in her trigonometry book. As if Seung could help. How stereotypical. I wanted to yell, "Just because he's Asian doesn't mean he's good at math." Maybe I'm overly sensitive.

Bea is popping up this week more than usual. Unannounced. Even in my dreams. She glares when I pass Seung's locker and stares when I wait for him in the hall. She mouths "Trailer Trash Bitch" a couple of million times in class, one million more than usual. She thinks I care for all the wrong reasons. I want to say, *Bea, we have more in common than you know,* or *Bea, vulnerability is a place of strength.* But I don't think of these things until after I've mumbled how much I hate her, then yell at myself the remainder of the day.

I turn off the computer and collect my blank paper. Nothing's worth noting on the blog except homecoming. The only buzz at Hinderwood High surrounds the royalty ceremony. I scratch down a title: Who Will Be Our Next King and Queen? Then I draw a line through the words and scribble, Who the hell cares?

I flip the page of my notebook and write my name at the top. Linden Rose, Editor. I draw five bullet points to make Mr. George smile.

I stare blankly at the white space that should be filled with research notes. It's not that I'm ungrateful for the scholarship opportunity. I'd love to win, especially if it makes Mr. George beam with pride. He'd feel satisfied as a teacher and I'd feel the burden of paying for school lift.

I scratch the words Gender-Based Violence beneath my name and eyeball the letters, forcing them to sink into my brain. I rapid-blink to block the words from blurring. Only Violence loiters on the page.

Linden? Would you hand me that necklace, those earrings? I'm going to be late.

Where are you going tonight, Mama?

On a date. Can you believe it? A real date. With someone sweet. Maybe even special.

Who's the lucky guy?

He's in my new computer class. Asked me to go to the library, of all places. I guess I'll take my books.

Will you be out long?

I'll be back before you wake.

The library, huh? Wear these. They're library approved.

You're sweet, Linden. Sweet like honey.

I love you, Mama.

I love you more.

If only my mother had made it to the library that night. If only she'd left early.

I doodle stars on my paper that turn to spirals, and within moments my eyelids drop and I drift to sleep.

I wake to someone clearing her throat and saying, "Shouldn't you sleep at home?"

I wipe my chin and instinctually zoom in on my backpack at my feet, zipped and secure. I scoot my bag between my legs and squeeze it tightly in place.

"Shouldn't you be anywhere but here?" I ask.

Bea turns her back to me and snatches an umbrella hanging on the wall. "Forgot this," she says in the most normal tone she's ever used while speaking to me. No hiss, no snicker.

My mouth should be filled with words. I'm Linden Rose,

Editor. Words are my job and the subject of my story is in front of me, alone, and speaking in a half-normal tone.

"You going to homecoming?" I blurt out. It's the only question willing to jump from my mouth.

Bea frowns.

"You'll no doubt be queen. Right? Queen Bea." *Bad joke, Linden. Incredibly bad.*

Bea tilts her head and slow-nods. "Why do you care?"

I flick my notebook. "Story. You know how Hinderwood loves homecoming."

Again with the slow nod. Then, "I assume you're going with Ham?" she says flatly.

I laugh. "Well, actually—"

Bea interrupts, "I don't have a date."

My eyes widen. "You mean, yet?"

She shrugs. "So who's Seung going with, and don't tell me you?"

My eyes are literal plates. And when I'm about to ask, *WTF?* Mr. George bursts through the door and marches to his desk.

"Linden," he says, opening and shutting drawers. "You were asleep."

"Uh, yeah, sorry."

Bea scoffs at me, then turns and leaves.

Mr. George picks up a stack of paper from his desk and heads back toward the door. With a hand on the light switch he says, "Do you want the room dark?"

I shake my head. Not at Mr. George, but at the thought of Bea and Seung. Is Bea planning to ask Seung to go to homecoming? She has a boyfriend. A larger, meatier boyfriend, who's already tried to assassinate Seung for no reason. Why actually give him a reason?

Mr. George smiles and winks and squeezes the door shut softly.

I tap my phone two hundred times. I should be thinking about the broken railroad tie I need to wedge beneath the fire-escape door. But Bea's words buzz in my brain, make me second-guess why Seung hasn't spoken to me since yesterday. Maybe Seung changed his mind. Maybe Bea knows exactly who he's taking to homecoming, and maybe it isn't me.

I draw an oversized *X* on my notes. Why even consider this article? Bea triggers something, that's for sure, but not inspiration. This whole idea was Ham's, not mine. I slap my notebook closed. At least I have the weekend before Mr. George begins breathing down my neck for research notes and outlines.

"Hello?" a voice says at the door. "I'm looking for Mr. George."

The bouncy blond reporter from Cheese Country stands in the doorway, her blown-out bangs popping inside the room before the rest of her body. The back of her hair is twisted high on her head in the shape of a hoagie, and her lips are the color of cherries.

"Hi. Hello. Mr. George went to class."

She taps her phone. "No problem. I'll wait." She strolls

beside Mr. George's desk and unloads a compact tote. She glances my way. "Ignore me. Don't want to interrupt your work."

I scoot closer to the computer and try not to stare. "Editor of the school blog. That's me," I say with my back to her. Time to fish for information. "Sort of on assignment right now. You?" I shift sideways so I can watch her.

She half smiles and tilts her head. "Assignment? Not really. But maybe." Her shoes clomp until her silhouette shows up in my computer screen. "What's *your* assignment?" she asks, crouching over my shoulder.

I shift sideways to get a closeup of the woman who's been asking questions about me. I want to say, *I'm Linden, the girl you've been asking about,* but instead I rattle off words I'm trying to avoid, like I'm an expert in the subject. "Gender-based violence. A big problem at this school."

She arches an overpenciled eyebrow and says, "Hon, it's a problem everywhere."

I nod and there's silence. She smiles and looks comfortable, like she lives for the long pause.

"Shouldn't you be getting ready for homecoming? My sister said it's kind of a big deal around here. Right?"

I laugh. "Believe me, I have plenty of time." Then I ask, "So, Principal Falsetto—I mean, Principal Falls—is your sister?"

Now it's her turn to laugh. She holds a finger to her lips and whispers, "Don't let it get out," then smiles and picks at her plum-colored tights.

"You look nothing like her."

She chuckles. "Sweetie, I adore my sister, but you've made my year."

"How long are you visiting? Your sister, that is."

She licks her top front teeth and adjusts her lipstick. It's as if she's readying herself for the camera to switch on. Last-minute touch-ups, preparations. She puffs air up to relocate a loose strand of hair slipping into her eyes.

"Not long." She pecks her phone screen with her finger. "So, do you have a name, Editor of the School Blog?"

I suddenly feel like I'm being interviewed, maybe inter-rogated. Principal Falsetto's sister swirls her phone with her finger, waiting, checking email with eyes locked on her screen. She's showing me she's not really interested in my answer, or at least pretending not to be. I don't need a college journalism class to be an expert on that old interview trick. I decide to wait until she makes eye contact, force her to work harder at her job. My mouth shapes my name and she looks up, all ears, and Ham barges in the door.

"Why aren't you home getting pretty?" he shouts, and plops on top of a table, swinging his backpack between his legs. Ham glances at the journalist and nods. "We meet again, Miss Sunshine." He holds out a hand.

She nods and says, "Franklin."

I jump to my feet and announce we'd better go and get ready.

Ham says, "You're probably the only girl on earth who'd rather work on a story than get ready for homecoming." He holds his phone in my face. "Three hours until go time and you need three hours of work."

I tug at Ham's sleeve and pull him toward the door. He looks over his shoulder and says, "Good-bye, Miss Sunshine."

She wiggles her fingers in the air, still staring at her phone. "Good-bye, Franklin. Let's talk soon, Linden."

My chest tightens. She knows my name. Is this a big-city-journalist tactic, or is she just being coy?

"You know who I am?" I ask at the door.

She unlocks her eyes from her phone. "Linden, right? Editor. Isn't that what you said?"

I nod. "I'm the one you were asking my friends about?"

She smiles, and there's another long pause.

"Was there something you needed to talk to me about?" I run my fingers along the doorjamb. Now it's my turn to act coy.

Again, the pause. "Nope," she says. "Not today. You're getting ready for homecoming. Maybe the next time I'm in town. We can chat about journalism. According to my sister, you're damn good."

I snap my fingers. "Sure. Journalism. Next time you're in town."

She waves, still smiling. "Until then." She glances back at her phone.

I swing the door shut and slap Ham's chest. He falls against the lockers like he's been shot.

"What the hell, Linden?" he shouts, and rubs his chest.

"That's Principal Falsetto's sister. Miss Sunshine? Is that really her name?"

"Nickname I gave her," Ham says, his arms beginning to whirl. "Fitting, I think. When I first met her, I was like, 'Damn. What's that smell?' and she was all, 'My perfume, perhaps.' She has a scent like oranges and caffeine and something else I can't quite figure out."

"Sunshine?" I mumble, my annoyance meter plunging off the chart.

Ham snaps his finger. "Exactly. If sunshine had a smell—"

I shush Ham's lips with my finger, the way a mother hushes her infant. Only my big baby won't take the hint.

"She's that lady on TV. KOIN 6. You know, that Portland news station with the slogan 'Watching out for you.' Like if they don't, who will?"

I interrupt Ham's ramble. "What do you mean when you first met her? Why did she meet with *you*, and not me?"

Ham's cheeks droop and his voice rises. "Are you being condescending? Like I'm not good enough to speak to Miss Sunshine? Like I'm not the blog editor, so why is she talking to me? Nice, Linden. Real nice."

"Hammy." I tap his shoe with mine. "That's not what I meant."

Ham stares at his feet and shuffles his steps.

"I'm sorry," I say to his back.

Ham turns sideways. "Well, I was going to have my dad

156

take you to Seung's, but now maybe I won't."

I chase after him and snake my arm around his waist. "I'd love your dad to take me to Seung's if it means spending more time with you, buddy." I tickle his stomach and he giggles. "Can we talk about this later? I just didn't understand why Falsetto's sister was talking to you and Kristen about me. Why didn't she just talk to me?"

"She didn't talk to me about you, Linden. Wow! Your ego. She asked me about me."

I nod, somewhat satisfied with Ham's answer. Maybe she wanted to know who the journalism team was at Hinderwood High. Maybe her sister was the one who started the conversation. Principal Falsetto's always been the biggest supporter of the school blog. Maybe I'm worrying for nothing.

The front doors of the school blow open and wind whips my hair. I shove my hand into my pocket and jam my nail on metal. *Shit.* Could I be more forgetful?

"Wait for me, Ham. There's something I need to do."

Ham grunts, but I'm already racing toward the gym, skipping up the stairs.

At the top landing, I shove the metal shank into the fire-escape door and fold my hands like I'm saying a prayer. I need this door to stay cracked so sneaking in after midnight is a cinch.

On the way down the stairs I stomp on an unopened pack of fruit snacks, reach down, and smile. I tuck the packet into my bag for later. I don't even care that they're grape flavored.

At the front of the school, I'm met with a white SUV parked beneath the overhang. Ham's dad beeps the horn twice to signal he's here, although he's the only car in the entire parking lot.

Ham's already in the front seat, so I slide into the back.

"Hello, Linden," Mr. Royse says at the rearview mirror.

I smile and mouth, "Hello," slightly out of breath. My mind's smacking me with questions I could have, should have, asked Miss Sunshine. But Ham's right. I need to settle down and focus on homecoming.

"Take Linden to Seung's," Ham orders in a stern dad voice. "She's getting ready there."

Mr. Royse nods and puts the SUV into drive. We turn onto the highway and Ham flips around in his seat. "I have plans for tonight."

I slow-nod and say, "Yeah, Ham. We all do. Homecoming."

Mr. Royse interrupts: "Ham says he has a date tonight. How about you, Linden?"

Ham slams the side of his head into the headrest. "Interrupting, Dad. Please stop."

Mr. Royse chuckles.

I tap Ham's shoulder and mouth, "Who's your date?" and he shakes his head like an animal.

"Homecoming is such a memorable event," Mr. Royse rambles. "Who'd you say your date is, Linden?"

Ham shouts, "No! Nobody's talking about dates, Dad. We just need you to drive. You have one job."

Mr. Royse smiles at Ham, although I'm not sure why. I sort of feel sorry for him, but then Ham says, "Sorry, Dad," and pats his arm. "I just need to talk to Linden and you pretend you're not listening."

Mr. Royse's mouth droops. "Sure, Son."

"Look," Ham says as he turns around, his seat belt cinching across his neck, "we're going to make Toby Patters wish he'd never fucked with me, I mean, with us. The whole Triangle."

My face scrunches and Ham amps up.

"Don't give me that confused look, Linden. He's already tried to kill Seung." Ham points at his dad. "You're not listening, remember?" Ham yanks the seat belt and inches forward. "He tried to kill me when I was a kid, and we're pretty sure he's trying to kill Bea. Am I right, or am I right?"

I nod.

Ham sighs. "It's time we get him back. Make him pay for all the pain he's caused us."

"Interrupting," Mr. Royse announces, and Ham and I break our gaze. "Your destination, Linden."

I swing my bag over my shoulder and Ham grabs my arm. "Are you in?"

I stare at Ham's shiny face, the sparkles in his eyes. "Sure. I guess. I'm in." And suddenly, uneasiness settles in my stomach.

Ham slaps the seat. "I knew it, Linden. You're always on my side."

As I slip out of the SUV, Ham motions me to his window.

"So," he whispers, "I do have a date. But I need you to just be cool." He reaches for my hand on the door and squeezes. "Don't overreact. In fact, don't react at all." He pats the top of my hand and winks. "We'll chat more tonight."

I hitch my bag over my shoulder and say, "Thanks for the ride, Mr. Royse." I pat Ham's hand and head toward Seung's house.

Ham shouts, "You guys don't be late picking me up! Remember, Dough Boy in tux!"

When I wave at Ham from the steps, he's drawing a heart around his name written on the fogged-up glass.

CHAPTER ELEVEN

MRS. RHEE OPENS THE DOOR before I ring the bell and sweeps me away to the master bedroom. The borrowed black mini-dress is spread on the bed, complete with three pairs of shoes in different sizes and an odd-looking strap that's supposed to attach to my bra, then make it disappear on my back.

On the bathroom vanity sits a makeup bag full of color. A curling and flat iron are near the sink. Seung shared more information than I thought he knew, because everything, I mean everything, is here in the bathroom, waiting for me. I feel like Cinderella minus the mice, pumpkin, and prince.

I ask Mrs. Rhee if I can shower, and she scurries to a cupboard to retrieve two towel sizes, both full and fluffy, not lifeless and limp like the overbleached ones from the locker room. She promises to return to help with my hair if

I want her to, and of course I do.

My plan for Kristen and me to put on makeup together didn't pan out. It took convincing for Kristen to even agree to join us at homecoming. She said she had decorations to fuss over, last-minute tickets to sell, and chaperones to direct. Finally I promised her one dance with Seung, and she agreed right away to meet us at Ham's place.

The shower is hot, steamy, everything a shower should be. I smell like a lemon soaked in vanilla, different from the mildew freshness that sometimes lingers on my skin after a locker-room shower. Water streams massage my shoulders instead of jab at my muscles like pins and needles, and I feel like I could stand here, on this one square foot, forever.

After a full body scrub and leg shave with a brand-new razor, I shut off the water, wrap myself in a towel, and sink my toes into the memory-foam bath mat. The scratches on my feet from gritty floors and occasional fights with foot fungus immediately heal. The rug is like aloe.

I gawk in the mirror, unsure which body part to tackle first. I decide to dry my hair so my dress won't drown. When I'm done, my hair flops onto my shoulders, except for the few snapped strands shooting straight up from the crown of my head. Mrs. Rhee left a glass bottle on the vanity filled with something that looks like honey or liquid gold. I pump three drops onto my fingertips and rub oil into my split ends.

I fumble through the makeup bag. Three kinds of costly blush, four mascaras, five lip liners with matching sticks.

There's also the complex eyeliner I'm afraid to uncap.

I crack the bathroom door and peek to make sure I'm alone. The bedroom door is shut, so I walk to the foot of the bed, pick up the lace dress, and let the towel drop to the floor. The dress doesn't fit as sexy and snug as I imagined. I guess I've lost a couple more pounds than I thought. I pinch the back of the dress to draw it tight at the waist and stuff my fist into the cups that are hunting for boobs.

Mrs. Rhee taps the door with her fingernail.

"Come in," I say, turning around.

Mrs. Rhee's smile reassures me she can, and will, reconstruct the dress, my mop of hair, and my face. She kneels and pins, fluffs and curls, paints and brushes. Her hands, which normally help heal the sick during the day, have transformed into those of a sculptor, turning life magically into art. I won't say I'm a masterpiece, but when Mrs. Rhee applies her last stroke of lipstick and scrawls her signature with a puff of eau de toilette, I feel as beautiful as a Botticelli painting. I'm afraid to blink or smile big, because if I move a muscle, my face might crack.

"You're ready," Mrs. Rhee says, tucking in a loose strand of hair that snuck out of the side braid. She smiles, and so do I. It's more than homecoming, or Seung seeing me in makeup and a dress. It's Mrs. Rhee's affection, the warmth of her fingers and care from her hands. It's the touch of a mother I fight to remember.

Mrs. Rhee links my arm around hers and walks me to the

163

full-length mirror. She straightens the neckline by gently tugging on the cap sleeves. When I make eye contact with myself in the mirror, my chest tightens. I want to glance over my shoulder and shake the imposter's hand behind me, the one who should take credit for the beauty I see.

"Thank you, Mrs. Rhee." I flicker my eyes to prevent tears from destroying her canvas.

"You like what you see?" she asks, and I nod. "You should, Linden. You're stunning with or without all this." She circles her hand at my dress and hair.

Mrs. Rhee snatches the towels from the floor and folds them over her arm. She walks to the chest of drawers and opens a miniature door on a wooden box. She says, "One more thing," then drops the towels on the bed and reaches around my neck. The cold metal tingles my warm skin, and I catch a shimmer in the mirror. "This," she says, "belonged to Seung's grandmother. It's from Seoul."

I run my fingers over the baubles and stones that cluster into three tiny lotuses. "It's gorgeous," I say, "but should I really wear it? I mean, it's *just* homecoming and this looks priceless."

Mrs. Rhee laughs. "It isn't replaceable, but it's no Harry Winston." She straightens the pendant. "Wear it. It needs to be taken out once in a while. Given a night to remember."

And only because it's Mrs. Rhee do I hold the poker face. Her sentimentality is contagious and makes me feel like I fit, somehow, into a family. If Seung were in the room, I'm sure he'd make me laugh or tell his mother to quit embarrassing me, but I don't want her to stop. It's obvious that the necklace means so much. And to me, it means a connection to family I no longer have.

"Seung's grandparents were Buddhist," she says. "They believed the lotus, *padma*, is a symbol of our true nature."

Between her words and whispers, I'm overcome with the feeling I get when I first walk indoors following a freezing night outside. I'm fuzzy and warm from head to toe.

"The lotus flower grows in shallow, muddy water. It rises above the surface of the muck to bloom and show its beauty to the world. When night comes, the flower closes and sinks underwater. But it always rises and opens at dawn."

"Why does it sink?" I ask.

"To remain untouched by impurity." Mrs. Rhee smiles. "There's so much symbolism in Buddhism and Korean culture. Seung and I don't get the chance to discuss his father's family. We're all so busy. Maybe when he's older and has kids." She smiles again, that affectionate, motherly smile. "Now, let's go see if Seung's ready. He's been a fidgety mess this week and a bundle of nerves tonight. Something's definitely gotten into that boy." Mrs. Rhee winks and blood rushes to my cheeks. Instant blush.

I round the corner of the hall and pass the main bathroom. The door is shut, and Seung's on the other side.

When we reach the family room, Mrs. Rhee announces my arrival like she's heralding a queen. Mr. Rhee says, "All hail the queen," and I don't know whether I should twirl or curtsy, so I jokingly do both. Mr. Rhee plays along, reaching for my hand and kissing the back of it.

"Doesn't she look beautiful?" Mrs. Rhee says.

Mr. Rhee smiles and bows. "Our homecoming queen has arrived."

Seung struts in and clears his throat. My cheeks flame up and my hands start to sweat. I mean, he looks like Seung, only hotter. Cheeks glowing in the yellow light, hair shining almost blue. Thanks to the fabric of the tux, his shoulders look even wider somehow. I glance at my feet, then back at Seung. We finally lock eyes and stare at each other until Mrs. Rhee tugs at Mr. Rhee's arm and says, "Honey, I need you in the kitchen," and they bolt.

I nod. Seung nods.

I smile with the side of my mouth and Seung matches my move. It's a slow game of chess until I finally blurt, "You look fucking hot!" Checkmate.

Seung exhales as if he's held his breath since entering the room. "This old thing?" He thumbs at the lapels and his shoulders relax.

"So, dinner?" I say, switching subjects. "I'm starving."

"Change of plans," Seung says, still staring me in the eyes. I mean, he won't look away. "We're eating at Ham's. He says he needs us." Seung flashes the text from Ham on his phone screen and I step forward.

Seung takes a step back, then realizes he moved in the

166

wrong direction. He practically jerks his body forward. "So," he says.

"So," I say, and smile.

His eyes bounce around the room, finally landing on me, or should I say my cleavage. I mean, holy shit, Mrs. Rhee is a miracle worker. She created cleavage and I'm not even offended by Seung glancing at it.

"We should probably get going," Seung says.

I spin my heel on the carpet and watch the indentation it leaves. "Yeah. Yes. We should."

Seung and I bump into each other scrambling for the doorway. "Sorry," we both say in unison. Then Seung remembers he has parents and should probably say good-bye.

He bangs the kitchen door and Mr. and Mrs. Rhee bounce back into the living room.

"We need pictures before you leave." Mrs. Rhee opens a buffet drawer and presents an oversized camera and lens longer than my shoe.

Seung rolls his eyes. "Really, Mom?"

"You'll thank me when you're older," she says, turning toward Mr. Rhee's already nodding head. She glances around the room. "Kids, stand in front of that cabinet. The backdrop looks nice."

Seung and I shuffle to the picture spot like two first graders being told where to stand for school photos.

"Seung?" his mom asks. "Where's Linden's corsage?"

Seung doesn't move. He doesn't answer Mrs. Rhee, either.

Instead, he stares at me as if I'm privy to its whereabouts. I shrug my shoulders. Seung reciprocates.

Mr. Rhee launches from the footstool. "Saw it in the refrigerator." He darts into the kitchen and returns with a clear plastic box. "Chest or wrist?" he says, kneeling before me. Talk about awkward.

"Honey," Mrs. Rhee says, "let Seung fasten it."

I gulp and Seung's eyes go wide. His chest, too, literally expands before me as he sucks in air. His eyes pinball until he finally fixes on the plastic shell clutched in his hands. He squeezes the top until the box bends and the lid pops open. We jump.

"Be careful not to poke her," Mrs. Rhee says.

I refuse to make eye contact with Seung and instead tuck my lips around my teeth to prevent the push of a nervous smile.

Seung stands in front of me stone faced. Our eyes are glued on the plastic. "Wrist or . . . ?" Seung taps his chest and I tap mine back. He lifts the flower out by the stem and stares at the pin. "I have no idea how to do this."

Mrs. Rhee pops her head over Seung's shoulder. There are now four eyeballs staring at my chest, six if you count my own. I hold my breath as Seung's cold knuckle grazes my bare skin. I shiver, then feel the pinprick.

"Ouch."

"Sorry."

"All good."

"Try not to move."

"Okay."

"You're moving."

"I am?"

The back of Seung's hand brushes my collarbone. He slides two fingers beneath my bra strap and I slowly sip air.

"Be careful not to stick her, Son." *Ohmygod, Mr. Rhee.*

Once the flower is in place, Mrs. Rhee wiggles her finger at Mr. Rhee to start snapping pictures.

Seung shakes his head and says, "Okaydonelet'sgo," and Mrs. Rhee points at the buffet table.

"We need one more of you two together," she says.

Seung groans. "Come on, Mom. It's just Linden."

My chin drops. I stare at my feet. When I'm brave enough to glance at Mrs. Rhee, I see the *just Linden* comment hit her, too, deep in the stomach. But Seung's right. We're just Linden, just Seung. Two best friends going to homecoming, together. And I guess I'm okay with that for now. I mean, he found me a dress, a flower, a mom to pamper me.

Then Seung contradicts his words and shoves his phone at his mom, saying, "Take a picture with this." Seung hooks my waist and yanks me next to him. I'm pretty positive the photo displays my mix of jolt and joy.

Mr. Rhee hands Mrs. Rhee a small container.

"Seung," she says, "we forgot yours." She passes me the box.

My face freezes. What do I do with this?

Seung snatches the box from my hand. "We're going. Good-bye."

"Yes. Yes." Mr. Rhee pats his son's back. "Go on. Get out of here. And don't return until it's really late." Mr. Rhee winks, but Seung is too busy rushing to the door to notice.

"Honey, if you don't want to wear your boutonniere," Mrs. Rhee shouts, "give it to Ham!"

"Leaving!" Seung yells halfway out the door.

By the time I step onto the porch, Seung is already in the car. I round the back of Gold Nugget and hear Mrs. Rhee say, "They make a stunning couple."

I pause and wave. Seung's parents wave back with so much force, it looks like their arms might snap at the elbows. Mr. Rhee snakes his arm around his wife's waist, and they turn to walk inside. I'm still staring when Mrs. Rhee twists around for one last glance. I mouth, "Thank you," and she says, "You're welcome." She blows me a kiss and my throat tightens.

If only my mother could see me and how happy I am tonight. I imagine her standing on the other side of the yard, opposite Mrs. Rhee. Her curls blow away from her face, and her skirt whips against her knee as she fixes her earring post back into place. She waves with her fingers while Mrs. Rhee nods in her direction, as if to say, *Look at our babies. Look how happy they are.* My mother smiles and nods at Mrs. Rhee as if to thank her for all she's done for me. When my mom looks my way, my eyes fill with tears and I blink. She's gone. I pause for a second, a minute, and whisper, "Mama, I love you. I don't know how, but I'm going to be okay. I promise."

In the car, I wiggle up and down on my seat, smoothing my

dress. I attempt to sit in a way that defies wrinkle-making physics, which means when I'm finished, I'm practically standing on the floorboard, bridging my body with both hands. Seung shifts into drive and my hands slip. I plop onto the seat and bounce. Seung glances over and smiles.

"You okay?"

"Yeah," I say, "I actually am."

"You forgot your coat," Seung says, still smiling. "Put it in the back for you."

"Thank you, Seung."

"You are most welcome, Linden."

The ride to Ham's quiets us. Instead of talking, I wring my hands, pop three knuckles, and smack my lips. Seung drums the steering wheel to the beat of whatever notes are playing inside his head. Neither of us speaks until Gold Nugget creeps into Ham's circular drive. Six vehicles line the curve leading up to the steps.

"What's with all the cars?" I ask.

"Ham's grandparents?"

I shrug. "You know Ham has a date, right?"

"Is that what he called it? Specifically?" Seung tilts his head. Could he be any more gorgeous tonight?

I shrug again. "Has Ham talked to you about Toby Patters? Some revenge plot?"

Seung snatches the small flower box from the dashboard. "Ham hasn't talked to me about anything," he says, slamming the car door. "Should I be concerned?"

"Only if you're Toby."

We stomp up the steps and pause in the archway of the door. "Sorry about my mom," Seung says, rubbing his neck and yanking at his collar. "She kind of overdoes it, you know."

I smile. "I know. And I love that she does."

Seung opens his mouth like he wants to say something, then snaps his lips shut and chickens out. He holds his finger on the doorbell, hesitates, then drops his hand and stuffs it into his pocket. He draws a deep breath, turns to face me, and reaches for my hand. I offer both. He quickly unstuffs his pocketed hand and grabs all my fingers. His Adam's apple bumps up and down while he gulps and swallows. Finally, he says, "I've been meaning to say this all night."

We lock eyes.

"You look fucking hot, too," Seung blurts, his face beaming beneath the porch light.

Hello, goose bumps.

I'm all smiles when I bump Seung with my hip and reach for the doorbell. He's all smiles, too, as I push the button. Any worry I had about Bea and Seung just jumped ship. I mean, we are definitely together tonight.

As soon as the bell dings, Basil and Thyme, the Royses' Welsh corgis, yap.

I shout, "Remember to spread your feet!" when Mrs. Royse opens the door. We crouch like quarterbacks ready for the ball as Basil and Thyme weave between our legs, dribbling dots of urine.

"Basil, Thyme: Retreat." Mrs. Royse claps and the dogs scurry off toward the kitchen, where a delicious family dinner bakes in the oven. "We're almost ready, kids. Come in. Come in."

Mrs. Royse disappears around the corner into Mr. Royse's office, shouting, "Ham's been in the bathroom for hours."

Seung laughs. "Yeah, and I doubt he's getting ready."

Mrs. Royse bounces back into the hall. "Could one of you knock? Tell him we're all in the dining room."

Seung and I stare at each other, drawing mental straws, flipping the proverbial coin.

Mrs. Royse lowers her voice and cups her mouth. "I'd rather not interrupt a teenage boy in the bathroom, if you know what I mean."

We slip out of our shoes and park them in the entryway, house rules, and follow the lines on the hand-scraped hardwood toward the dining room.

As soon as Mrs. Royse disappears, Seung whips around and I slam into his back. "The *button ear*," he says. "Will you give it to Ham?" He shoves the box with the boutonniere into my hands.

"No. You should give it to him after dinner." I push the box back at Seung and slip up the stairs toward Ham's bathroom, wondering when and how I drew the shorter straw.

I rap on the door, hoping Mrs. Royse is wrong about teenage boys.

"Go away!" Ham shouts.

"It's me, Linden."

The door swings open and slams against the wall. Ham grabs me by the elbow and yanks me inside.

"Jesus, Ham!" I slap my hands over my eyes. "You could have gotten dressed first, you know?" Ham snatches a white robe from a hook and swings it over his back like a cape.

"I can't do this, Linden." I peek through my fingers as he cinches his robe.

"Do what? Eat dinner? Are you sick?" I reach for his forehead and a temperature check. His face is rosy, his eyes are puffy, red.

Ham untwists the towel from his head and tosses it at the sink. His hair springs in all directions.

"I'm not sick, Linden, I'm nervous for the first damn time in my life." He grips the vanity for balance, wobbling for effect.

"Does this have something to do with Toby Patters? Your plot for revenge? Getting him back for all the terrible things he's done to you and Seung?"

Ham chuckles and slices the air with his hand. "He's not my concern now. He'll get what's coming to him in due time."

"What, then? Why are you nervous?"

Ham finger combs his bangs. "Do you remember the moment you realized Seung's the only guy you want to see naked?"

"Well, uh, you kind of ruined that moment for me." I wink and Ham tightens his robe.

He clears his throat. "Yeah, sorry about that."

Someone knocks on the door. "Franklin, honey." Ham's mom. "Are you ever coming down? And is Linden in there with you?"

Ham stomps to the door and shouts, "Of course Linden's in here with me!"

"Well, um, I hate to interrupt, but, um, please . . ."

Ham whips the door open. "Jesus, Mother, get your mind out of the gutter. There's more that goes on in a bathroom than *that*."

I wait in the hallway while Ham slips into his tux. He emerges from the bathroom with his chest puffed. He smiles and says, "This night belongs to us, Linden."

Arm in arm Ham and I step inside the dining room and the crowd erupts. Parents, grandparents, aunts, uncles, cousins, Seung, and Jarrell. Cheers. Accolades. Affection. Seung waves at me with a what-the-eff face and I flash a perplexed yet bring-down-the-house grin. I mean, Seung oozes sexiness, and thanks to Ham I'm actually picturing Seung naked, at the table, in the middle of a Royse family gathering.

Ham's dad stands and taps his champagne glass with a tiny fork. Hurrahs hush as Mr. Royse thanks everyone for coming. Ham interrupts, saying, "Move over, asswipes," to his male cousins, and squeezes into a chair beside Jarrell. It's the first time I've seen Jarrell in anything but a well-worded tee or football jersey.

"This is for you," Seung says, all hot potato with the flower box. He chucks the boutonniere across the table to Ham.

I glance around the room at the familiar faces. Grandparents smile. Cousins giggle. Aunts and uncles pat each other's backs. Ham's parents beam with affection for their son, their family, and the love that's filling up the room.

I pick up a toasting flute and tip it at my lips, then realize I sipped champagne, not cider. I smile at Ham and his big, amazing family. He sits like a stone while Jarrell pins the flower onto his lapel.

Then I remember Ham's date. That he actually has one. I jab Seung with a tiny spoon and he raises his eyebrow. *Enough with the sexiness, Seung.*

"To my son," Mr. Royse continues his speech.

More relatives cheer and Ham yells, "Hear! Hear!" to himself.

"Shall we eat?" someone says, and Ham reaches for the mashed potatoes. He's the first to dip the spoon, but not the first to take a bite. He plops a pile of spuds onto Jarrell's bare plate.

I sit up straight. Squirm in my chair. Glance at Seung, who's busy scraping the bacon off his green beans. Ham said he was nervous. The first time in his life. Am I imagining things? Drama Jarrell? But Ham hates football.

"Thanks for the spread, Mom," Ham says with his mouth full.

No. Not Ham. He would have told me. In the bathroom. But his mom interrupted.

"Yeah. Thank you, Mrs. Royse," Seung says, and I piggy-back the gratitude. Seung knuckle punches me under the table. I swear his fingers linger on my thigh. My stomach goes weak, and electric pulses shoot up my leg. I playfully jab at him with my fork, then let my finger graze his knee.

We scarf dinner like it's our last meal, and it could quite possibly be mine until tomorrow evening, unless I count the pack of fruit snacks I found as breakfast. I grab a second roll from a platter passing by and tuck it into my napkin.

"Do you think you'll win tonight, Franklin?" Mr. Royse asks.

Ham's mouth is crammed with pineapple-glazed ham, but it doesn't stop him from saying, "Win? As in football? Sorry, Jarrell, but who the hell cares? You know I hate football, Dad."

Ham's hardly acting nervous now. Is he trying to impress Jarrell?

Ham's dad nods. "No. You've never been much into sports." He turns toward Seung. "How about you, Seung? You a football buff?"

Seung wipes his lips with his cloth napkin. "No, sir. I'm not really into sports I can't play online. Sorry, Jarrell."

Jarrell laughs and picks a crumb from Ham's cheek. Am I the only one watching a budding romance unfold? I glance at Seung again, but he's back to babying his green beans.

"When Franklin was little, he and Seung used to pretend they were brothers. Told everyone they were family." Ham's ears perk at his mom's nostalgic biography. "They've always had so much in common, those two boys."

"Still do," I say, and Mrs. Royse sits up and begs for more tales about her son. "Ham, I mean Franklin, and Seung, are really into mob movies," I say. "You know, the Mafia? They spend hours critiquing mob movies together. Are you into mob movies, Jarrell?"

Jarrell gulps his milk and says, "Nope. Too much violence."

Ham looks like someone slapped his face. I hold my breath for Jarrell. Nobody insults Ham's mob movies, even if unintentionally.

Ham dabs at the corners of his mouth before unleashing on Jarrell. "Excuse me. You play football. Could there be any more violence?"

Jarrell smiles and says, "And *you* don't play." He drops his chin and I swear he's giving Ham puppy-dog eyes. I squint. Are those puppy eyes?

Ham scoffs and says flatly, "We should go."

"Yes. Go." Seung scoots his chair back. "Wouldn't want to miss a minute of that real-life game."

The sarcasm in Seung's voice is obvious, but I don't have time to joke back. Instead, I decide to turn on my journalism skills and confirm what I think I already know.

"I hear there's a possibility of two homecoming kings this year." I wait for Ham's ears to perk like his corgis', but he's busy putting Jarrell in a headlock.

Mr. Royse pops his head over my shoulder. "That's

wonderful, Linden. Especially for a town trapped in a time warp."

I nod and Mrs. Royse interrupts. "Let's snap photos by the fireplace before the kids leave."

Seung wedges between Ham and Jarrell like a third wheel, straightening Ham's floral bow tie. Jarrell picks lint from Ham's tuxedoed chest, and Seung sweeps Ham's shoulders with his hand. They're a pack of grooming birds.

We file into the living room, white from mantel to carpet. I plop into a silvery velvet chair and absorb the only color in the room. All eyes are on the boys, including mine.

"Linden, get in there!" Mr. Royse shouts.

I spring to my feet and link arms with the boys. We smile big for the five million cameras.

Ham steers Jarrell toward the chair I was sitting in, pushing at his chest until he falls onto the seat. "Take one of the Triangle, Mom. Sorry, Jarrell."

We link arms. Me in the middle. My eyes sting for a moment, all this family and friendship. It's hard to breathe when you're smothered by love. I squeeze my arms, drawing Ham and Seung closer to my sides. I want to hold them tight, never let them go. Neither knows it, perhaps never will, but they've supported me like a buttress, held me up when I neared collapse. Seung's more than a crush and Ham's more than a best friend. They've given me hope in spite of the darkness. They're my brightest stars, shining even when the lights go out.

"Now a couple pictures of Jarrell and me," Ham says, shoving me out of the way. I mean, he pushes me so hard, I practically stumble. I shake my head, settling my sentimental thoughts, and shoot a look at Seung that says, *Ham and Jarrell?* He blows me a kiss. *Ohmygod, pay attention, Seung. But please, blow me another kiss. First.*

"Done," Mr. Royse says, waving his hand. "Now go. Have fun. Stay out all night." He pats Jarrell's back as he walks us to the door. "And good luck to you, son. Hope you and the team kick ass tonight."

Jarrell smiles. "Thank you again for dinner."

Ham waves his arms. "Yes. Good luck with the *violence*."

Jarrell ruffles Ham's hair and Ham stiffens like a soldier.

We exchange good-byes and fall back against the door when it shuts behind us.

Jarrell leans against the wrought iron railing and says, "Man, your parents—"

"Are fucking weird!" Ham blurts.

"Love you," I say. "Consider yourself lucky." And even though I believe luck is made, perhaps there's an exception to my rule. When you're born into a loving family, shouldn't there be a slight advantage?

"If I don't leave now, Coach won't let me play," Jarrell says.

In unison, Ham and I snap, "Fuck Coach Jenkins." We burst out laughing.

Jarrell jogs toward his car and shouts, "I'll see you at the dance." He's pointing at Ham while patting his chest . . . or

180

heart? We all wave and trot off toward Gold Nugget.

Ham calls shotgun and mocks my feeble attempt at pulling the ladies-first card. "When you find a lady," he says, and winks, "let us know."

Seung's mouth twitches, but words are nonexistent.

"I'm in a freaking dress," I say, waving my arms in protest.

Ham shakes his head. "No go."

A horn beeps and Kristen rolls alongside the curb in her mom's minivan.

"Oh, no!" Ham shouts. "What is *that* lady doing here?"

I sigh. "Remember when you made me promise I'd find your one true love?"

Ham winces and scrunches his face. "Not who I had in mind."

"Well, I wasn't sure you really had a date."

"She's not my date," Ham insists. "Not tonight. Not ever."

I pat Ham's back. "I'm sorry. Truly I am."

Kristen rolls her window down and shouts, "I'll follow you there!"

I shoot a thumbs-up. It's not like Kristen knew she was Ham's date for the dance. I just didn't want Ham to be alone. And I'm still not one hundred percent sure he's with Jarrell tonight.

I flop into the backseat of Seung's car like a mermaid and wiggle my shoes until the borrowed heels hit the floorboard. I rummage through my backpack for sneakers and slide my feet into them like a runner at home plate, flipping my body on the side and using the hump in the backseat to dig my heels deep. I wiggle the cramp free from my toes. Ah, home.

"Any chance you can drive slightly above the speed limit and lose Kristen?" Ham snaps.

Seung shakes his head. "No chance."

Ham sighs. "Well, I'm going to need a slushie before the game."

Seung makes a sharp left in the direction of the convenience store. I glance in the rear window to make sure Kristen's still behind us.

"I am not, I repeat *not*, slurping a slushie in this dress."

Ham flips around in his seat. "I meant to tell you, Linden. You clean up well." He punches Seung's arm. "Doesn't she, Seung?"

Seung's eyes flicker in the rearview mirror each time he steals a glance. I've counted eight so far.

I fondle Seung's grandmother's necklace. My fingers dance along the stone petals. Everyone's been so good to me. Mrs. Rhee, the Royses, the ladies at the nursing home. And what do I do for them? Keep secrets and steal food. I'm even lying to my friends, lying to their parents. The only real thing is my love for them all.

I straighten the dress wrapped tight around my thighs. I shouldn't be thinking about my past now. But that image of my mom and Mrs. Rhee sticks. Tonight I plan to live in the moment, forget my worries and uncertainties or how my future will unfold. I don't want to think about anything but the here, the now. It's the moments I've truly lived that I'll remember. Tonight isn't about homecoming or this beautiful damn dress. Tonight is symbolic. Just like Mrs. Rhee said. If I live in this moment, it could chisel and carve out my future. Maybe, just maybe, when the sun rises, I'll rise, too. Out of the muck, unaffected by my past. The only way to survive the unknown, the tomorrows that haven't arrived, is to appreciate where I am today, experience the moment, and live within it.

Seung parks in front of the convenience store, and Ham rattles off his order like we're at a drive-up window. Large suicide slush, three packs of M&M's, and mints.

"Get 'em yourself," Seung says, climbing out of the car.

Ham lifts a paper bag to his lap and says, "But I'm getting the elixir ready."

I lean over the seat and witness an oversized glass bottle emerging from Ham's bag. "What's that?" I ask, knowing full well what *that* is.

"Why, *that*," Ham says, "is Mr. Royse's premium bottle of scotch."

Seung falls onto the seat with his hands. "There is no way in hell you're drinking tonight, Ham. You know my rule."

"Ham is not allowed to drink in the presence of Seung Rhee," I say on behalf of Seung, and on behalf of Seung's Rule.

"Ham is not allowed to drink in the presence of me," Seung repeats, tapping his chest.

"It's been a year, guys," Ham says. "A lot happens in a year. A man grows up. A man matures. A man grows hair on his chest, his balls. A boy becomes a man. Besides, that episode you're thinking of didn't even involve alcohol."

I fake gag as Kristen walks over to the car and says, "Hey, everyone."

Ham tucks the bottle back into the bag and kicks it under the seat. "Revenge plot, Linden, remember? No need to worry your pretty faces." He bumps into Kristen as he climbs out of the car, leaving the door open. "I guess you're my date, huh?" Ham winks and marches into the store.

Kristen ignores Ham and asks if she should meet us at the dance.

"Yeah," I say, glancing into the store window as Ham zigzags between candy baskets. "He could be a while."

"I'm sure I'm needed for setup," Kristen says, "but text me when you get there."

She heads toward her van, and I shout, "Why don't you come to the game with us?"

She stops, pivots on her heel, and marches back to the car. "Are you inviting me to hang out?"

"Um. Yeah," I say. "I think I already did."

Kristen grins. "I want to. I do. But I'm always needed inside for last-minute preparations."

"Give yourself a rest, Kristen," Seung says, tapping his phone screen and checking the time. "Haven't you delegated enough?"

I smile at Kristen. "He's right. Have fun! You deserve it, especially tonight."

Kristen shifts her hips once, twice. "You're right." She snaps her fingers.

"Time to enjoy your hard work." I smile and glance over at Ham, who is now juggling mints.

Kristen skips toward the van, shouting, "I'll find you at the game! I promise!"

When she drives off, Seung says, "You and Kristen are becoming close?"

"Yeah. Might be nice to have another girl around."

We watch Ham through the glass as he meanders up and down the four store aisles. He lingers at the slushie machine, working his cup like a potter at the wheel, oscillating back and forth, crafting the perfect swirl. Once he's added every available flavor, he smiles at his cup and scoops some slush from the spoon-straw. He pours the icy mess into his mouth and flashes us a grin. We wave.

"Did you notice Ham and Jarrell?" I ask.

"He did say he was making new friends."

Headlights beam from behind the car as I'm about to scold Seung for his inability to detect details. The blinding glare and sound of a revving engine sink my stomach. I lean forward, over the seat, but I can't reach Ham's door quick enough to shut it. The truck bumper hits the door and bends it backward until the hinges creak.

"What the hell?" Seung shouts.

Toby climbs out of his truck like a monkey, first hopping onto the step and swinging off the mirror. He's parked so close, he has to circle around the back of his truck to get to the store.

"Watch where you fucking park!" T.P. shouts at Seung, although he's looking at me. *Hey, Asswipe. I'm not the one behind the wheel.*

I slink lower in my seat when I hear the soprano giggles of Bea and Beth. They scurry toward the door, Beth's hand against Bea's back. They pause in front of Gold Nugget and Bea whispers something to Beth. They both wave, at Seung, not me. Seung nods and my stomach sinks a second time.

Toby whips around, probably making sure his concubines are in tow. He points two fingers in our direction until he reaches the store doors.

"He wants us to know he's watching," I say. "He's sending a message."

"Yeah," Seung says. "And the message reads, 'I'm Toby Patters. Town's colossal asswipe.'"

Ham walks to the counter, taking his own sweet time. His head bobs when he moves, while he looks for Bea. His obsession since ninth grade. Her hair. Her clothes. Her flawless skin. But I wonder if it's Toby he's really searching for.

Ham backs away from the counter when Bea flounces from the aisle. Ham says something, Bea says something back. Beth joins the duo, then Toby walks up and they form a square. Ham jabs T.P.'s chest and I hold my breath. Then he patty-cakes Toby's triceps and laughs. There's a whole lot of patting and laughing and turning and jabbing.

"Shouldn't Toby be at the game?" I ask.

"Suspended for fighting," Seung says.

"So he has nothing to lose tonight," I mumble, biting my lip, wishing I had more details surrounding Ham's revenge plot.

We stare at the window. It's impossible not to be bothered by Toby's towering trunk shading Ham's stumpy one.

On cue, Ham shoots his thumb toward the car, and my nerves settle.

"What could they possibly be talking about?" Seung asks.

"This is the closest Ham's been to Toby in years," I say.

Ham steps to the counter with his slushie, candy, and five packs of mints. He holds up a finger to the cashier and jogs to the back of the store, returning with several rolls of duct tape.

"I'm extremely concerned about Ham's revenge plot. You?"

Seung scrunches his nose and hugs the steering wheel for a closer look.

Bea dumps her gum and soda on the counter and Toby pushes a dozen meat sticks at the cashier. Ham pays for everything and they walk out of the store together, looking chummier than they should. Ham shouts something to Toby and jogs over to the car. He reaches beneath the seat and grabs his duffel bag and his dad's scotch.

"Ham, explain yourself," I say.

He digs into the duffel and I spy a roll of twine and what appears to be hair dye—orange.

"All part of the plan, Linden." Ham stuffs the booze into the duffel bag.

"Not good," I say. "Not a good idea for Ham." I whack Seung's chest. "Tell him this isn't a good idea."

Toby revs his engine and shouts, "You got the booze, or what?"

Ham hikes his bag over his shoulder and says, "I'll be drinking with my *new* friend tonight." He winks and races for the truck, which suddenly looks like the most monstrous of monster trucks I've ever seen.

"Ham! Wait. . . ." My voice is muffled by the engine. Toby points his two fingers at us as he backs up. His stupid stage direction is getting old, fast. The door of Gold Nugget springs back, then snaps shut. I lean out the window and watch my best friend ride away with his enemy.

"What was it again that Abe Lincoln said?"

Seung sighs. "Ham's made his enemy his friend."

We sit quietly and replay what happened in our minds. After a couple of minutes, I break the silence. "So, I guess this means I'm riding shotgun."

Seung smiles, but a worried look swathes his face. "I guess this means you are."

CHAPTER TWELVE

MY FIRST GLIMPSE OF HAM is during the last five minutes of the game. The score is zero to zero for what seems like forever. Seung tracks back to the car to grab a blanket. He tosses it over Kristen and me, and the three of us huddle and laugh and blow on each other's hands for warmth. I couldn't care less about the plunging temperature or the possibility of sleeping beneath the stars. Tonight I'm focused on having fun with friends. Feeling like I finally fit in.

It's the end of fourth quarter when I hear a chant of what I believe to be Ham's name. It starts as a dull hum and hits a high note thirty seconds deep.

Ham-HamHamHam.
Ham-HamHamHam.

It sounds like a fraternity drinking game and quite possibly Ham's demise.

I elbow Seung and point to the far corner of the field. We stare in awe as our bare-chested, formal-trousered friend pirouettes across the football field. A dad behind us shouts, "Hey, Chunk from the *Goonies*," and a mom, who should be ashamed of herself, yells, "Do the truffle shuffle, kid!" The crowd erupts with laughter.

"Oh my God!" Kristen shouts. "That's Ham!"

I jump from the bleacher for a better view, and Seung steps beside me at the railing. "What the hell is he doing, and why is he doing it?"

"I don't know," I say, "but I wish he'd stop."

The referee whistles and waves his arms in the air like he's swatting gnats. One oversized, overstuffed, truffle-shuffling gnat. Ham grips his belly and twists the skin to synchronous chants from sidelined players.

Ham-Ham-HamHamHam.
Ham-Ham-HamHamHam.

"Stop laughing!" I shout at the row of parents behind us. "Stop laughing now!" I want to jump over the fence and wrap Ham in my blanket. Order everyone off the field. Scream that the show's over. Time to head home.

A referee lunges at Ham, and he sprints toward the crowd. He sidesteps the yard lines, passing front and center at the fifty-yard line. He drops his belly to wave wildly at us with both hands.

Seung cups his mouth and shouts, "What is wrong with you?"

"Having fun!" Ham yells, now pounding invisible drums. "You should try it sometime." Ham flashes his teeth and blows me a kiss. "Love you, guys!" he shouts.

"Be careful!" I holler as Ham's foot slides switch to full-fledged crisscross scissor steps.

"All part of the plan, Linden! Remember? And I'm just getting started!"

"What plan?" Seung yells.

Ham answers by pointing in our direction, and that's when I see T.P., leaning against the chain link fence, signaling Ham to spin like a top. I nudge Seung and he says, "Toby's making him do this nonsense."

I shake my head, unsure who I'd rather be in charge of Ham's *nonsense*, T.P. or Ham. But beyond the surface, Ham seems to be maintaining control of the situation.

The crowd cheers as the referee closes in. Ham trips over his feet and sprawls flat on the field, back first. The mob explodes, first booing the referee, then cheering for Ham. Jarrell drops his helmet on the field, sprints toward Ham, and lifts him up—but Ham drops to his knees, then speed-crawls off the field.

Seung senses that my worry has returned. "He said he's just having fun, Linden. It's what Ham does best."

I point at Toby's fist pumping at the moon. "I hope this is part of Ham's plan."

"I'm sure it is," Seung says.

Kristen jumps up and down with the cheering crowd, shouting, "I'm having fun, too!" her blond curls loosening and spilling from their clips. I've never seen her relax like this before. Maybe Seung and I should learn a lesson from Ham and Kristen, and stop standing here like stiffs.

Seung smiles and I link my arm through his. I reach for Kristen's hand and join her in jumping. It takes Seung a minute, but before long he's hopping, too.

We watch while T.P. slinks down the side of the stadium to meet up with Ham. They race behind the bleachers as Toby yelps, "Shit was awesome! Now time to get my drink on!"

The next time we see Ham is in the gymnasium.

Kristen scurries off to talk business with Principal Falsetto, and Seung bumps his head on a low-hanging pagoda. I swat the paper away and we stop and stare at the carnage that our high school gym has become. Mistletoe. Everywhere. In the shape of upside-down artificial bonsai trees.

"Holy shit," Seung says, his eyes wide and twinkling under the red flashing lights.

"Whispers of the Orient."

Complete with kimonos, plastic trees, and fake-gold-leaf dragons. The homecoming committee outdid themselves by stuffing every stereotypical Asian trope into one room.

Everything they could shape out of paper and plastic, that is.

I don't know whether to laugh or vomit. I nudge Seung with my elbow and he chuckles. Then reaches for my hand.

"It's about time my people receive recognition. Especially at this school." Seung waves his hand, the one unattached to mine. "Even if it is *this*."

My hand slips from Seung's grip and our fingers fumble against each other's forearms until they lock back in place. I swallow hard and we walk deeper and deeper into Hinderwood's Orient.

When I see Ham he is shirtless, except for the "cape." Well, Ham is technically wearing a shirt, if one calls a tuxedo vest a shirt. His jacket sleeves are tied around his neck and flop in rhythm to the music as he twists and turns. Where his white button-up went remains a mystery until Bea and Beth circle Ham and link arms like they did with Reed in the Pajama Day photo. As they walk center stage, I notice that Beth's hips are wrapped in Ham's shirt. Ham performs what I believe to be a slow dance but looks more like a mating ritual for a sloth.

Seung groans and repeats his earlier rant. "What the hell is he doing, and why is he doing it?"

I shake my head. It's not so much Ham's dancing, which I've grown to admire, as the affectionate groping between Bea and Ham, Ham and Beth, and Ham and Ham. He's literally dancing with himself, arms wrapped tightly around his shoulders. The three are all smiles and seem to be enjoying each other's company. I'm damn suspicious.

Seung and I discuss dancing, but since neither of us dances, in public or private, we stare at Ham until Bea's laser-beam eyes target my other best friend.

First she glances over Ham's shoulder and a smile spreads across her face.

She beelines toward Seung, with so much force that I actually step back, out of her way, immediately regretting my move. Bea twists to her side and blocks me from my space next to Seung. He squeezes my hand but our grip weakens, slips. Bea tugs him into the crowd, and I'm left with a shit-ton of jealousy stacked on my shoulders.

I'm alone with my green-eyed monster for only a few seconds before Jarrell appears beside me. He watches Ham do-si-do with Beth, twirling her in circles. I belly laugh and plop onto a foldable chair. Jarrell sits next to me.

"Good game tonight."

"Until we were interrupted." Jarrell points at Ham and leans forward with elbows on his knees. "Please tell me he hasn't been drinking."

Poor Jarrell. He's remembering last year's episode. The one that prompted Seung's Rule. Jarrell was there to pick up the pieces. And by pieces, I mean chunks. After Ham blew a few on the hood of Jarrell's car following an emotionally complicated night of what appeared to be beer guzzling but was later revealed as an energy-drink overdose. Ham said he needed to blow off steam, so as Ham does, he called a few near-strangers and asked them to come over to his house. Jarrell was the only one who showed. Seung and I were already there because we're not strangers and don't count. By the time Jarrell arrived, Ham was uncontrollable, uncontainable. So, basically, he was Normal Ham.

"I don't think so," I say, then remember the scotch, the revenge plot, and Toby's "get my drink on" comment. It's not like Ham requires liquid courage, though. But maybe this preplanned prank is bigger than Ham or his personality.

Out of the corner of my eye I catch Bea draping her arms around Seung, then plopping her head onto his chest. She runs one hand up and down his jacket, causing Seung's spine to stiffen. He moves like a robot. A rather constipated robot in desperate need of grease.

"Where's your date?" Jarrell asks.

I point at Seung.

"And yours?" I ask, ears perked and poised for confirmation that he and Ham might just be an actual thing in need of confirmation.

Jarrell shrugs. "Well, I thought I had one, but I guess not. . . ."

I want to ask Jarrell if Ham's his date, but I don't want to butt in where I don't belong. I mean, shouldn't Ham be the one to tell me who he's dating? Besides, Ham insisted I not react.

Principal Falsetto squawks into the microphone, informing us the votes are counted. Hinderwood High has chosen its royalty. Winners to be announced within the hour. Kristen squeals from the stage.

The music bounces from country to pop and the crowd begins to bob their arms in the air. I bump Jarrell and wave good-bye. He nods as I race toward the bleachers. When I reach the bench, I slide down the back row toward the exit, to avoid Principal Falsetto. Kristen's talking to Falsetto's sister, which makes me pause longer than I should. When I reach the side door, the one that will lead me to the fire escape, a hand squeezes my bare shoulder.

"Where do you think you're going?"

I whip around and my nose digs deep into Reed Clemmings's shearling jacket. I position myself to answer truthfully, mouth open and eyes wide, but something stops me. I don't need Reed knowing about my trips to the outdoor fire escape.

"Nowhere."

"Sure about that?"

Yes, Reed, I'm sure I'm going nowhere you need to know. I bite my tongue and hold on to the words.

"Well, wherever you're going, I'll join. I need air to breathe."

I snicker at the obvious and slide past him, out the door, saying, "I really need to go."

The fire escape beckons—otherwise I'll be spending the night in the windy outdoors.

"Good idea." Reed winks, twice, or maybe the red lights

196

make it hard for him to focus. I'm unsure if he's complimenting my plan or planning to join, so I step into the grass to find out.

The door shuts and Reed marches behind me.

Here's me, living in the proverbial moment, the place I swore I'd be tonight, staring at the stars with Reed, while Seung slow-dances with Bea. Could this night complicate my life more?

The only way out is to straight-shoot the truth. So I say, "I need to check something," and stomp off toward the metal stairs.

"I'll come with you," he says, and jogs after me in the dark.

I pound through the tall-weeded grass near the corner of the school. Blades brush against my calves, making me happy I slid into my own shoes and out of Mrs. Rhee's.

"Wait up!" Reed shouts as I jump a knee-high bush.

Wait up? For you? I'm sort of surprised he's still behind me.

When we reach the bottom of the fire-escape stairs, he asks, "Where are you going?"

I point. "Up there."

He smiles and his snow-bright teeth sparkle. He's probably never missed a brush, floss, or dental appointment in his life.

I skip the last two stairs and lunge for the top, pouncing on my makeshift metal doorstop like a cat jumping on one of those rubber mice. I forget all about Reed, or the tight dress riding up my ass. I forget the fact that he followed me up the stairs and is observing everything I do. I slide the shank with my foot and yank the door open.

"What are you doing?" he asks as I bend over to secure the railroad tie beneath the door.

Good question. What *am* I doing here with Reed? Letting him see where I live, what I do. I won't even let Ham or Seung get this close.

"I might need to get in here later." The words fly from my mouth before I can stop them. I jerk the door handle to make sure it's secure, then walk toward the stairs.

Reed blocks the exit with his arms. "Wait. Can't we stay here longer? Look at the stars, or something?"

I choke out, "Sure. I guess," but the words squeak and I slap my hand to my lips. Maybe it's the fact that I'm standing two stories high beneath the stars with Reed, or that he witnessed my preparations for breaking and entering. Possibly it's the question he asked . . . because when he said *we*, my response was faint, my voice trembled.

"They're going to announce the royal court, and I am so over it." He slaps the rail with his palms. "I'm over this whole fucking place."

Of course you are. You're Reed Fucking Clemmings.

I stare at him, at his jacket. I wonder what it smells like, all wool lined and warm. A football dipped in deodorant, probably.

I think about Seung and Bea and wonder if Toby interrupted their dance. I wonder if Seung's nose is bloody from the beating he took for "stealing someone's girl." I wonder if Seung's smiling while he dances with Bea like he smiles at me when I insult his driving or tell him he's hot. I wonder who makes him smile more.

"Aren't you excited to be king?"

Reed scoffs. "I'm not king."

"How do you know?"

"Because Bea and I argued."

Bea. That explains everything. Why Reed wanted to go outside, why he needed to escape. *Bea.* Slobbering all over Seung, patting his chest, probably pretending to know the geographical difference between North and South Korea. *Bea.* Paying attention to Ham so that she could pay attention to Seung.

I shiver and attempt to mind-control Reed into handing over his coat, because the chill is inching up my spine and crawling over my limbs. I need Seung's blanket in the worst way, but he stuffed it in the car before heading in to the dance. I also need Reed to transform into Seung.

"So you and Bea haven't been together for a while, right?"

"Define *together.*"

"She's with Toby Patters now."

"Something like that."

"So shouldn't Toby be king? I mean, logistically, he is with Bea, and she's always the queen." I clamp my lips together to prevent my teeth from chattering. Wind whips against my bare back.

"Who knows what the future might bring," Reed says, using his sexy voice. Okay, his normal voice.

There's a smile in Reed's eyes, or maybe a reflection of the crescent moon. I should turn around, but I don't. I'm instantly warm from my nose to big toe. Reed doesn't pick up on my heat, though. He slithers out of his jacket like the rock-star, sexy gentleman that he always acts like, and says, "Here. You're cold."

He drapes me in suede and shearling. The scent of football, cocoa, and—I'm not going to lie, it's either beer or B.O.—inches up my nose. Not quite the smell I expected. Reed is his own tailgate party. He smiles again and I'm positive now, it's not the moon's reflection.

"Who's your date?" he asks as I stand drowning in suede, empty sleeves tapping my thighs.

I crinkle my nose, fighting to remember. For a while tonight, at Seung's house, with his mom, later huddling and jumping with Kristen, and then when he reached for my hand and led me deep into the dance, I felt like I was on the biggest date of my life. But now Seung is dancing with Bea. And though he looked like an in-need-of-a-laxative robot, he did ask his mom for pictures of *us*, even after the *just Linden* comment.

"My best friend," I whisper.

Reed nods and puckers his lips. It's his kiss look, I know it.

I flop back toward the fire escape, jacket arms swinging and slapping me on the hips. "We should go back inside before we get caught."

"I don't care if I get caught."

I smile. I like his style, but arguably, risks aren't my thing.

200

Remaining unnoticed is. "I do," I say. "I care if I get caught."

Reed groans but tags behind me, down the stairs and to the side door of the gym.

It is the third time I see Ham.

Spinning in circles, puking, hands on his hips, half naked, and alone. Several strips of duct tape stick to his stomach like markings for a runway.

"Ohmygod, Ham!" I sprint toward him. "Are you okay?" I reach over his shoulders to stop him from spinning.

"I don't feel so well, Linden." Ham drops to his knees. "I need a mint."

I dig my hand into his front pocket.

"Whoa, whoa—easy, Linden." Even Ham's laughs are slurred.

I pop a mint into Ham's gaping mouth. "What have you been doing?" Knowing full well what I've seen him doing, but more concerned about the moments missed.

Ham grabs my arm for balance and whispers, "Gaining trust."

I wipe spit from his mouth and ask, "Are you going to be okay?"

"I am now that you're here, Linden. Just cold. So very cold."

I tear off Reed's jacket to cover Ham's bare chest but am stopped midremoval. "No!" Reed snaps. "That's fine shearling. I don't want puke on it. Someone should get towels."

I huff and grunt and shout, "Towels! Now!" and point to

the door. Reed jumps and disappears into the gym, along with his jacket.

"The sky is spinning," Ham moans.

"Kneel down." I push on Ham's shoulders and his knees bend. "What happened? Did you drink your dad's scotch?"

"It was something I ate."

I rub Ham's shoulders. "You sure? We ate the same things."

He groans and holds his stomach. "Bad meat sticks or something."

I remember the convenience-store loot and ask, "Where's Toby? I haven't seen him since the game."

Ham laughs. "And you probably won't see him again. He's a little tied up right now. Or should I say taped up?" He flops over on his back.

"Ham? What have you done?"

He rolls over, shuts his eyes, and moans.

"You're cold." I glance back at the door. What's taking Reed so long? "Let's get you inside."

"No." Ham swings his arm, then kicks his legs like an over-turned beetle. "I don't want to go in there, Linden. I want to go home."

"Okay? Okay." I pat Ham's chest. He's right. Going into the gym would be a bad idea, especially if a teacher witnessed his condition. "I'll get Seung. We'll get you home."

Ham grumbles and moans and grabs his stomach. "Hurry, Linden. Please." There's worry in his voice that causes hesitation.

202

"I hate to leave you. Maybe you should just come with me."

Ham straightens his arm, points, and shoots. "GO!"

I race for the gym.

Inside, lights flicker and horns toot like it's a new year. I follow the glow-in-the-dark court lines toward the locker room, glancing around for Reed and his promised towels. Midway, the crowd splits into a gap and at the head of the aisle, I see Seung, his crown, and his ear-to-ear smile. The crowd claps as Seung moves toward me. His eyes dart around the room and take in everything but me, his arms locked with his queen—Bea.

A forearm snakes around my neck. "I told you I wasn't king." His breath, hot on my ear. "Let's get out of here."

A part of me wants to leave. Run. Flee far from this scene. Seung and his smile. Bea, staring at Seung as if he could smash away her problems. But another part of me is left outside, spread-eagled on the grass, nearly naked and alone.

"Towels." I snap my fingers. "Where are they?"

Reed points to a stack on the bench, and I race for the pile. At least I can wrap Ham in towels and scoot him to the car before the dance ends. Seung would never leave without us. I drop a towel on my way to the door but don't stop to pick it up. I hit the side exit at full speed and race toward the gar-bage can. There, on the ground, lie his ripped-up vest and a tail of duct tape.

But no Ham. He's gone.

"Ham!" I shout, spinning 360 degrees. "Where the hell are you?"

I jog to the front of the school, circle around, and run to the back of the building. He could have crawled off, passed out, fallen behind a bush. But he's nowhere I look.

I run back to the place I first saw him and snatch his vest. The back fabric torn, the bottom frayed and frazzled with loose threads. I didn't notice the rips before, but then again, Ham didn't have it on. He wore duct tape instead. I step on something plastic and it squirts brown liquid onto my shoe. I pick up the bottle and squint to read the front: ULTIMATE BRONZER GUARANTEED TO COVER EVEN THE BLOTCHIEST OF SKIN TONES. *Oh, Ham. What have you done?*

I scour the entire perimeter of the school before heading back inside. Ham couldn't have crawled far unless he had help. My stomach turns. Ham said Toby was taped up, but I can't help wondering if the tape is strong enough to hold a monster.

When I open the gym door, the music is loud and everyone's dancing, including Seung. He's still smiling, too. Having the time of his life. Enjoying this moment without Ham, without me.

Jarrell stands at the opposite door with his coat draped over one shoulder. I dart and weave through the crowd, forcing my way to him.

"Hey, Linden," Jarrell says when he sees me.

I slap his chest. "Ham? Have you seen him?"

He frowns, eyebrows fold. "Indeed." He rubs his forehead. "Pretty sure Ham left. He said he had to check on Toby." And the way he spits out *check on Toby* slugs my stomach.

Shit. Left? How? Was one of them sober?

Jarrell glances behind me as two heavy arms cloak my shoulders. "Let's dance," Reed says in my ear, although it's more of a command than a suggestion.

He pushes me toward the middle of the room, guiding me with his arms, while I insist, "I can't. Must go. Have to find Ham. Need to speak to Seung."

Reed points at the newly crowned couple and says, "Seung's a little busy right now."

Seung's wrapped in Bea's arms, dancing, more relaxed and fluid and all Seung 2.0. He doesn't see me dancing with Reed. He's forgotten I'm here. And it hits me: I've been searching for Ham like a good freaking friend, and Seung hasn't even bothered to find out where I went.

I twist Reed around so I have a clear view of Seung. I yank, then push hard to steer him, because he's twenty feet tall. That's when I notice, just for a moment, everyone watching me. Noticing me. Seeing me.

I'm the girl.

The one others long to be.

At least right now. In this moment. Which has nothing to do with me, only Reed. Sure, it feels good to wear a fancy dress and dance with the guy everyone worships, but I don't really want to be that girl, the one hanging on his arms and

205

every word, for more than this instant. I want to be mopping Ham's face and laughing with Seung. I want to be poking fun at plastic pagodas while stuffing my pockets full of egg rolls. That's who I really am.

I tug Reed toward Seung. We half dance and half walk, weaving through the crowded floor. Reed inches with ease toward Bea and Seung, and I realize they're his target, too, and I'm not the only one aiming the bow.

We turn left, right. We walk more than we dance until we reach the head of the crowd. Only one couple between us and the homecoming king and queen, and when the song ends and a new one begins, there is only space between us.

As soon as we land next to Seung and Bea, Reed rubs his hands up and down my bare back. This is the moment when I'm supposed to get turned on. And maybe if I could let my guard down, or if Reed weren't so hell-bent on making Bea jealous, I would enjoy this moment. *But news flash, Reed. You picked the wrong girl.*

Seung's eyes dart my way and he scowls.

I act like I don't see him at first and desperately wish I didn't. Bea rubs his chest and Seung twitches his shoulders. We move beside them and Reed shoulder-bumps Bea. She whips around and laughs. Okay, to me it's more of a cackle.

"Nice date," Bea snaps, and as I prepare to mouth the words *nice crown* to Seung, Reed snatches my chin with his thumb and forefinger and shoves his lips into mine.

I expect his tongue to force its way between my lips,

206

pushing and probing to get what it wants. What I don't expect is a warm, slow stride, his mouth matching the movements of his body. I also don't expect his fingers to graze my neck and web the back of my hair, or my stomach to wobble like Jell-O.

When Reed opens his eyes, he finds mine never closed. He smiles and rubs my cheek with the pads of his fingers. I draw short breaths while my lungs fight for air and my stomach falters. The feeling is pleasant, and I can't help myself, I don't want it to stop, but when I see Bea's bare leg hook around Seung's clothed one, and her mouth stick to his like a lamprey, the poke jabs. Hurts. Bleeds. Bea, sucking the life out of Seung, which means I'm dying, too.

I twist away from Reed and his weighty arms and tap Bea on the shoulder. Okay, jab her on the shoulder. She whips around and I shout, "Cutting in!" She shakes her head *no* and I bump her to the side. Reed steps in for backup and whisks her away. Bea's the girl he wanted anyway, not me. But the way Bea looks back at Seung, her eyes brimming with hurt, tells me Reed is the wrong guy.

"Where have you been?" Seung says, no longer dancing, his hands on his hips, pissed.

"Oh my God. Are you serious?" I slap his chest and hold my hands there for a few seconds. Okay, a minute. He looks at his chest and I drop my arms.

"Why didn't you stay?"

"Why would I want to?"

He thumbs at his crown. *Yeah, I've seen it.*

"This is weird," he says, eyeballing his forehead.

"I guess Bea pulled some strings." I smile, although it's forced. I'm happy for Seung and his awkward confidence, just not settled with the fact that Bea's involved.

"Yeah." Seung smiles.

"Well, glad you're happy, but celebration time's over. Ham's MIA."

Seung's face scrunches. I tap his chest. My fingers like magnets drawn to his damn chest armor. "Found Ham sick outside. But now he's gone. Missing. And Toby Patters is unfortunately involved."

"Ham will turn up. He always does."

I shake my head with force. "Jarrell said he might be with Toby."

Seung pauses. A hint of worry spreads across his face; then Bea reaches between us and snatches Seung's arm. "Royalty's leaving," she snaps. "Come on. Let's go."

Seung turns back with saucer eyes. "Follow us!" he shouts over the cheering, clapping crowd. "Please, Linden."

I raise a finger. *Sure. I'll get right on that. Follow you, following Bea.*

Principal Falsetto announces that the royal court will meet in the corridor for pictures and the rest of us, *peasants*, are free to leave. I half smile at Seung when I slip by him toward the exit. He's standing like a scarecrow, straw stiff.

At the front of the school, a pack of smokers join forces beneath the awning.

208

"Hey," a girl says from the step.

I smile and say, "Hey," back.

A guy with curly bangs bubbling from beneath a knit hat lifts his hand in my direction. "Want one?"

I shake my head. "No, thanks." Then I fall against the concrete pillar to wait for Seung.

"What's up with you and Man Bun?" a girl asks. She's wrapped in a poncho and boots I'd die for.

It takes a minute to register that she's talking about Reed. And me. "Oh. Yeah. Reed. Me. Nothing's up."

"Yeah," she says, "that'd be weird," and I wonder what she means exactly by *that* and *weird*. Lately, I seem to be misinterpreting what people think about me. How they view me. I mean, Toby tells the story like he sees it. Bea never shuts up. But people like Jarrell or Kristen or Reed seem genuinely interested in me. Sure, Reed has a motive, but when he kissed me, I felt it in my ankles. You can't fake that. Can you?

"Have you seen Ham?" I ask, not directing the question to any particular person.

"Saw him on the field," a guy says. "Stellar moves." He jumps to his feet and shimmies back and forth.

"Wasn't he dancing with Bea?" someone asks.

"I saw him with Jarrell. Looked like they were arguing."

Huh. Jarrell didn't mention that detail.

Knit-hat guy says, "How'd Seung swing homecoming king? Thought he was better than that."

I chuckle. "It's a fluke. He doesn't really care about the whole king thing." At least I don't think he does.

"He cares," a girl says in middrag off her cigarette, "about one thing, anyway." She smiles, and I know exactly who she's referring to.

"Bea would be okay," hat guy says, "if you duct taped her mouth."

"That's vile."

"And wrong."

"That's what she's into. Isn't it?"

"Again, a horrible thing to say."

"Seung wouldn't treat her that way," the girl with the cigarette says.

"Seung's hot," a girl says.

"Agreed," a guy says.

"Extra hot," they both say.

I roll my eyes and try not to barf, even though I heart-and-soul agree. I decide to try my question again, forage for more detail. "So where did Ham go? Anyone see him leave?"

Hat boy says, "He was in the parking lot with Jarrell. I told you."

Uh, no. You forgot that detail.

He puffs his cigarette twice before I snap my finger and motion for him to pass it to me. I take a drag and cough like a barn animal.

"Ham's probably at Beth's party," a girl says. "Isn't that where everyone's going tonight?"

The front doors open and laughter surges. Voices suck away the second-hand smoke and my questions.

"Make way for Hinderwood's King and Queen!" Complete with entourage in tow.

Seung's eyes widen, and his mouth drops open when he sees me. He wiggles his hand loose from Bea and I wave my cigarette in the air, pretending not to see their webbed fingers.

I bump shoulders with members of the court and force my way inside the group.

"Linden!" Seung snaps, and points. "Smoking? That shit will kill you." The crowd rolls down the steps like a wave and I glance at my hand still clutching the cigarette. I wave it in Seung's face and ignore his alarm over lung cancer. It's not like I'm inhaling correctly, anyway.

The group ripples into the parking lot. "Where are you going?" I shout.

Seung walks backward. "Bea and Beth's party. Come with!"

I suck on the cigarette, cough a few more times, and toss the butt into a soda can.

"Vape, Linden. Heard of it? That shit's so unhealthy."

I want to shout, "So is Bea and Beth's party!" but instead I sprint toward Gold Nugget.

Bea cuts me off at the driver's-side door. "You're not going," she snaps. "Unless, of course, you're going with him?" She points to Reed strutting down the steps.

I shake my head. "Whatever. Move over."

"The whole school saw you attack his mouth," Bea says. "Go with Reed. You guys are perfectly matched."

Seung, shocked by Bea's words, says, "You kissed Reed Clemmings?"

Oh my freaking God, Seung. Where have you been?

I lift my arms, and Seung snaps, "Yeah, Linden. Maybe you shouldn't go with us." He sounds like a puppy, all whimpers. He has no reason to be hurt. It's not like I asked Reed to kiss me. It's not like I kissed back. Besides, Seung is the one marching around with his fingers wrapped around Bea's.

I scoff. "Yeah. Well, if you see Ham, take care of him. Better yet, find me so I can make sure he's okay."

"Ham *will* be okay, Linden. He always is."

I hope Seung's right, but he's hard to believe. If only he'd act like himself, or at least who I think he should be.

"C'mon, Seung," Bea calls from inside the car.

Seung bumps me, scrambling for the passenger's-side door to sit next to his chauffeur. He won't even let *me* sit behind Gold Nugget's wheel.

The engine revs and Seung rolls down the window and shouts, "Come with us! Ham's probably already there. Plenty of room in the back."

News flash, Seung. I prefer shotgun.

The car windows are dark, but light enough for me to see my bag, the blanket, and my belongings piled in the backseat. *Dammit.* I reach for the handle as Bea kicks the car into

212

drive. Gold Nugget's tires spin and squeal and I'm left with the scent of rubber and a hint of rejection.

There, in the parking lot, dressed to the nines and decorated with Grandmother Rhee's lotus, surrounded by smokers and small-town hipsters, I scream at the top of my lungs.

"Fuck. FUCK it! FUCK IT ALL!"

The crowd behind me cheers.

Maybe it was the applause that shot me with moxie. Normally I'm not a girl who seeks danger on purpose. I plan. I schedule. I prefer to know what's happening next. It's what living homeless has done to me. I adapt to change yet fight to keep everything the same. However, tonight is anything but normal. So when the guttural crack of a motorcycle pops behind me, I weigh all options: (1) eliminate regret, (2) rescue friends, (3) all of the above.

First I wave for Reed to hand over his prized sheep. Then I button his coat to my neck, wrap my legs around his hips, and squeeze. I need to feel safe.

We race down the highway, free of helmets and horse sense. I'll admit it's not my smartest moment, but I'm on a mission to save my friends. I shut my eyes as we climb the hill before Triangle Park, when I begin sliding in the wrong direction. Away from safety. Seatbelts should be regulation on motorcycles. That's what Seung would say. One bump and I could break open, spill all over the pavement. I press my knees into Reed's ass and clench. He mistakes fear for flirting, and shifts

213

sideways and smiles, but who cares? If clutching his ass with my knees prevents me from hitting concrete, squeeze I will.

We slow alongside a 1950s brick rambler overlooking the park. Cars block the drive but Reed manipulates the bike toward the tiny porch and parks horizontally. He lifts his hand to help me out of the straddle, and winks.

He opens the front door without ringing the bell, and music booms from the basement. We walk downstairs, bumping into three guys passing in the opposite direction. They hold red plastic cups and splash beer with each stomp. At the bottom of the stairs, we're met with low lights, beer bottles stuffed in coolers, and the smell of feet. I glance at couches in search of Ham or Seung, while Reed scans the room, too, but for different reasons.

"Want something to drink?" His breath tickles my ear.

"Yeah, sure," I say, soaking up the ambience. There's nothing more appealing than being one of the few sobers in a space full of drunks. "I want something to drink, something strong, maybe something to smoke, too." If for no other reason than to clutch weaponry. . . . I may need to crack a bottle over someone's head, send smoke signals with a lit cigarette.

Reed strolls toward a cooler, opens the lid, and grabs a beer. He ignores two girls saying, "Hi, Reed," and beelines back to me, twisting off the bottle top and flicking it onto the tile. He hands me the beer and I slurp bubbles off the top. Too much, too fast. Here's me gagging, wiping my tongue, and looking damn desirable.

Reed snatches the bottle from my hand and gulps. Apparently we've reached bottle-sharing status. I mean, we did kiss and my thighs clutched his ass, but there's something more intimate about sips from the same bottle.

"Want to dance?" he asks. My answer is a firm *no* in my head, but I reach for his waist and push him to the center of the room. His eyes go saucer big, but he's reading me wrong. My mission is to circle the floor to search for Seung and Ham.

So here I am, dancing with Reed Clemmings, and his crotch is rubbing my stomach, and all I'm thinking about is finding my friends. I promised myself I'd live in the moment tonight, ignore probability, welcome possibility. I'm free from worrying about security or whether I'll make it back to school in time to sleep indoors.

Reed snakes his hips from side to side and I laugh in my head. If Seung and I were on the sidelines, watching him dance, we would remark on how ridiculous he looks. This mating ritual. And me, his mate.

He bends in for the second kiss of the night and I consider closing my eyes, letting it play out the way it should, but I can't even blink. He pushes his neck forward and parts my lips with his tongue. I let him poke around until he finds what he's looking for, but my arms are stiff and his lips are warm and sticky, and smell of beer. After a few seconds, my eyes shut and a picture of Seung and Bea flashes in my mind, her hand on his ass, their fingers intertwined. Then Ham, bouncing about the dance floor, all pink cheeked and smiles while

215

the crowd eggs him on. I run my fingers through my hair and remember the gentle tugs of Mrs. Rhee braiding with her warm, soft, motherly hands.

Pagodas, dinner rolls, and pink powdered soap flash through my mind.

There's pounding on the door, then my mother's voice winds up.

Linden. In here.

Where?

The closet. Put your headphones on.

More banging on the door.

Now, Linden. Go!

Mama?

She should have been gone before he arrived. She had a date. She was happy. Happier than I'd ever seen her. The wrinkle between her eyes showing signs of smoothing. But in an instant, fear flashed in my mother's eyes. I crouched and scooted toward the door, glanced over my shoulder, and witnessed relief on my mom's face when I nodded and climbed into the closet. Into my safe place. This is where I went, where I was told to go, when he knocked and demanded money. She never let me see him. Never let him know I was here. This man who showed up unannounced every time my mother made changes to make our lives better.

I wrapped my knees to my chest, cuddled my legs, and was asleep when the police came, headphones still hushing out sounds. I fought not to see my mom's lifeless body. The busts,

216

cuts, and broken bones. I pretended not to hear their assumptions. When they called my mother a dead prostitute. When they whispered that I was the daughter of someone who didn't matter. Why didn't I stand up for her? Tell them she wasn't who they thought she was? Why didn't I do something? Fly out of the closet, protect her from pain? My mother promised nobody hurts you when they don't know you exist. But she existed. And so do I.

I jerk back from Reed and he draws a deep breath. "What's wrong?"

I shake my head, settling surfaced visions, the ones fighting for their rightful space in my mind. Pictures from the past grabbing at me, jabbing, tapping me on the shoulder to remind me they're still here, every time I lift my foot to take a forward step. My eyes pool with tears. I blink and unwind from Reed's grasp.

I shift left and immediately see Seung.

Alone.

Staring at me from the bottom step.

For how long, I can only guess. But from the look on Seung's face, I'm guessing it was long enough to see me close my eyes and kiss another guy.

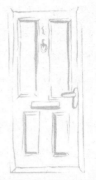

CHAPTER THIRTEEN

I WANDER THE HOUSE, SEARCHING for Seung. I'm looking for Ham, too, but he's a mere spark compared to the blazing inferno separating Seung and me. The Triangle always sticks together, but now we're falling apart.

I've been tapping on doors and circling Beth's house for fifteen minutes, maybe longer. I've seen naked people I never wanted to see naked, and smelled enough vomit to last five lifetimes.

I open a bathroom door and notice another door connecting to a closet, maybe a room. I jiggle the handle. It's locked, which means a bedroom is on the other side because who locks their closet? I double-check the outer door and flip the lock. I really have to pee.

After I spend a minute on the toilet, voices seep through

the crack. A guy. A girl. Sounds like arguing. Sounds like Bea.

Seung?

No. Not his voice. Too much anger.

"You're trash. Nobody gives a fuck about you."

Definitely not Seung.

My hand lingers on the toilet handle. I close the lid gently and hold off flushing.

The girl's voice shouts something incoherent. Then a few hundred f-bombs fly. Something bumps against the wall and I jump and clutch Seung's grandmother's necklace.

Okay, Linden. Do not involve yourself. This has nothing to do with you. Tiptoe out of the bathroom and continue searching for your friends.

The girl says, "Leave me the hell alone," and I freeze. Hold my breath.

The dude's voice booms. "You're cheating on me, you bitch!" Then there's a slap. A scream.

Damnitall, Toby Patters. When will you ever learn?

Guess Ham's tape didn't hold after all. If only Ham could see me, what I'm about to do. Carry out this much-needed revenge plot.

I pound on the door, shouting, "Unlock it!"

Someone scrambles around the room; something hard hits the floor.

I pound and kick, but the door won't budge. I throw open the vanity drawer and search for something sharp. Nothing. I

219

pat the top of the doorframe and find the wire door key, then shove it through the hole and pop the lock.

I'm not thinking about my next move, only getting the damn door open and stopping that asshole once and for all.

The door swings wide and I shout, "What the hell is going on?"

Bea's huddled in the corner, crying. Her head tucked between her knees, hair covering her cheeks.

Reed Clemmings slinks out the bedroom door.

"Go after him!" I yell.

But Bea won't move.

"Call the cops!"

But she's can't. She's frozen.

"Bea? Get up! Do something!"

How can she? She's petrified.

CHAPTER FOURTEEN

BEA FORBIDS ME TO CALL the police.

She says, "I'll handle it."

I say, "Like you've done before?"

"You don't understand what it's like," she says. "To be the girl others need, look to, for all sorts of things."

I shrug. I know more than she thinks, but now isn't the time to argue about our similarities or differences. She's gone through hell and I'm in the middle of it with her. There are few places I'd rather be.

We don't run after Reed. Bea says he won't be back now that there's a witness. I'm not as confident.

I ask her if it was Reed all along. If he was the one hurting her. She nods and tells me Toby is the only other person who knows what Reed's like. He's known for a long time. But I don't understand why Toby doesn't do something.

She says, "He tries, but it's not really his fight. Is it?"

"Toby dwarfs Reed. Sheer size alone should solve your problem. Can't Toby just kick Reed's ass?" It seems simple, but is it?

Bea says, "He's tried. But they used to be friends, and they're on the same team. It's not his fight, though. Ultimately, it's mine."

When it hits me that I'm still wrapped in Reed's coat, I can't tear it from my body fast enough. Bea tells me Reed wasn't always this way. He snaps sometimes. I tell her she shouldn't make excuses for him. She repeats, "You don't understand." I nod. She's right. I'm not her. I can only understand what she chooses to tell me.

Before we leave the room, Bea stuffs the sheepskin in the toilet, splashing my piss water with each shove.

I sponge her brow with a washcloth and find cola in the kitchen to dab on the blood staining her dress. The damage to her beaded neckline looks worse than her eye. But the pain inside her probably drowns out everything else.

"Are you going to be okay?" I ask when we reach the front door.

She nods. "Probably."

"Stay away from him."

She sighs. "I try."

"He doesn't own you."

"He just thinks he does."

I reach for her hand. "There are people who can help. Like Mr. George. Principal Falls."

We both smile because it sounds so clichéd.

I tilt my head to the side and say, "I should have done something that day I was at your house, cleaning for your mom. I should have gotten more involved."

She shakes her head. "Not your job."

I pause and examine her face. "Are you sure you don't want me to call someone?"

Bea nods. "I'm sure."

"Do you want me to find Beth?"

"I'll find her myself."

We stand facing each other for what seems like an hour. I lean in to hug her and am okay that she doesn't hug back. She shouldn't have to do shit.

I lock the door on the inside before squeezing it shut. I have to help her in some small act, even if she won't let me.

When I reach the driveway, Seung's car is gone, which means my belongings are gone, too. I don't have the energy to walk to Seung's house, especially not now, after my adrenaline dumps. I'd rather eyeball Triangle Park for Ham. Maybe Seung's there, too. I cut through Beth's backyard, down the hill toward the park.

Before crossing the street, I check to make sure there are no motorcycles or monster trucks. I guess it was wishful thinking that Seung would be on the swings, waiting for me, or Ham would be snoozing on a picnic table awaiting rescue before a deputy arrives to arrest him.

I rock back and forth on a swing, shivering and staring at the sky, shoving thoughts of Seung aside. Like the look on his face, seeing me kiss another guy. I cringe. Reed had his tongue in my mouth. I suddenly have the urge to spit. I don't feel right thinking about Seung. I should be thinking more about Bea. What would have happened if I hadn't been in the bathroom or banged on the door? These thoughts make me shudder.

I tap my phone, but the screen stays black. I have no idea if Ham made it home or if Seung will ever speak to me again. If only I had my license and a car, I could have avoided this entire mess. Taken Ham home and put him to bed, made sure everyone was safe. It wouldn't have helped Bea, though. And now I'm worried I made her mess worse.

I jog across the street and climb the dirt hill beside the main road. Avoiding traffic, or a motorcycle engine whining my name, is in my best interest. Halfway up, my leg slips and I slide all the way down to the base of the hill, landing against a pile of tumbleweeds mixed with sagebrush. The plants scrape my legs and dig into my bare back. When I reach the top of the hill again, the ground that's jagged with rocks, I step sideways on an uncovered root and my ankle rolls. I land flat on my back. And when I sit up: *Rrrrrip.*

The back of my borrowed dress opens wider and wind whips against my skin. I pinch the fabric like a bath towel and hobble toward Hinderwood High.

Few cars cruise the main road, and the only traffic light in town blinks yellow, signaling that the clock has struck midnight and my houseguests, at school, have vacated.

I slink through the chain link fence and pass by the baseball dugout on my way to the back of the school. At the top of the fire escape, I lean over the railing and stare at the parking lot dotted with the flickers of streetlights refusing to center against the black asphalt. Lights bounce and dance, even when I squeeze one eye shut. My teeth chatter, but I feel like standing here, catching my breath, at least for a moment.

It was easier when I first arrived in this town. Money and a grandmother were what I had to lean on. I ignored the fact that my grandmother had dementia and every day another piece of her mind and memory vanished. It's not like she knew who I was anyway. But she didn't have to know me to expect me. Every day after school when I arrived to brush her hair, paint her nails, or tuck an extra blanket over her lap, she didn't know I was her granddaughter, but she knew I cared. I didn't need her to know me. I needed her to connect me to family. When she died, the only person left to lean on was myself.

A motorcycle engine whirs in the distance and reminds me to seek safety, fast. The last person I want to face is Reed, especially after he saw me wedge the door. I should never have let my guard down. Tomorrow, in the daylight, life will look better, brighter. It's these dark spaces that mess with my mind.

There should be several hours before the homecoming cleanup crew arrives. Time enough to clean the dirt from this dress, then maybe sleep, if I'm lucky enough to turn my mind on mute.

I feel my way along the stairwell to the gym. The black room looks nothing like it did during the dance, except for outlines of pagodas and a dragon that appears more cartoon-ish than Asian. A figure at the door causes me to jump. It's a plastic Buddha, life-sized.

I imagine Buddha saying:

Peace comes from within.

No one saves us from ourselves.

If you light a lamp for somebody, it will also brighten your path.

I shout, "You're a flipping statue!" and push the locker-room door open.

Spooked by the statue, I punch the light switch and flip the deadlock. Just in case Statue Buddha or someone else decides to join me.

I beeline for the mirror, and my eyes target my borrowed dress and Mrs. Rhee's necklace. That is, what's left of it. One blossom, no stones, the chain wrapped up in my bra strap, barely holding itself together. It must have broken when I slipped and fell down the hill. My chest tightens, my stomach aches. This necklace meant so much to Seung's mom, to their family, to me. I unwind the metal and undo the clasp. I dig my hand into the back of the towel cabinet for my emergency bag

226

and slide the necklace into a plastic bag. I'll need to figure out how to replace an irreplaceable piece of jewelry.

My eyes fill with tears as I slip into my spare change of clothes. Sweats and a T-shirt. Tomorrow I'll scrub the dress clean and figure out how to mend the rip, but tonight it stays in my locker. I'm exhausted, mentally and physically, so I won't shower; besides, after the time I spent in Mrs. Rhee's bathroom, the grayed-out locker room suddenly looks like shit.

I dab wet paper towels in soap and wipe away the dirt and debris, then mop up the sink, making it cleaner than when I arrived.

As I'm leaving the locker room, I notice something fixed to the wall. A piece of duct tape with a clump of cantaloupe-colored hair stuck to the back. Orange dye dots the floor and leads me to a stall. I pause. Nobody's in here with me. Are they?

I jump back and listen, then drop to my knees—the scratches on my legs remind me they are there—and peek beneath the door. No feet in sight, so I kick the stall open and witness the carnage of what I think is Ham's revenge plot.

The supposed-to-be-white-now-yellow toilet seat has turned a showy shade of tangerine. Whoever busted out of here did so with rage, because the toilet's tilted and the seat's on the floor.

I haul ass out of the locker room and walk straight into a fake bonsai. I'm met by Statue Buddha again, so I mutter a prayer for Ham, his safety, and imagine the statue shutting its eyes, nodding, and saying, *Yes, my child.* Maybe one right tonight will cancel out so many wrongs.

I open the main door that dumps into the corridor (my foyer) and pat the walls so I don't bump into another tree. The check-in table is now gone and the photography backdrop dismantled. I wiggle the locked library door handle. Guess I'll sleep with the theater curtains tonight.

I wish I were at Seung's or Ham's or someplace with at least another breathing body. A comfortable couch, where I hear barking dogs instead of clanging water pipes. I wish Kristen was working on a late-night project, or Bea, even Bea. We could talk about what happened, or talk about everything *but* what happened. I can't imagine what would have happened had I ignored the voices from the bathroom. As much as I didn't want to care, how could I not? Bea said it wasn't Toby's fight. Does that mean it isn't mine, either? Because the last time I hid from something, my whole world fractured and fell and dropped straight to hell.

I picture Statue Buddha waving a red flag, signaling me to stop before I cross the line from caring too little to caring too much. Maybe Statue Buddha knows what he's *not*-talking about. Maybe he knows I've reached a crossroads.

At the back hallway, my foot crunches, and when I step again I crush glass. A draft whips at my hair. Wind hits my face. Stomp. Crunch. Stomp. Crunch.

My foot slips on something hard. Glass? Maybe metal? I

strain my eyes but can't even see my shoes in the dark. The only things visible are outlines of lockers and trophy case frames. I shuffle around the corner and slide against the wall. My shoulder hits something big, hard, and not supposed to be here. I pat my way to a front grille, bend down, and come face-to-face with the front of Toby's truck embedded in the wall.

Ham?

My foot slips when I take off sprinting down the hall to the nearest light switch. I scramble to the lockers, running my hand along the metal until I reach the end of the row. If I turn the light on, I'll signal the cops for sure. But there's no alternative. I need to know if Ham's here. I have to see what the hell happened.

One. Two. Three.

I punch the light.

Seconds pass until my eyes adjust.

Definitely Toby's truck. Definitely poking through the wood-and-glass wall. Windows on both sides are smashed and the trophy case shattered.

I race for the nearest exit, shouting, "Ham! Ham!" and once I am outside, I see the truck, stuck in the wall, driver's door ajar.

Someone's on the ground, rolling back and forth. "Ham?" I spring toward the body. "Ham? Are you okay?"

It's Toby. Duct tape wrapped around his arms, legs, and stomach. His hair is darker than normal and his face looks like it's smeared in blood.

I drop into a squat at his side. "Toby? Are you okay?" He moans and swats the air, his breath bitter and ripe. "Ham!" he groans. "Did I kill Ham?"

I gasp. "Where is he?"

Toby slaps the air again, and I have to jerk back to avoid being hit. That's when I see Ham's shoe wedged beneath the truck tire. I run to the hood, drop down on my knees, and check under the cab.

It's hard to see in the dark. But on the other side of the truck, a body sprawls in the bushes against the building. Half naked, flat on his belly.

I race toward the familiar body, the one I care about more than myself. I know exactly who it is. It's when I reach him that I haven't a clue what to do. Tears shoot down my cheeks.

Do I run? Scream? Get more damn towels?

"Get up!" I whisper-yell, brushing glass from his back, pushing and poking his shoulder. "Please. Please! Get up!"

I'm shouting now, but he won't move. He won't do anything he should. He's piled on his stomach, cold and bloody, with a gash at his ear, another on top of his head.

Near the truck, Toby moans, "Help! Somebody help!"

My body shakes. I can't breathe.

I rub my best friend's back, his flesh like ice. "Ham! Ham! Please move. Please get up."

I push at his side, breathing in and out, not for myself but for him. He won't budge. He won't make a sound.

"Why aren't you moving?" I'm sobbing now. "Why won't you get up? Don't you know how much I love you?"

"Is he dead?" Toby moans. "Oh God! Did I kill him?"

I drop my head to Ham's waist and groan from my gut. "I should never have left you alone. I'm sorry! So fucking sorry!"

I fall onto the bushes splattered with broken glass and scream.

CHAPTER FIFTEEN

I SPEND THE NIGHT IN a shallow hole I scooped with my bare hands. In the dirt. Behind my school. Far from the dugout, but close enough to pay homage to my best friend. It is the least I can do after abandoning him, twice. I tuck myself away in the hills behind the building, where the only things alive are dying tumbleweeds. My life, my loss, my guilt battle my brain for space. Each talking over the other.

Why did I leave Ham alone? Why didn't I stay with him, make sure he got home safe? Friends don't leave friends. They hold them close to their heart, even when they're away.

Only hours have passed since I rubbed Ham's back and told him I was sorry. I want more minutes, hours, days. More time to waste with my best friend. All those nights at Seung's, watching the world's worst Mafia movies. All those mornings waiting for my Ham sandwich. If only I could ruffle his hair, kiss his cheek. If only I could feel his arms squeeze my shoulders one more time . . . but time makes no promises. You're never guaranteed how many minutes you'll enjoy with the person you love before they disappear from your life and the only things left are memories.

All I have are memories of those I love.

All I have are thoughts about those I've lost.

Everyone leaves me. Everyone close to me, gone.

I didn't think there were any pieces to my heart left to break. But like shards of glass, even the innermost chambers have shattered and smashed.

After placing an anonymous call from the emergency phone in the school hall, I nuzzled Ham's cheek, covered his shoulders with a towel, and told him we'd be together again, someday. I whispered to him the same shit I tell the nursing-home residents. All the same shit I don't know now if I believe. I told him how sorry I was, two thousand times. That I only left to get towels but should never have abandoned him. I should have stopped him from leaving the convenience store with Toby. If I could rewind the clock, go back in time, start over, none of this would have happened.

Principal Falls and Deputy Boggs were the first to arrive on the scene. I turned my head when the ambulance showed. I listened for its siren, though, and watched as the paramedics drove in the opposite direction from the county hospital.

Construction workers arrived this morning and unloaded piles of wood and plastic. I'm watching, waiting for the flag to lower, but it's flapping at the top of the pole like it doesn't give a damn.

I wish I could speak to Seung, but I'm afraid to hear details. Images brand my brain every time I shut my eyes. The glass. The truck. Ham's half-naked, blood-spattered body.

Moving myself from this hill is hell, but I can't sleep here another night, even though I want to punish myself somehow. Guilt from leaving Ham consumes me. I should have held his hand and waited until they carried him away on a gurney. That's what a good friend would do. Risk all that they're hiding for a friend.

I trudge toward the road to wander the town like the true homeless girl I am. No longer pretending, no longer keeping up a charade.

I don't care who sees me in blood-speckled sweats. I'm hiding in plain sight and no one is looking because they're focused on the details of their own lives. If they listened, they'd hear. If they looked closely, they'd see. The charming guy who's really a monster. The pretty girl forced into thinking she should take his abuse. The homeless girl who lives among them.

The next two nights I spend in the broom closet at Nowhere Near Like Home. Eva, the head nurse, refuses my explanations. She knows I'm there to sleep. She's never asked many questions, and I never overstay my welcome.

I force myself to eat a plate of chicken-fried steak soaked in white gravy and let my mind drift into the dark places. The space where my mother lives. Where Ham is.

There's Mama, stirring oatmeal and asking how I slept last night. She smiles, tucks a strand of hair behind my ear, and kisses my forehead. I reach around her waist and squeeze. There's Ham, shutting his locker and telling me he's in love. I ruffle his hair and peck his cheek. I'll never hear about his one true love. I'll never see him adored and cherished and doted on like he deserves. I'll never witness my mother's happy ending. Ham's, either.

When my thoughts become more than I can bear, I imagine that my life is a dream and none of these tragedies happened. I sleep more than I've slept in a year.

On Monday something inside my gut pushes me, shoves me, yanks me forward. I'm up. Awake. Sure, I'm going through the motions. But I'm ready to face the hard reality, and I long to see Seung.

Eva runs her fingers through my hair and stuffs my hand with buttered toast. She says, "Come back tonight if you need to. I'll keep the closet door unlocked." I thank her and tell her I might.

Engines rev in the school parking lot. Voices greet other voices.

I pass Statue Buddha on my way to find Seung. Someone moved him to the front of the hall to watch over students. His head is bowed. Arms folded. He's probably praying. I imagine him tossing a supplication up for me. For my mom. For Ham.

The buzzer rings and the crowd scatters. Seung stands at

235

his locker, frowning. He looks like he could use a friend right now, or maybe someone to kick him while he's down.

I slap my hand against Seung's locker. "Where were you?" I shout, holding back the tears. I don't want to be angry with him, but I am.

Seung's eyes light up—not like they should. They're brighter, focused. "Linden? Where have you been? I've searched this entire town for you."

"Liar!" I hit the lockers again, this time with my fist. "Where were *you*? We should have stayed together. We should have been with Ham. Together!"

Tears run down my face and pool on my collarbone. It is the first time I've cried since I kissed Ham good-bye. It's the first time I've felt anything but regret.

"They found him," Seung says. "You know that, right?"

I pound the locker in rhythm with my words, "I know! I know! I know!" and fall to my knees. Seung drops his books on the floor and falls with me. He wraps his arms around my shoulders, and all my weight pushes against his chest. He sits back on the floor, squeezing me tight. No more numbness. I feel everything there is to feel. And for some reason, right now, wrapped in Seung's arms, I feel closer to Ham and everyone I've ever lost.

A second buzzer rings. Someone says Seung's name, but I don't look up. The sobs go deep, hollow me out.

"Are you going to be okay, Linden?" Seung whispers in my ear. He rakes my bangs to the side and flicks a tiny twig across the hallway.

I grab a clump of my hair and twist. I'm not okay and I don't know how to be. Ham needed me and I wasn't there. I should have fought harder for my friend. I shouldn't have stopped searching for him. I feel like I'm an accomplice to this disaster. And it's not the first time I've had the job. Only this time, I hid afterward, not during the killing.

I'm not okay, I never am. I'm always hanging by a thread just to survive. Wearing masks made of sarcasm and jokes that make it easier to hide. That's what I do best. Hide and survive. Hide to survive.

Linden?

Yes, Mama?

Don't come out. No matter what.

Okay?

Listen to me. You hide. Always stay hidden.

Okay.

Nobody hurts you when they don't know you exist.

I love you, Mama.

I love you more.

She was wrong, though. People hurt you whether intentionally or not. The pain comes when you're aware of how you feel. The pain comes when you love.

Seung lifts my chin and scoops tears from my cheekbones with his thumb. He swipes my forehead with his finger and says, "My parents said I could go see him. I don't want to go alone. . . ."

I hold my breath. What does he mean? The thought of seeing Ham's body causes every cell in my own to freeze. I want to tell Seung I've already seen Ham and I can't handle another visit. But Seung's eyes are teary, too. He needs to say his good-bye, and for that reason alone, I nod.

"Meet me here after school." Seung hops to his feet and snatches his books. "You sure you're okay, Linden?"

When I look up, Bea is standing beside him, clutching her math book at her chest. "Are you okay?" she asks with care in her eyes.

There's that question again. *Are you okay?*

I'm sitting on the floor of my school, wearing blood-spattered sweats, making plans to do something I swore I'd never do again. No, I wouldn't say I'm okay. Had I avoided Beth's house and searched for my best friend, left Bea alone to handle her own affairs, Ham would be at school with me. History rewritten.

Bea tugs at Seung's shirt and whispers, "We should probably go."

Seung's posture stiffens and he wiggles his arm loose from Bea. His face is twitching when he turns and says, "Meet me here, Linden. After school. Don't forget."

If only.

Instead of going to class with my books, I walk empty-handed to the newsroom, where I find Mr. George sipping on coffee and staring at a magazine from New York. I walk to the computer and flop into a chair. I'm breaking all the rules for living homeless. My rules, that is. I'm in need of a nap, carrying too much stuff in my bag, and authentically looking the part of a stereotypical homeless person.

If anyone could miss the clues, though, it would be Mr. George. He always looks for the bright mark on a dark horizon, always finds the positives in a negative picture. I am nothing but muck.

"Linden," he says. "How do?"

I say nothing.

"Can I get you anything?"

My best friend?

"There are water bottles beneath my desk. Help yourself to the snack drawer, too."

I slump over a desk chair, and the hum of the computer lulls me to sleep.

When I wake, Mr. George is gone and two freshmen are in a heated discussion about vegetarianism as spiritual practice. My face is flushed and there's drool pooled close to my chin. I wipe my forehead and let the spit hang from my lip while I command the two guys to move far from my Realm of Existence. They grab their books and scurry out the door. Weird homeless girl, pointing and shouting, is a lot to absorb, especially for freshmen.

The world won't pause for anything. The carousel of life continues with or without you. No one cares that Ham's not at school. No one's concerned about the accident. It's unreasonable, unjust, un-fucking-fair.

I walk over to Mr. George's desk and plop into his padded

chair. I prop my feet on top and close my eyes, grabbing and grasping for nostalgia and times-when, but every detail I remember about Ham rips my heart. His springy hair, belly-ful laugh. His sarcasm in the most serious of moments. I imagine him saying, "Linden, zombies look more put together than you. Can't you at least comb your hair before grieving my good-looking ass?"

I rake my fingers through my hair and scan Mr. George's desk to prevent my eyes from dripping all over his magazine.

One oversized coffee mug-jug. One French press in need of rinsing. Picture of Andrew, Mr. George's handsome hus-band. Rechargeable batteries. I open a drawer and see six different protein bars that all look unappetizing. There's that scholarship packet from Willamette University's School of Journalism. The one labeled with my name. The school I was supposed to go to with my friends. I want to shred the papers now that my heart's ripped in two.

Mr. George walks in and clears his throat. I sweep my feet off his desk and refuse to look him in the face. The letters on the envelope blur into a block of black ink behind tears. I was supposed to help Ham get into school. It was my job, my duty.

"You're not yourself today, Linden," Mr. George says.

"How could I be?" Whatever myself even is.

"No classes?"

"None for me."

"You'll need a note."

"Will you write one for me?"

Mr. George nods and tells me to make myself at home. *Already on that, Mr. George.* If he only knew how at home I was.

I spend the day in the newsroom. I drop fifty cents in a cup on Mr. George's desk to pay for the apple and piece of turkey jerky I ate. Munching on the snack Mr. George's husband packed is a five-star restaurant experience.

Before school lets out, I check two bulletin boards near the administrative office, searching for an announcement or acknowledgment or assembly in honor of Ham. It's as if he didn't matter at this school. But he mattered to me.

I sit beside my locker and stare at a candy wrapper, lifeless on the floor. There's no sign of Toby, either. I wonder how bad he's hurt, or if he's even hurt at all. Don't some drunk people walk away from accidents unharmed?

Seung greets me in the hall, his happiness colliding with my sorrow. I glance around for Bea, likely the source of Seung's glee, but she's not with him. For a split second I want to ditch Seung, make him go alone. But only for a second.

"You ready to go?" Seung says at my locker. His eyes dart around the hall. He wrings his hands, fidgets, and glances over his shoulder.

I can't resist. "Watching for your Queen Bea?" I snap.

Seung glares. "What about you? Shouldn't you be looking for Reed?"

Oh yeah. Reed. The kiss. There's so much Seung and I need to talk about. So much he doesn't know. But the only energy I have is focused on Ham.

I stare at Seung's face and will it to look as blank and formless as mine feels, but there's always a light in his eye that refuses to dim. The carousel spins again. Picks up speed. Never stops for grief, for pain, for loss. It's bright and showy. Flaunting how life goes on even when you're no longer around to live.

CHAPTER SIXTEEN

TWENTY MINUTES ON THE ROAD and the silence inside Seung's car consumes me.

"Why are we on the highway? Why are you driving so fast?"

"Seeing Ham, Linden. Remember?"

"Shouldn't you slow down?" I say. "Drive like an old man? Yourself?"

Abide by rules of the road. Adhere to etiquette. Drive the proper speed while traveling to see a friend's body.

Seung ignores my questions, so I toss another.

"Where is he, anyway?" Because not only are we speeding, but we are driving in the wrong direction, away from the town's only funeral home.

"Bend."

"Bend? That's an hour away. Why Bend? What about Ham's parents?"

Seung side-eyes me and says, "Ham's parents are in Bend, Linden. Been there since the accident."

I drop my head against the seat. Of course Ham's parents won't leave his side. Maybe it's a religious thing. Maybe it's what they want to do for their one and only son.

I stare at the blur of pines and sagebrush moving at sixty miles per hour. Within seconds the greens and browns become hazy blobs and I free a much-needed moan.

"You don't look so good," Seung says.

"I look how I feel."

"I don't mean you look bad. You never look bad. I mean you look sick."

And then I am. It crawls up my throat and sours my mouth. I slap my hands on my lips and fill them with vomit.

Seung doesn't yell, *Oh, shit!* or laugh or swerve. He checks the rearview mirror, signals, pulls over, and flips on the hazard lights. He jogs to my side of the car, opens the door, and lifts me by the elbow. He pours a half gallon of water on my hands and dabs my face with a dingy blanket from the trunk. Supplies reserved for emergency situations.

We drive to a rest stop a few miles away and Seung waits while I wash my face and hands. When I reach the car, he is leaning against the passenger's-side door. All four windows are down, welcoming fresh air. I smile and his slouch goes straight. "All better?"

I shrug.

He opens the passenger's-side door and says, "Let's go see our buddy."

Seung smiles at the road. Either he is in denial or he's mastered the art of coping. His eyes blink and his lips mouth words to the song playing on the radio. I want him to be angry and sad and queasy like me, but in actuality, I appreciate his still and stable mood.

"So, you and Bea." Once the words spit out, I know I've ruined the stability.

Seung shakes his head. "No. No."

"Yes."

"It's not how it is."

"You're the king and she's the queen. It's what it is. How it works at this school. Isn't it?"

He smiles. *Damnitall*. He smiles.

Minutes pass while I stare at the dashboard, afraid to look anywhere but straight ahead. The green blur in my peripheral vision makes my jaw squeeze tight, bringing back the sour taste in my mouth. I push my head into the seat and close my eyes.

"So, you and Reed," Seung says, re-ruining the moment.

I finger part the back of my hair and scoop it forward. "There's something you don't know about our beloved Reed Clemmings," I mumble, my eyes still shut.

"Do I want to know?"

"You might. I mean, it could affect things with your queen."

"Would you please stop calling her that."

I open my eyes. Too tired for more sarcasm. Besides, Ham hated when Seung and I argued, claimed it was cover for sexual tension.

I drop my head to the side and whisper, "Sorry."

Seung sighs and stares at the road. "So what about Reed?"

"We had the wrong guy. Reed's the one who's been hurting Bea, not Toby. In fact, as surprising as it sounds, Asswipe's been trying to help her."

I fill Seung in on homecoming night, postkiss, and he insists that we talk to Mr. George or Principal Falsetto when we return to school. He's typical overprotective Seung, but I think he's right. No matter what Bea says, she needs our help.

"Is Toby okay?" I ask.

"Define okay," Seung says, and chuckles.

"Not the best time for jokes," I whisper.

"Sorry, but yes. Well, Asswipe's never going to be okay, by our definition, but physically he got off easy. I'd say the crash into the school wall was minor compared to what happened to him earlier."

"Minor?"

"A bit concussed, but he left the hospital with only a bruised chest and ego. Despite a few hair-related items missing from his body, he got off easy."

I chew the inside of my cheek, enough to start a canker sore. Yeah. Toby got off easy.

Traffic picks up. Some of the buildings I recognize from

my visits to the city—and I use that term loosely because a population over 80,000 in central Oregon equals city—with Seung's parents. If anyone wants to shop for anything besides milk and bread, they travel the distance to the only mall on this section of the state. I always ride along for the comfort I get from Seung's family. Today, I am here for Seung. He needs me. I need him. We need to say good-bye to our best friend, together. I just wish Seung showed more grief.

An urge bubbles up and I blurt, "You know I saw my mother die?" All of a sudden I feel like I need to assist my lungs to function, when all they want to do is close up and constrict. I don't know why I chose now to tell Seung about my mom. But it feels right to share something personal now, something I've kept hidden.

Seung glances at me, and then the road. He taps the brake and slows. "Do you want to talk about it?"

I stare at the road, lines, bumpers. My head shakes *no*; my mouth says, "Yes."

"Well, I didn't actually see it happen." Does it count if I was in the closet, hiding, refusing to look, even though I knew she was there? My mother never woke up. She never moved. She never saw her daughter grow up, get hips, start her period, or take the SAT. It's what happens when you're beaten with a fist and the end of something hard and sharp.

Seung glances over, looking like he does when fighting for answers on trig problems. But all he says is "I bet your mother was beautiful."

And all I say is "Bettie Page pretty."

Seung drives, without a word. He continues to glance at me, wondering if I'll share more, but refuses to probe. I decide now is not the time to discuss my mother. This moment belongs to Ham.

Seung flexes his forearm as he steers and I can't lure my eyes away. I force myself to stop because I feel like I'm disrespecting the dead. He slows and we turn left, then right. We pass medical buildings and doctors' offices before pulling into a hospital's parking lot.

"Hospital?"

Seung stares at the building without speaking. Either he doesn't want to see me cry or doesn't want me to spot his tears.

We walk toward the main entrance. Seung takes the lead. Not on purpose, but I'm dragging my feet, shuffling them on the tile, mentally preparing myself for arrows pointing to the morgue. White sheets and metal drawers big enough for mothers, fathers, sisters, and brothers. Steel tables with metal body scoops that reach down and turn your loved ones. The last time I was in a morgue, I ran. Death doesn't discriminate against age. Neither does body identification. And when you're young, and the body is your mother's, a part of your brain and heart dies. When you see your mom on a stainless-steel table, marked with a tag, you run, hide, and never look back.

Seung punches the wheelchair button and the doors open.

I watch my feet to make sure they're still moving. We stop at the elevator and I'm breathing like I do after running from security. My chest tightens. My stomach shifts like it's rising to the top floor. "Seung!" I shout, and cup my hands over my mouth.

"Linden?" He pushes me toward a drinking fountain and twists my hair around his wrist.

I wipe my face with my knuckles and Seung hands me a ball of paper towels he grabbed from the restroom. I rub the sandpaper over my chin and dab at my lips.

"You okay?"

I shake my head.

"You want to sit before we see Ham?"

My jaw tightens. I inhale-exhale before another wave of nausea hits. Then I shoot Seung a thumbs-up.

"You sure?"

I nod. I'm as ready as I'll ever be.

The elevator opens, and a man steps out with a yellow bucket and biohazard bags. *Sorry, dude.* I lean against the wall and grip the rail until we stop. "This can't be the basement," I say, following Seung off the elevator. "We went up instead of down."

Seung says nothing, and I'm too focused on not puking to argue. We pass the nurses' station and round an open room lined with carts and IV stands. We walk toward the back of the wing until we reach the last door on the right. Ham's grandparents are sitting in the hall on stools. His grandmother's face is dark and droopy, and his grandfather looks like a gloomy gray sky. The sides of their mouths hang. Grandma Ham swirls her forehead with her index finger, probably sketching a cross.

"Seung!" Grandpa Ham shoots out of his stool and drapes his arms over Seung's shoulders, squeezing him like an orange. "Good to see you, boy."

Seung says, "Okay to go in? Is now a good time?"

As if any time is good. But at least Ham is in a room and not somewhere cold, like the basement. I promise myself I'll focus on Ham's sweet round face and big heart, not the tag on his toe or the gauze clamping his jaw closed. I'm happy Ham's family is Catholic, offering access to him for long good-byes. At least I think Ham's Catholic. He mentioned chatting with Jarrell at Mass once.

We walk into the room and I stare at the back of Seung's shoes. Mrs. Royse reaches for Seung while tears cover her cheeks. I'm motionless and dizzy at the same time. My head spins. I stumble backward. I want to run, hide, go anywhere but here. I want to replace the images of Ham in my head, but I'm afraid the new ones might be worse. I slap both hands on my mouth. *Damnitall.* I leap into the bathroom, kicking the door shut behind me, and spill my guts into the toilet.

The heaves pause, and I'm breathing regularly again, so I shuffle to the door and let my hand linger on the handle. Ham would want me to hold my head high and march with shoulders back. I'm the vertex of our triangle, not the leg. It's time I act the way Ham saw me. The way I pretend to see myself when others are watching. I swallow, twist the knob, and face the most wonderful friend I've ever known.

And . . .

He faces me back.

Eyes wide, chest moving, breathing, doing everything it's supposed to do.

"Ham? Ham. Ham!" I scream, shout, roar.

"Linden," Ham whispers. "You came."

I hop on the bed and straddle his waist. I squeeze Ham's face, then mash mine against his cheeks. I crawl alongside him and pat his chest. It's too much, I know, but *whothehellcares*.

"Ham. Ham. Ham!" I'm on repeat. His laugh is Chopin to my ears, and I can't stop singing his name and listening when his mouth makes a melody of words, with air in his lungs and a beat in his chest.

"What the fuck, Linden?" Ham says, his face flinching, showing signs of terror.

"Franklin," Ham's mom says, "your friends are happy to see you."

Happy? There's not even a word to describe the emotion I feel. I can't stop squeezing Ham's body to make sure he's alive and well and here in this world with me.

After many seconds of pawing and pinching and patting, Ham swats my hand and tells me it's enough. I ignore, squeezing his belly one more time, and he yells, "Ouch! Not my side! It's still tender."

"Oh, Ham. I'm sorry. But I thought you were dead. I thought you left me. Left us." I glance at Seung and he's wiping his eyes.

Seung says, "Would have brought you flowers, buddy, but you know I'm broke."

Ham smiles. "I prefer candy, anyway."

I flop against Ham's pillow and snuggle next to him in the hospital bed, careful not to bump his side. I rest my head in the crook of his neck and my tears soak the pillow.

"I'm glad you're here, Linden," Ham whispers.

"I'm glad you're here, too, Ham."

"Revenge plot backfired. But I guess you already know that."

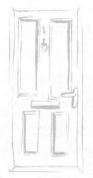

CHAPTER SEVENTEEN

WHEN WE PULL INTO TOWN, it's dark. I insist on spending the night at Seung's. Mrs. Rhee deserves to know what happened to the dress and heirloom necklace, and I need to make plans to pay her back.

I start in about my fight with a tumbleweed and Mrs. Rhee holds up a stiff hand and refuses my apology.

"But Mrs. Rhee," I say, "I'm so sorry about the necklace. I want to repay—"

Mrs. Rhee wraps me in a hug, her arms made of honey that soaks into the cracks and holes in need of patchwork. For a moment, I remember what it's like to have a family, or at least the structure of one. To feel loved, cared about. Connected to at least one other person you trust with life because they gave you yours.

"I'm sorry," I whisper.

Seung's mom slides my hair behind my ear and whispers back, "Don't be. It was an accident. My friend's a jeweler and she owes me a favor."

She unwraps her arms from mine, punches a throw pillow back into shape, and grabs a blanket from the closet. She leaves a stack of bedding on the couch and walks upstairs. Seung follows his mom, but midway up the steps, he turns and announces he's going to crash on the couch, as long as I don't mind. *Mind?* Since when does Seung ask for permission to sleep on his own couch, in his own home?

We start a movie but turn it off twenty minutes deep. We watch TV but decide we're bored with network television. We settle on staring at our feet while listening to music. Tonight, talking is overrated. Besides, I'm still reeling about Ham's *resurrection*.

After Seung sighs three hundred times, I finally say, "What?"

He flinches.

"Your sighs," I say softly. "Do they mean something other than you're tired?"

Seung tilts his head. "They mean something," he whispers, and returns to staring at his feet.

I know what's bothering Seung. It's obvious. I wish he would just ask me about the Reed Clemmings kiss. What it meant, if I liked it. I figured once he learned what a dick Reed was, is, has always been, he would forget all about the

254

kiss. But his lips have tightened, his arms crossed. He's even tucked his feet beneath a pillow to avoid touching me.

We fall asleep on the sectional sofa in the shape of the letter L, our feet inches apart.

When I wake in the morning, I pat the couch, expecting Seung to be asleep, but he's in the chair reading something on his phone, sunshine-eyed with wet hair falling into his lashes. The aroma of warm biscuits and dryer sheets makes it impossible to even pretend to sleep.

I exaggerate a sigh, hopeful Seung's forgiven me for kissing Reed, but he doesn't look up from whatever he's reading. He furrows his brow and grunts, so I swing a blanket over my back like a cape and march toward the bathroom.

At the door, Seung snaps, "Who the hell is 'Anonymous'?"

I whirl and the blanket flaps. "Huh?"

He holds his phone into the air. "What is this shit?"

Seung looks like his ghost, the color drained from his face. His lips twitch and his hand, the one gripping the phone, trembles and shakes. I stomp toward the chair and snatch the phone from his fingers, then rub the corners of my eyes into focus. The headline on Hinderwood's blog reads:

What You Don't Know, by Anonymous

"What's this?" I ask, rereading the title. My eyes scan the text, then the comments that mention my name. "What the hell is this?"

CHAPTER EIGHTEEN

BY THE TIME WE ARRIVE at school, the blog published by Anonymous has been deleted from Hinderwood's Facebook page, Twitter feed, and Tumblr. Thank you, Seung, for believing me over blog comments. But just because Seung logged into a few social media accounts and deleted the article doesn't mean the entire school didn't swallow its words. Lies at a small-town high school travel at warp speed. Even late risers know someone who memorized key points.

> Reed Clemmings = Monster
> Anonymous = Victim

The article punches Reed where it should, but the comments don't. They split the school in half and say things like

"She should have signed her name. Owned up to shit." *Owned up?* Some call the article blasphemy. Others call Anonymous a hero. "Burn the jerk at the stake." "Take him to the chopping block."

The article shares what kind of person Reed used to be. In his past life. Before he became a monster. There's mention of his tender touch and the first time he and Anonymous had sex. Then there are the words describing the first time he slapped her face, seven times in a row, each hit with more force. The article reads, "How could someone so flawless become so fucked up?"

But there's also that comment at the top. The one responsible for the rumor rage and giving Anonymous her name. "Linden Rose didn't seem to mind kissing Reed Clemmings at the dance. Who's the monster now?"

When Seung and I plow through the front doors of Hinderwood High, we're met with a frantic principal and rabid school counselor. Apparently they read the comments, too, and have arrived to rescue me. News flash. I don't need a rescue mission, or at least not for the reason they think.

Seung loops his arm through mine and waves his hand like he's swatting away paparazzi cameras. "She can't talk right now!" he shouts. "She needs to see Mr. George."

As we storm the newsroom, Principal Falsetto's sister walks out.

"Hey," she says. Not the most professional salutation for a journalist.

"Not now," Seung snaps, struggling to shut the door on her.

The journalist smiles and grips the handle. "Nice article," she says, *"Anonymous."*

"No further comment!" Seung shouts, and slams the door in her face. He twists the lock, then rushes Mr. George's desk.

He logs on to the computer and pounds keys. Mr. George isn't in the room, but I'm certain he'll be here soon, ready to talk.

"Everyone thinks it's me," I say. "Even Miss Sunshine."

"Miss who?"

I shake my head at Seung. "Never mind."

"It's because of that comment," he says, his voice climbing. "One comment spawned fifty more. What the hell is wrong with people? Don't they know the rules? You *never* read comments. Ever."

I step beside Seung and accidentally bump him with my hip. His eyes open up and I smile to myself. Seung notices, too. Right away.

"Why are you smiling like that?" he asks. "You should be mad, not smiley."

I tuck my lips around my teeth. It's hard to stop grinning when you thought your friend was dead, then find out he's alive. All else seems trivial. "I know the truth," I say. "Why be mad?"

"Because everyone thinks *you* wrote the article," he says. "Everyone thinks you're Anonymous."

"Well, it's not me. You and I both know that. Obviously, it's Bea."

"And you're not mad at her?" Seung rubs his forehead, confused.

"Why would I be mad at Bea? She can't control the comments."

I don't feel anger toward Bea. If anything, I'm relieved. She finally stood up for herself, even if she did it anonymously, even if I was indirectly implicated in the process of telling the truth. This has nothing to do with me.

I neaten a stack of notebooks on Mr. George's desk, unsure why I'm compelled to organize shit. I suppose I could be raging mad, pissed at Bea for eliminating her name from the article or forgetting to disable comments. But why? I know the truth. Seung knows the truth. Everyone at school now knows the truth about Reed. Who cares if Bea refused to sign her name and shine a flashlight in her face? Maybe she wanted to fly beneath the radar. Maybe it's her way of getting revenge.

"You don't care if everyone thinks you had sex with Reed?" Seung asks, and I can't help but notice him recoil and squirm.

"I can't control what others think."

Seung cares more about my reputation than I do. But he believed me without question. And I've done my fair share of lying. Everything else seems minor-league.

I bump Seung with my hip again, only this time I don't hit his hip, I hit the front of his pants. By accident. My head is instantly twenty degrees warmer than the rest of the room.

"I'm glad you don't care," Seung says, and bites his bottom lip. "And I'm glad it's not true. I mean, not you."

"Did you think it was?" I match Seung's move by chewing my lip. Only when it makes a slurping sound do we both smile and stare at each other's face, lips, feet.

"Never." Seung taps my thigh with his knee, then clears his throat. "You snored last night."

I chuckle. "Well, of course I did. I was tired."

"It was cute."

Now it's my turn to bump him with my knee. "You're cute."

"Shut up," he says, playfully.

"Make me," I say. *Make me?*

Seung opens his mouth as if to offer the world's greatest comeback, then says, "You make *me*."

But I don't. I freeze. Because it's the world's greatest come-on.

Seung eyes me. My knees lock. The corner of his mouth hikes up. I can't stop looking at his mouth until I realize I can't stop looking at his mouth. We stare at each other for eight seconds. How do I know? Because the room is so quiet I hear the wall clock tick eight times.

Seung moves first. And by move, I mean combs his hair with his hand. The sudden movement makes me whip around and head toward my bag. Why I insist on pilgrimaging to my bag at a moment I could be kissing Seung is beyond me. I hear Seung exhale halfway across the room, and the sound makes my eyes blink long, squeeze hard.

"Mr. George. Hey," Seung says, and I whip around.

Mr. George throws his keys at his desk. "Sit down. We need to talk."

I'm sure he means me, but Seung drops into a chair and says, "We need to talk to you, too."

A shine of sweat beads on Mr. George's brow. He dabs it with a yellow handkerchief. "Who wrote that story, Linden? The one unapproved to publish. Was it you? Is it true?"

Mr. George points at me and I struggle with my answers. I mean, no, the story isn't mine because I didn't write it, but yes, the subtext is fact. My name is nowhere on the piece, only in the comments.

I need to say something. But what? *Well, Mr. George, the story is true, but I didn't write it? I'm not Anonymous?* Seems simple, plausible, but for some reason I can't form the right words. Those explaining the facts. Instead, a familiar jab pokes my gut. The sting of sympathy. This isn't my story to tell. If Bea didn't want her name known, I sure as hell won't reveal it.

I shove my chair back and it squeaks across the floor. My bag is out of reach, so I extend my leg and loop the strap over my foot. Mr. George is still waiting for an answer I won't give. He's tapping his pen on paper, and his patience is at a low level.

I lift my bag with my foot and swing it toward me. Breaking rule #2 from beginning to end.

My backpack tips, falls, spills.

"Whoops," I say, stepping on my deodorant and stumbling to one knee.

"Linden," Mr. George says. "Are you listening?"

I yank at my bag's strap to settle my belongings to the bottom. Then, because I'm distracted, unfocused, too busy thinking about Seung's mouth and how it would feel against mine, I swing my bag over my shoulder, upside down.

Hey, Linden, there's your other bra.

Beans.

Balls of brown paper towels.

Your toothbrush.

Plastic bags packed with bacon.

And biscuits from breakfast.

Dumped on the floor in front of me. The rest behind, and off to the side.

I'm on all fours, scooping everything I own into my backpack. Everything I wish I didn't see. Everything that screams *Linden Rose = Homeless.*

Seung squats to help, and I snap, "No!"

He jumps up, twirling my underwear around his index finger.

Here's me, trying to keep my shit together after I failed to keep my shit together.

I reach for my underwear and Seung jerks his hand back. I watch for a smile, wink, or wisecrack. Silence. Until the cogwheels whirl in his head.

"Linden?" Mr. George says. "For God's sake. Time to spill it."

I already did.

I yank my underwear from Seung's fist and stuff it into my bag. This time I remember to zip.

"Can we talk later?" I ask, refusing eye contact with Seung, who is refusing to look anywhere but dead into my eyes.

CHAPTER NINETEEN

SEUNG TAGS ME IN THE hall. I pick up speed and lose him at the turn.

I'm already dodging Mr. George, or at least prolonging our meeting. Mr. George said we needed to talk about why my name came up in response to that article, but I told him I needed to speak with someone else first. I patted Mr. George's hand and told him not to worry. This isn't my story to share, and it's unfair to Bea for me to share anything. And now Seung demands answers, too, but for more personal reasons.

I go left. Seung darts right. "Linden!" he shouts.

"Seung!" a voice calls from down the hall.

It echoes again. "Seung. Seung."

I turn and see Bea, waving her arm. Seung stops, pivots, and plunges into a chemistry classroom. He has trig. Bea turns around, her nose pointing at her ballet flats. When the crowd clears, I charge after her.

"Bea!" I shout.

She looks over. Her eyes are wet. She starts to shuffle away.

"Bea?"

"Not now," she snaps.

"Please. Now," I beg.

I watch as Seung bounces out of the wrong classroom and scoots along the wall toward trigonometry. He glances over his shoulder, sees Bea, and picks up speed. Basically, Seung's walking faster than he drives. Bea watches me lose interest in her and whips back around. As soon as she sees Seung, she sprints after him, shouting his name.

"Need to talk!" I yell after her. "Mr. George has questions."

She turns the corner and I pound the locker with my heel. My foot slips on paper, and when I look at the ground, there's another ten-dollar bill stuck to my shoe. I check to see if anyone is watching, then stuff the money into my pocket and race to class.

The beginning of first period is full of whispers.

I notice right away that Reed is absent. I also see that Bea didn't make it to class. I wonder if she found Seung. I wonder if he's hiding in the restroom, knees tucked to his chest on a toilet seat, while Bea calls his name.

Kristen races into the classroom and jabs my shoulder with her pencil. "Ohmygod, Linden," she says while whisking by me. "Whatthehellishappening? Whatthehelliswrong?"

I hold up my hands. "It's not what you think," I whisper.

"Just stay away from the comments."

Shoulder jabs continue. First from Jarrell. Then from Toby.

Only Jarrell is gentle when he taps my back with his finger. He says, "Do you want me to walk you to your next class?" He motions to the students with cupped hands, whispering my name. They wonder how and why I'm singlehandedly taking down their hometown hero. I shake my head, and Jarrell shrugs his shoulders and smiles. He says, "Can you tell me how Ham's doing? He hasn't returned my calls."

Toby taps my shoulder hard, then pounds his fist on my desk. "Is this a sick joke, Linden? You're fucking with Bea on purpose?"

I exhale and turn toward T.P. I jump when I'm met with a giant ball of fire. "Holy shit! What, uh, what the hell happened to you?" In the light of day, his face is striped like candy corn. White forehead, bright orange face, yellowish chin.

Toby glares, but his beady eyes don't strike the fear they once did. How could they? They're missing outlines, punctuation, or as most people call them, eyebrows. His hair, or at least what's left on his head, is neon, and even his neck looks sun kissed.

"You know what happened," Toby says with a grunt. And I do, somewhat, but Ham's going to need to fill in a few details. Like how he was able to shave the initials T.P. above Toby's browline.

Mr. Dique taps the board with his pointer as a cue to sit down, shut up. I decide to do the opposite. I stand and say,

"Mr. D., I have to go. Mr. George needs me." I don't wait for his answer. I'm too busy racing for the door.

I slip into the vacant newsroom, ready to process my thoughts, alone. I don't know what to do, or if I should do anything at all. So what if people think I'm the girl Reed hurt? The truth causes me no pain. The lies hurt her more.

Seung barges through the door, shouting, "Bea won't leave me alone. I can't take it anymore, Linden! I'm a hot-girl magnet and I can only handle one hot girl at a time."

Seung swings his backpack into a chair, on the other side of the room, and continues his rant. "I can't handle this, Linden. Bea's everywhere I look. And it tears me in half because I know she needs a friend. I'm just not the right guy for the job." Seung holds his hand to his chest. "Besides, I have *you* to worry about. I don't have time to care for Bea. She has a boyfriend. A rather big, Cyclops-ish boyfriend who's been dipped in orange dye thanks to Ham and his revenge plot. And don't even get me started on that psychotic, poetry-puking ex-boyfriend—"

I interrupt Seung. "What about 'time to stand up and fight'? Isn't that what you proclaimed after T.P. tried to run you over? Destroy your enemy and make them your friend? What about Seung Freaking 2.0?"

Seung rolls his eyes, his head. He mumbles, "What *about* Seung?" He spins around on his heel, saying, "Linden? I said I have *you* to worry about. I've always had you to worry about."

I swallow, knowing what's coming next.

Seung frowns. "Why do you carry so much shit in your backpack?"

Now it's my turn to roll my eyes, head, everything.

I clench my teeth and the word "preparedness" pushes its way out. I clamp my mouth shut before another lie slips and slithers. Lying to Seung makes me weak. And while there's an assumption that homelessness falls upon the weak, it is not *for* the weak, or the unprepared.

"What are you preparing for, Linden? End of days?" Seung's eyes smile but there's something in them, a flicker, a flash, a snapshot of this moment that prevents me from smiling back.

I turn around in my chair and stare into the blank computer screen. Seung exhales and I shut my eyes. I refuse to say anything for fear it will come out as a lie. I'm sick of lying, hiding, withholding the truth.

Seung deserves better. He deserves the truth.

The truth that will set me free, piss him off, or maybe both.

I want to share my past with Seung. Tell him about my mother. That a monster killed her, because he wanted to and could. My head tells me my past is irrelevant to my future, that it merely paved the way. But I feel it gripping my ankles and dragging me behind with every step I take. I shouldn't be afraid. My past made me who I am today. But the fear of losing my future to my past terrifies me.

"No comment?" Seung pushes.

No words escape. They're huddled in the corner, shivering, shaking, afraid to crawl out.

Seung sighs. "Being truthful won't get you a lot of friends, Linden, but it will always get you those who matter most."

I wait for my tears to draw lines on my face. When I turn around, he's gone.

The one who matters most.

CHAPTER TWENTY

"WHAT IF I TOLD YOU my parents think I'm gay?" Ham's announcement in the food line at Cheese Country is anything but subtle. In fact, when I look around the restaurant, all eyes stick to Ham. He's alive and loud and oozing everything I love about him. My big, juicy Ham. "Are you listening to me, Linden? Gay."

"I'd say you have perceptive parents?" Ham notices my uptalk, and his eyes widen.

I step to the counter. "I'm buying. What do you want?" I wave two ten-dollar bills, found outside Mr. Dique's door.

Ham waves. "I have a fifty burning a hole in my pocket. Besides, I need change for the soda machine." He shoves in front of me and orders two chili dogs, two baskets of cheesy fries, and two sides of ranch dressing. "What do *you* want, Linden?"

"No thanks. I'll get my own." I'll also figure out another way to pay back the debt I owe. What price do you pay for leaving your best friend naked, alone, and presumably dead?

When we find a table that isn't covered in crumbs, Ham revs up again.

"Want to know what I told my parents?"

I do, but I can't stop thinking about the secret I'm keeping from Ham, from Seung, from those who matter most.

"They think Seung and I, you know, we're together." Ham chomps a fry with force.

I smile. "But Seung's not your type."

Ham slaps the table. "Exactly!" He launches a fry at my chest and grins, all teeth, until I pick the fry from my sweatshirt, dip it into the communal ranch, and shove it into my mouth.

"They're clueless, though. I mean, they think they have me all figured out. But I'm multifaceted, Linden. I've many secrets they'd love to know."

"So I've heard." I smile and my eyes start to sting. "God, Ham. I thought I lost you homecoming night."

Ham groans and holds a palm to my face. "Not again, Linden. Go back to smiling. Your tears are beginning to make me self-conscious."

I chuckle. *Ham*, self-conscious?

He smiles, reading my mind. "I know. Foreign concept. But stop. Now."

I dunk another fry in dressing. "So I finally saw Toby, in the light of day, looking like an oversized Cheeto. Tell me, how did you tape Toby to the toilet?"

"Scotch," Ham says. "And a lot of it."

"And the plan backfired when he sobered up?"

Ham shakes his head. "It was a backfiring that almost killed Ham." He pops another fry into his mouth. "Actually, it was when I returned to the scene of the crime, after I saw you. Remorse overtook me. I should have known not to go back, Linden. Those movies we watch misled Ham."

I roll my eyes but could not care less if Ham refers to himself in first, second, or third person. I'm in love with every layer.

"I thought duct tape held the universe together," he says. "It's used in practically all Mafia movies. But it couldn't hold a drunk Toby Patters to a toilet, now, could it? He nearly made me a pancake when he escaped and tried to pin me to the building with his truck. Thankfully I'm quick. I was able to dart, fast. He only clipped my side, but the impact slammed me into the wall, knocked me out. Can you imagine if he'd actually hit me head-on, Linden? The irony. Ham, a pancake."

I smile. "I'm just glad you're alive."

"Had Toby not risen from his drunken slumber, he'd be bald instead of blotchy."

"He sure is orange," I say.

"Hair dye works wonders. So does bronzer."

I smile and repeat, "So happy you're alive."

Ham nods. "Lived to tell the tale. Didn't even need to execute the entire plan, thanks to my near death."

272

"Don't tell me there was more."

"Photos taken but not needed. Going to keep them safe, though, just in case. But the accident seems to have made Toby remorseful. I don't think he'll be bothering any of us anymore."

The bells on the door jingle.

"Buddy!" Ham yells. "We were just talking about you. How you're *so* not my type."

Seung glances in our direction, but he's staring at Ham, avoiding me. Bea and Beth file behind him. Jarrell follows, but he's not with Bea. I wonder if Seung is.

"Scoot over. Make room," Ham says.

"You scoot over." My words hiss.

Ham stuffs a scoop of chili minus the dog into his mouth and frowns.

Seung slides into the booth next to me and bumps my leg with his. I plaster myself against the wall. Seung hasn't said more than three words to me since he declared he was the one who mattered most . . . or that I was the one who mattered most. All I know now is that he matters more than I'm willing to accept, and I'm not sure how to handle my next move.

Jarrell walks by and knocks on our table. Ham jumps up and follows Jarrell to a booth in the back of the restaurant, leaving me alone with Seung and piles of food.

Bea and Beth walk over.

Bea smiles at Seung, waiting for him to look up and invite her to sit down, but he's busy swirling ketchup and mayo, watching the drips and drops hit his plate. Seung's channeling Jackson Pollock, refusing to look up.

Bea taps her foot, clears her throat, and smiles larger than should be physically possible. Seung stares at his plate, mixing media, perfecting his condiment masterpiece.

"Hi, Bea," I say to snuff the awkwardness out of the atmosphere. "Had a chance to talk to Mr. George yet?"

She shakes her head.

"Talk to him about what?" Beth asks.

"I'll take care of the misunderstanding," Bea says.

"What misunderstanding?" Beth asks.

I nod, wanting to believe Bea. I mean, I know what it's like to wear a mask, hide in plain sight, but who am I to ask her to clean up a mess she never made in the first place? People assume I'm the girl, Anonymous, because of a single comment. Is it Bea's job to come clean, for me?

"You know," I say, "forget about it."

"Forget about what?" Beth asks.

Bea's eyes lock on Seung, and pity punches my gut. Bea's never made things easy for me. A part of me hated her for treating me the way she did, but then that other part—the part that found her in the bathroom dabbing at broken skin, the part that found her in the bedroom huddled against the wall—experiences the same pains and hurts she does. I was there, huddled against the wall, while my mother died. My pain may not be external, but it's real.

Bea ogles Seung, willing him to rescue her. I drop my head,

sad that Bea doesn't know she already initiated the rescue mission herself when she published that anonymous article. She doesn't need someone else to do the job.

Seung stares at his plate, stiff armed and not at all ready for his knight-in-shining-armor role.

The scene is agonizing to watch. Bea staring at Seung. Seung staring at his plate. Bea sighing. Seung tightening. Finally I toss a half-eaten fry onto the table and say, "For shit's sake, sit. Seung, scoot your ass."

I yank Seung's pants, pulling his leg toward mine. He plants his feet and grips the table, unwilling to budge. Beth drops onto the edge of the booth opposite us, while Bea stands by Seung, waiting for him to move. I admire her persistence but wish her affection were directed at someone else, someone other than Seung.

"Seung," I whisper and tug at his pants. "Scoot over." As much as I'd prefer Bea buzzing at a different table, the disappointment in her eyes makes me pull harder on Seung's pants. "Move. Seung. Now."

He tilts his chin toward me, still staring at his plate. That's when I see the tear. Right there, balancing on his cheek.

Whatthehelliswrongwiththisboy?

Here's me, saving the one who matters most from his most embarrassing moment. Consider it debt recovery.

I slide my hand toward his and he locks his finger around mine. Under normal circumstances, my body would heat, ignite, combust. Frankly, I'm surprised by the finger hold. It's nice, but Seung's terrible with timing.

I climb onto my knees on the bench and shout, "Hey, Ham!" and motion toward Bea and Beth. Ham mumbles and I point, signaling him to move ass, now. He does, after a thirty-second hug with Jarrell.

"Your food's getting cold," I say as Ham slides into the booth.

"Not hungry," Ham says, and if Seung's finger wasn't hooked around mine, I'd beckon the marching band to play in Ham's honor, because Ham is never not hungry.

I shove Seung to the edge of the seat and slide out of the booth. He becomes an uncaged animal. First pausing, unsure what to do, then sprinting to the door looking like a completely cute dork. I jog backward, yelling to Ham, "Meet us at Seung's later! SAT prep, or something."

"I think I'm getting kicked out of school. Remember?" Ham shouts back. "Screw the SAT!"

I ignore Ham's remark because I'm trying to reschedule his upcoming three-day suspension for after the SAT, and his parents are already on top of purchasing pricey reclaimed wood and floor-to-ceiling windows to rebuild the wall, bigger and better and more Ham-like. "Meet us anyway!" I shout, and head out the door.

When we reach Gold Nugget, I ask Seung if we're skipping class, and he answers by opening the car door and revving the engine. We drive beside Cheese Country's glass windows and I crane my neck at Ham having lunch with Bea and Beth.

Jarrell sits in the booth. Beside Ham.

We drive for five minutes before I decide it's safe to speak. "Were you crying back there?" The words belly flop from my lips. Seung can't deny it, but I'm fairly certain he will.

"First Ham. Then Bea. Then you. Then me."

I ignore Seung's Dr. Seuss-ish sentiment. "Maybe go easy on Bea."

"Linden, she follows me everywhere I go. And I know I should like it because the rules of being a guy say I should, right? She's beautiful and vulnerable and seems like she's into me. But it's too much. I already have pressure figuring out you and me, and the SAT."

"You and me?" I tuck my hair behind my ear and wait for Seung to answer. He leaves me hanging.

We stop for slushies and I suggest we pick one up for Ham, but Seung suggests Triangle Park because Ham has two more classes—those we're skipping—and a meeting with the principal to negotiate his suspension.

We drive to the park, and as expected, no one is there because they're where they should be. School. We teeter and totter and try to balance our drinks while bouncing up and down. I ask Seung if he's really going to go away to college.

"Not if I bomb the SAT," he says.

I laugh, but he's wearing his serious face.

"They say it could impact your future."

Seung chuckles. "No one cares about your SAT score, Linden."

277

"College admission boards do."

I dig my heels into the dirt and try to balance our weight on the teeter-totter.

I inch higher into the air. "Seung Rhee, your score matters more than you know."

When I reach the top, Seung jumps off his seat and balances it in his hand so I don't crash to the ground. He pushes the totter until it teeters parallel. "You matter more than a score. And for that reason alone, I'll study."

I suddenly feel like ripping off my coat. I mean, it's forty degrees Fahrenheit and hot as hell.

Seung lowers the teeter-totter to the ground and I bounce gently on the dirt.

"Let's go to my house before Ham shows up on the step."

He snatches my hand and we jog toward the car.

Seung's house is silent. Mr. and Mrs. Rhee aren't home from work. No warm welcomes or hello-how-was-your-day? Just two truant teens exhausted and hungry and in need of head space.

"Food. That's what I need," Seung says.

He opens the refrigerator and unloads a tray of enchiladas, premade and wrapped in foil. He rips off the tin foil and replaces it with plastic wrap.

"It's Thursday," I say. "Shouldn't you be eating *American* food?"

"Enchiladas aren't American?"

"They're Mexican."

278

"Everyone in the world eats enchiladas," he says. "It's like saying pizza is Italian, fries are French."

The argument fizzles and I focus on the smell of cumin and cilantro piping from the microwave. The enchiladas would be better in the oven, crispy with burned cheese, but when it comes to Mrs. Rhee's cooking, I'm the least picky. Her food is five-star, no matter how it's heated.

We scoot into the dining room, where we wolf tortillas and scoops of cheese, chatting little between bites. The sauce is white and green and tastes like a garden of chives. I'd love to talk spices and how Mrs. Rhee should ghostwrite recipes for celebrity chefs, but Seung is deep in thought, and I'm sure the last thing he wants to discuss is his mother's cooking.

Seung tears off a chunk of tortilla and dunks it in sauce. He catches me staring. "What?"

I tap my mouth. "Right there. Cheese. Dangling from your lips."

I slide out of my chair and walk into the kitchen, shoveling four more bites of enchilada sauce into my mouth on the way. Seung follows me into the kitchen, and I wipe my mouth with my sleeve. He passes by me, then turns and grabs the plate from my hands. He rinses it off and loads it into the dishwasher, then reaches for a rag and runs it underwater. When he turns around, I snatch the dishcloth from his hands and walk to the table to wipe up our mess.

"You don't have to do that," he says.

"I know. I want to." And then I catch him watching me,

and I feel like I should move a certain way, wiggle my hips or something. I mean it's obvious he's staring at my ass and I'm not sure how to enjoy it. My thoughts smack me in the face, and I launch the rag at Seung. He catches it, tosses it into the sink, grabs my hand, and says, "C'mon."

We end up in the basement, crammed together on one section of the sectional couch. Our usual L shape changes to a hyphen. Head to head. My stomach feels fuller than it has in weeks, almost to the point of discomfort, which is something new. My heart? Yeah. It's jam-packed, too.

"Want to study for the SAT?" Of course, I don't mean what I'm asking.

"No."

"Neither do I."

"Want to watch TV?" Seung asks.

"No."

"Neither do I."

Seung rolls over and slides up the couch to a seated position. I stretch and stare at the ceiling.

"Thanks for rescuing me," he says.

"Thanks for believing me," I say. "Besides, I was just saving you from an embarrassing moment."

Seung pauses, then says, "Linden? You ever feel like you're suffocating?"

All the time. "Sometimes."

"This year was supposed to be different," he says. "I wanted to be different. To do things I'd never done."

"Which are?"

"Take no shit. Be me. And yet, I don't even know who I am."

"You're Seung Rhee. Homecoming king. I'd say you're off to a great start being different."

"Homecoming king was hardly my goal. I want to do what Seung Rhee wants to do. Not what everyone expects me to do, or what my parents think I should do."

I clamp my mouth shut, while Seung calculates who he is, who he wants to be, and I'm the last person qualified to chime in with advice. I won't even share who *I* really am. There's another long pause. I clear my throat. It's time to be honest, truthful, and show Seung he matters most.

"Don't you want to know about all that stuff in my bag?" I ask, and hold my breath.

Seung inches toward me. "Nope. Not now."

"But don't you want to talk?"

Seung reaches for my face, and his fingertips fall against my cheek.

"Not really."

"But don't you want to—"

"I'd rather do this."

Seung's head missiles at mine. His chin where his eyes go, his face upside down. When I stare at him all I see are nose and lips and the reverse face that forms when someone is topsy-turvy. He puckers, leans in for a kiss, and I start to laugh.

"What?" Seung freezes, his lips a millimeter from mine.

"Nothing."

"Are you laughing?"

"No."

"You are."

"I'm not. I promise."

"You're laughing at me?"

"No. No. Not you. Not even."

"You are."

"I'm not," I say. "It's just that you're upside down and I'm fixating on your nose, your mouth, and it looks like a tiny Seung face without eyes. You know when you look at someone upside down and their lips move but . . ."

Seung moves that missing millimeter.

His hands press against my cheeks.

"I'd like to kiss you now," he whispers. "Would that be okay?"

And here's me finally shutting the hell up because I'm kissing my best friend, and feeling it in every single cell of my body.

CHAPTER TWENTY-ONE

MR. GEORGE FORCES A MEETING the following day at school. And by force, I mean, he shuts the door, locks it, and says, "I'm forcing you four to stay. Don't like it? Call the cops."

Kristen says, "But I'm going to be late for class. Mr. Dique hates when we're late."

Mr. George says, "Mr. Dique needs to get out more. Live life. Have fun. Screw him."

Ham's eyebrows reach his hairline, a grin spreads ear to ear.

I open and close the clasp on my bag five thousand times until Mr. George clears his throat.

"Bea is no longer working for the paper," he says.

"What? Why?" Ham asks.

Mr. George shushes Ham. "We considered a corrective

story authored by Bea and published by Bea." He sighs. "But we won't be doing that."

"Wait. What?" I ask. "How do you know about Bea?"

Mr. George frowns. "She told me. She said everyone knew."

"Then why aren't you clearing the air?" Seung asks. "Move forward with a corrective story. Everyone thinks Linden wrote that article."

Mr. George nods. "Not so simple, Seung."

"Oh, yeah?" Everyone looks at me for more, which I don't have. So I simply shrug my shoulders and repeat, "Oh, yeah."

"I think we should let the story fizzle and fade," Mr. George says. "It's a sensitive subject. We have to examine things objectively, not emotionally."

"So ignore shit." Seung drops his phone on the desk.

Mr. George half smiles, but not in a happy way.

"What will Bea do?" I ask. "Will she be okay?"

"Bea's already done what she needed to," Mr. George says.

"Which is?" Ham and I ask in unison.

"Talked to me and met with a counselor."

"That's all?" I snap. "What about the police? Reed Clemmings can't get away with this shit. He's been hurting her for a while. That monster deserves punishment!"

"Would you settle for ridicule?" Mr. George says. "His cover has been blown. Word will travel. It always does. But it's up to Bea now."

I nod. "To tell her story."

Mr. George sighs. "Exactly. We all have stories. Don't we, Linden? It's up to us whether we want to share them or not."

I don't see Reed or his smile when I sit in front of him in class. I'm preoccupied with Seung's lips, his taste, and Mr. George's *last* words. My mind juggles subjects and bullet points, each fighting for first place in line.

I don't care if people think Reed hurt me. I don't care if those comments put my reputation on the line. It's not like I had some big rep to protect in the first place. Maybe I should be angry. It's no secret that Seung wants me to be. At least a little. It would help him forget that he watched me kiss that monster. But Seung doesn't know I have a backstory, too. Like Mr. George said, we all have stories.

My eyes are forward and I'm listening to Principal Falls talk about the SAT. Her focus is test anxiety and how to stomp its ass. I should be more concerned about the test designed to change my life, but my heart isn't here, and neither is my desire. I've always seen The Test as my ticket to freedom, college, a permanent address, but right now everything else weighs more.

A throat clears, and I make the mistake of turning around. Reed eyeballs me up and down and shifts his jaw to the right, then left. His eyes are bloodshot and he looks like he needs sleep. It irritates me that he's here in class, with Bea. He shouldn't be allowed to be here.

I shift in my chair and lean back to show him I'm relaxed, worry free. Sure, I know he punches female faces, but for all he knows, I'm the largest liar on the planet. If others believe I wrote that article, Reed might, too. He's probably wondering what other lies I'll spread. Maybe he thinks Bea and I planned the article together and are working as a team to expose him to the school. Let him wonder. Let him marvel. It serves him right.

Principal Falsetto chirps about positive self-talk while fingers slide into the back pocket of my jeans. In other words, someone's touching my ass.

I whip around and see Seung moving to an empty seat in front of the class, far from Bea. Way to stick up for your girlfriend, Seung. Because those kisses coated in enchilada sauce mean we arrived at a whole new level of friendship.

Reed clears his throat again and I make another mistake of looking into his eyes. He eyeballs my ass and shifts his jaw, again. I stare until I hear his teeth click. Then I fish for the note he poked in my pocket.

I stare at the back of Seung's head, five people in front of me. I wonder why he won't turn around and wave me toward him. There's another empty seat up front.

Why doesn't Seung rescue me like I rescued him?

"Open the note," Reed whispers.

I sigh, hard. "Piss off."

A coin hits my back. It's hard and it hurts. My mind screams, *Ouch!* but I'll never say it out loud. What I would say, however, is, this: "He's trying to hurt me again!" I shout it, loud and clear.

Here's me, Linden Rose, not giving a fuck what anyone thinks.

Principal Falsetto asks if there's a problem, which of course there is, but she's months late to the party to solve it.

I flip the coin at Reed's face and say, "Keep the fucking change," then swing my backpack over my shoulder and stomp toward the door.

Footsteps pound behind me, but I don't turn around. Seung would never let me leave alone. Not after that scene.

At my locker, I finally whip around, yelling, "You know what that ass—"

But my mouth can't finish the sentence. How could it?

Reed has his finger on my lips, shushing me. He's teary and saying, "I'm sorry. I don't know what's wrong with me. It's like I'm trapped in this body full of rage and I can't escape."

For a moment I wonder if he's plagiarizing Kerouac again, but his tears keep me focused on his face, cautioning me about his next move.

"Did you read the note?" he says with eyes wide. "Because I really need you to read that note."

I don't answer. His finger still mashes my lips.

"I never meant to hurt anyone. I don't like hurting people."

He's believable. Convincing. Maybe he doesn't want to hurt anyone. But it doesn't change that he has.

He says, "Everyone screws up sometimes. I need someone to give me another chance."

For a second I think he believes I'm that *someone*.

Then, for another second, I'm certain.

He says, "I want to kiss you again."

I nod, thinking, *Yeah, I'm sure you do*, and suddenly his face is on mine.

He whispers, "I'm sorry," but he's telling the wrong girl.

He says, "I can't stop kissing you," but he's forcing my mouth open and I'm clamping my lips shut.

"Stop," I tell him, but he's busy finishing what he started at homecoming, what he wrote in the note.

Linden Rose—I can't stop thinking about your taste.

He says, "You taste so good."

I push his chest and shout, "Fuck off!"

He says, "I'd never hurt *you*."

"Is that what you told Bea?"

He winces, but his face is stone.

He's Reed Clemmings. Perfection personified. At least that's what everyone has always thought. He keeps to himself, does what his coach tells him to do. He's become the brand our school wants him to be. Performing the way they tell him to perform, in class, on the football field. At least while eyes watch.

He pushes me against the locker and I shove back.

"You're not Bea," he says. "Bea's a liar. You can't believe anything she says."

He bites my lip and I imagine biting his. But my mouth won't budge. It won't even say, "Fuck off," again. Fear does that sometimes. It freezes you, stifles fluid movements, especially when

288

you've always been told to sit still, close your eyes, pretend not to exist. My face winces at his sour breath. I try to lift my hand to push him off me, but he grabs my wrist and slams it against the locker, above my head. His tongue dives into my mouth.

I jerk to the side, struggling for air.

Seung.

Standing at the end of the hall, sleeves pushed to his elbows, ready to accept his rescue mission.

Seung.

Staring at my hands, one flat against the locker, the other gripping an earlobe, ready to yank.

But he won't move. He won't rescue. He's frozen, too, but it's not Reed he's afraid of.

I want to shout, "Seung! It's not what it looks like!" but Reed presses his chest against mine and prevents me from budging. He hisses at my cheek, "Stay the fuck away from Bea." I squirm; he grabs my chin and kisses me long enough for Seung to watch everything we've ever had smash apart.

When I finally break loose, Seung's gone.

He doesn't see me knee Reed or punch below the belt. He doesn't hear me shout his name or Bea whip open the door and scream for help. Seung doesn't stick around long enough to watch an orange Toby Patters charge Reed like a man-padded football sled and slide him across the hall until his body folds like a tossed towel.

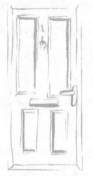

CHAPTER TWENTY-TWO

IT'S BEEN SIX DAYS SINCE I kissed Seung.

Five days since Seung watched Reed Clemmings kiss me.

Five days since Seung and I last spoke.

There is a correlation between kisses and Seung's icy shoulder, but I'm having a difficult time trusting myself since my mouth lies to friends. Don't even get me started on the way my lips freeze at the most inopportune times. I don't even know who they are anymore. I even BS myself, talking about my body parts like they're separate entities. Basically, I'm going bonkers from believing it was okay to hide my true self from the people I love.

"I'd invite you to Seung's house tonight to study," Ham says, carrying seven book spines on how to crack the SAT code, "but he says he's through with you and your lies."

I stop. "What about my lies?" I'm shocked at my defensiveness. Ham hears it, too.

"What about *you*, Linden? From what I hear, you're preoccupied with Reed. How can you kiss Seung, then immediately jump on that monster?"

"I knew it!" I jab my finger into Ham's chest.

"Knew what?"

"Seung refuses to hear my side of the story."

"What do you expect, Linden? Reed is a creep, a freak. And partially responsible for my limp."

"You don't limp."

"I have a dip when I walk. Had it since the monkey-bar incident when I was a kid. Some would call it a limp."

"Some would certainly call *you* something."

"Watch my ass when I walk, Linden. You'll see it."

"No thanks."

"Do it."

"Never."

I push open the front doors of the school. Gold Nugget greets us beneath the awning. Ham calls shotgun and I groan, extra loud. When I sidestep toward the back door of Seung's Volvo, a motorcycle engine pops behind me. I turn my head to watch a replay of the bad movie I starred in earlier.

The actual scene unfolds like this: Reed rips off his helmet. His bangs fall into his eyelashes and stick. He brushes dirt off the front of his pants and pats the back. He tilts his head before looking at me through a blanket of bangs. Then he shapes his fingers into a gun, cocks his thumb, and mouths, "Bang."

I gasp and reach for the car door handle.

Seung revs the engine and shifts from park to drive. The tires squeal and I'm left with the familiar scent of burned rubber topped with a cloud of rejection.

CHAPTER TWENTY-THREE
THE NIGHT BEFORE THE SAT

I SHOULD BE STUDYING WITH Ham and Seung, in the warm basement of the Rhee residence, not here in the dugout with moonlight reflecting the words typed on my SAT packet. The public library closed at nine, school doors locked earlier than expected, and with all my energy spent chasing after Seung, I forgot to slip the shank in the fire-escape door. I'm huddled on the wood bench, squinting to read about *Important Items for Test Day*.

Seung shunned me in the hall, even when I shouted his name. It's unlike him to avoid me this long. He'd normally cave by now. A smile, wink, tickle on the ribs, would cause him to crumble. But not this time. Not after seeing me kiss the same guy, twice. *I never kissed back, Seung.* But he didn't stay long enough to know that.

I lean back on the bench, shut my eyes, and picture my future. Brick buildings, bell towers, winding sidewalks, and warmth. Lots and lots of warmth. I rub my arms, then my neck. Tomorrow marks my moment to shine. Perform well on the SAT and take another step in the direction my mother wanted me to go. More distance, away from my past.

My mother would be proud. She wanted me to get an education.

"In order to get ahead in life, Linden," she'd say, "you have to read. You have to write. You have to finish school, no matter what. Don't do what your mother did." She'd dropped out of school when she couldn't conceal her pregnancy any longer.

"My mother made me do it," she'd say, "with a push and shove from school officials. Nobody wanted a pregnant girl shuffling the halls of a public high school. Not back then. Might give others ideas, they said. Cause a domino effect. A contagion."

I can still hear her giggle as she stuffed a pillow in her shirt and waddled around the living room like a penguin. "Can you believe you were once this small?"

My grandmother was the one who created the domino effect. She had my mother quit school, forced her to run away with the guy who got her pregnant. A guy who left us at the hospital with me still in the birth canal. But it wasn't my grandmother's fault. Had she known how I'd turn out, she'd have been proud of her daughter. I'd planned to show her proof when I arrived on the doorstep of her nursing home with a bag of cash and a photo of my mother. I'd planned to show her the kind of kid her daughter had raised. Resilient and resourceful.

I figured my grandmother would recognize her daughter from the photograph, even if she didn't know me. But a rosy reunion never happened. My grandmother's head was full of dementia and her mouth packed with gibberish. It didn't stop me, though. I wanted my grandmother to know her daughter did the best she could with what she had, which was nothing but a GED and me. I didn't need nostalgia or long-winded talks digging up memories of my mother when she was young. I needed one spark, one flicker in her eye to acknowledge my existence. And then it happened one morning, when I'd woken in the chair beside my grandmother's bed and watched as she swirled her bony finger around the frame of my mother's face. She pressed the photo to her cheek and held it there until she drifted to sleep.

When I woke again, the picture was on the floor and Eva, my grandmother's nurse, was shaking my arm. "Linden, Linden. It's time to go." She rushed me out of my grandmother's room before the doctor arrived and they pulled the blanket over my grandmother's head.

Eva took pity on me. I had no place to go. She let me bunk in a spare room stuffed with extra beds and brooms. "Makes more sense to sleep in a nursing-home living room reserved for visitors who never visit," she said, "but this will have to do."

She scolded other aides for questioning my stay. She said, "She's only here until school starts," which was a few weeks away. I cleaned toilets, dusted furniture, and smiled a lot. I don't know how, I'm not sure why. I guess I was happy to earn a roof over my head, and everyone was kind to me. But then school started and everything turned to shit. Eva told me her administrator was beginning to ask questions, but if I needed a place to stay, she could call the pastor of her church and see what could be done. Small-town churches barely have money to feed their own flocks, so I told her I had everything under control. She refused to quiz, even though her eyes begged for answers.

Answers to questions could disrupt my future. I wasn't ready, now or then, to bounce between strangers as a ward of a state. My mother leaned only on herself, and I was determined to do the same.

So what if the dugout was cold, hard, and filled with ants. It took me about a day to learn how to bunk inside Hinderwood High. Took another day to learn how to hide in plain sight.

In my heart, I know my grandmother caught a glimpse of the woman my mother had become, though they hadn't spoken in years. The strong, sturdy mother who fought for her life and her child, even while she was dying. I wonder if my grandmother remembered her daughter the way I remember my mom. I wonder how many years pass before your memories fog and fade. How she combed my hair and wiped food from my lips with her knuckle. How she smoothed my eyebrows with her thumb while she read to me in bed. How she made sure the tags were tucked tightly into my shirts. My mother wanted more for me than she ever had.

My promise to you, Linden, is that I'll always provide a choice. You won't be forced to do something you don't want to do. Not on my watch.

She left me with options. An emergency fund stashed in an envelope. Money she could have blown on herself but never did. She left me with choices. None of which I ever wanted to take.

It's hard, sometimes, to not think about the what-ifs. Like if there was $5,000 in the envelope to begin with and only $3,000 when I needed it. If I had taken off my earphones and screamed before the beating, would there have never been blood? If I'd stayed with the social worker at the morgue, would I have lived a better life?

I stop myself from remembering the past before I go the distance.

I quit before my mother's beating, before the blood.

My mother wanted to live. For me. For us.

She never deserved to die.

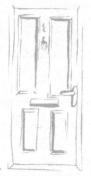

CHAPTER TWENTY-FOUR
THREE HOURS BEFORE THE SAT

MY EYES POP OPEN THIRTY minutes before dawn. My nose drips, acting like my alarm clock. I rub my arms and legs and check my pulse. Every day I wake, I'm alive. Today it feels okay to be alive.

I consider jogging a lap on the track to amp up my heart and fill my lungs with a burn. I immediately unconsider the lap when my stomach stabs and jabs and aches. After a few side bends, I massage my belly and inhale-exhale five hundred times. *Anticipation* is my word of the day. A day destined to form my future. So, to hell with stomach cramps. When I start to jog, the pinpricks punch. I diagnose the pain right away, and it sure isn't hunger. I tug at my waistband before bending over and checking my pants.

Oh, how lovely. My period and no tampons.

It'll be at least an hour before the school doors open and I can race to the bathroom to stuff toilet paper in my underwear. My stomach twists, pain punching me right below the belt.

Come on, Linden. Get your head in the game. This is your day. Your ticket to an education you promised your mother you'd get. I reach into my bag and dig for a ball of brown paper towels. I unbutton my pants, ready to stuff my underwear, when gravel crunches, like footsteps, behind me. I whirl and drop what was supposed to be my makeshift pad.

"Hey," Seung says.

I say nothing. I don't need to. My face says it all.

"What are you doing here?" he asks, his hand circling the dugout.

I gulp and stiffen my legs, my posture. My underwear sticks to my body.

Seung steps forward. "You're not talking? To me?" He shrugs his shoulders. "Figures, Linden."

What figures, Seung? That I love you?

"Why are you in this dugout?" His face scrunches like he's mad. Maybe confused. "Tell me, Linden. Now's your chance. Why are you here?" His face softens, his eyes wet.

I tried, Seung, but you didn't want to hear. And now I don't think I have the courage. I clear my throat. Kick dirt onto my shoe. Stare at my feet.

"Well?"

I inhale. "I guess I needed a quiet place to study."

Air deflates from Seung's chest. He turns around and mumbles, "That's what I thought."

"Seung?"

He waves his hand with his back to me. "You had your chance. A million chances"

"Seung."

He walks toward the road without turning.

"Seung!" I'm shouting now. "Please! I never kissed him back!"

Seung turns; his head won't stop shaking. "That's what you think this is about?"

Twenty feet separate us, but it could be twenty miles. That's how distant he feels. All I have to do is tell him the truth. Tell him why I'm here, in the dugout. Risk losing him over the lies or maybe shrink the gap between us.

But he doesn't wait. He takes off jogging until he blends in with the gray sky.

I walk to the corner of the dugout, sit, and bury my head in my hands.

I have to be real with Seung. Tell him where I live. Stop hiding from the truth. After the SAT, I'll answer his questions. Every single one of them.

I stand and brush the butt of my pants. A breeze rustles the trees. When I whip around for my backpack, a ten-dollar bill flutters like a leaf and lands in the dirt.

Seung?

CHAPTER TWENTY-FIVE
SEVENTY-FIVE MINUTES BEFORE THE SAT

I SHOULD BE AT SCHOOL, sitting on the front steps, cramming words my brain has no more capacity to contain. I should be preparing to take the biggest, most important test of my life. But today I question the validity of my beliefs.

Sitting on Seung's front steps, I legitimize myself to an audience of one. He won't talk, but I only need him to listen. Besides, I think he knows anyway. I just need him to hear the truth from me.

I unzip my backpack. "Dinner rolls I took from your kitchen. Bacon, wrapped in brown paper towels."

Seung stares at my hands filled with food, then slowly shifts to walk inside. I pause, unsure if he wants me to follow or never speak to me again. He hears my thoughts, cracks the screen door, and whispers, "Come in, Linden. You need to eat breakfast."

I trail him to the table and continue spilling truths. "I paid you back with help on chapter four's trig problems sixteen and twenty-four. It's what I owed you for the dinner roll and bacon slice."

Seung pauses and makes a popping noise with his mouth. He won't talk, but his eyes are warm and inviting, just like his home.

Mrs. Rhee bustles in from the kitchen and pushes a plate of cheesy eggs and orange slices in front of me. She suggests I eat and tells me the English muffin is on its way.

Seung keeps popping his lips. His eyes so fixed on the wall behind me that I almost turn around to find the spot he's staring at, through me. Mr. Rhee walks in with a miniplate of toasted muffins and sets it down in the middle of the table.

He says, "Want some honey?" but nobody answers. We're too busy not-staring at each other to reply. "Well, just in case," Mr. Rhee says, placing the plastic bear beside the muffin plate before disappearing into the kitchen.

Seung forks his eggs, holding them in the air for a moment before tossing them into his mouth. He overchews. He wants to say something, anything, everything, but says nothing.

Instead, I won't shut up.

"I found Ham homecoming night. Found him before anyone else did. I made an anonymous call and ran. I would've had to talk to the police, you know, about me. About where I live. I got scared and took off. I believed with all of my heart that Ham was dead."

I share how I held Ham in my arms, kissed his cheek, and hid in the hills behind the school. I discuss our drive to the hospital, how I thought we were going to see Ham's dead body. How I couldn't handle viewing another dead body after seeing my mom, my grandmother. I don't stop for air, or for eggs.

I'm starving, about to take the biggest exam of my life, and all I care about is passing this test with Seung. I don't know where I stand because he won't talk. The only things I know for sure are my eggs are cold, blood is beginning to soak my underwear, and I'm in love with my best friend.

Seung bites into a muffin, and the honey drips onto his plate. I watch him dip his finger into a pat of butter and put it into his mouth. I want to yell at him to listen, but I'm afraid if I do he'll shut me out, of his house, his heart. I want to tell him I love him and I always have, but instead, I keep chiseling away at truths. Digging my way out of the hole I created with my own two hands. Rescuing myself.

"I chose you," I say.

Seung looks at me this time, not through me.

"You, and Ham." I smile, remembering the day. "I saw you, Ham, on the first day of school. The way you hugged and patted and laughed. I wanted that kind of friendship. Simple and be-yourself." I stare at my eggs, my eyes stinging with tears. "I wanted you. I always have."

We don't talk. What else is there to say?

303

Minutes feel like hours, and then Seung whispers, "You need to eat," and I fork my eggs and take a bite, then another. Mrs. Rhee returns and squeezes my shoulders with both hands. "You two kill it today," she says. She sweeps my hair to the side of my neck, and I pinch the bridge of my nose. It's impossible to feel a mother's touch without my eyes burning. "Ten minutes until it's time to go."

I nod, wipe my nose with my sleeve, and ask Mrs. Rhee if I can talk to her in private. She looks surprised and pleased at the same time. When I tell her about my period, she presents me with six pads the size of pillows, then offers a fresh pair of underwear. I accept. Even the underwear. I slip out of my jeans and into a pair of Mrs. Rhee's jersey jogger pants. They're as cozy as she is.

When I return to the dining room, Seung isn't there, and neither are our plates. I grab the bear filled with honey and head into the kitchen.

"Why don't you just say it?" Seung says, scraping our plates into the garbage disposal.

"Say what?"

"I already know, Linden."

"Know what?"

He shakes his head, shuts off the water, and stands in front of me. We're three inches apart. "I don't get why you just won't say it. To me." He reaches for my hand.

I'm too weak to grip because all my strength is pushing my pride aside.

"The whole homeless thing, Linden," Seung says. "I've known for a while. It's obvious to those who look. We see."

Hearing someone else say your secret out loud hurts, in a good way. I blink and my eyes dump tears that run all the way into my mouth. I taste a mixture of salt and regret. Refreshment brewed with relief.

I turn around, incapable of facing Seung, at least for a moment while I catch my breath. I drop my chin to my chest. He drapes his arms over my back and plants his cheek against mine.

"I knew," he whispers in my ear.

"I figured you did when you dropped the ten-dollar bill at the dugout this morning." My head falls against his shoulder.

"Well, I wasn't certain until then."

CHAPTER TWENTY-SIX
THE SAT

SUPPOSEDLY THE BIGGEST TEST OF our lives.

We skip it.

Go to the park instead.

We kiss. We swing. We kiss.

We walk. We kiss. We hold hands.

We kiss.

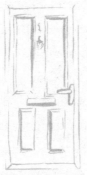

CHAPTER TWENTY-SEVEN

MR. GEORGE WANTS TO TALK. Code for *interrogation*. Code for
You skipped the SAT; prepare for shit to fly.

"You better have a good reason. Both of you." Mr. George
hits the newsroom door, mouth moving, words flying. "The
SAT, Linden, Seung. Your futures, Linden, Seung. Tell me
you have an excuse, Linden, Seung."

Seung and I look at each other and smile.

Once we calm Mr. George down and ease him into his
pastoral place with chatter about makeup test dates and with
his French press filled with coffee, he addresses my plans, my
future. He says, "Principal Falls saw your name missing from
the SAT roster. She asked me what your plans are after graduation." He clears his throat. "How's that scholarship piece
coming along, Linden?"

I flash a smile. A nod. Then shrug my shoulder, just one.

Mr. George frowns and I offer him his cup. He says, "Your shit, Linden. Do you have it together?"

Seung and I stare at Mr. George with eyes wide. It's almost comforting to hear him swear. His honesty oozes and flows, like his genuine care for us all.

I nod again and say, "Yes, sir. I have my shit together. It's just taken longer than planned."

A rhythmic knock hits the door before I have to explain that I'm not talking about the scholarship article, but my actual shit. How it's taken forever for me to get it together, but I believe I finally have, and now want to come clean, at least with Mr. George. He scurries to the door.

Principal Falsetto's sister enters, along with two guys in khakis and matching polo shirts. The men carry black leather bags marked with the KOIN 6 logo. The smell of a good morning fills my nose. Miss Sunshine sports a microphone clipped to her royal blue sweater. She says, "Mr. George. Good to see you again. I hope I'm not late for our meeting."

Mr. George cocks his head in my direction but refuses eye contact. "Yeah," he says. "They were just leaving."

"We were?" Seung asks.

"You were," Mr. George answers.

I linger at the door, cracking it to listen. Principal Falsetto's sister tosses twenty questions at Mr. George, giving him no time to answer even one.

"What's that about?" Seung asks.

"No idea," I say, but I pick up on buzzwords like *Principal Falls*, *SAT*, and *homeless shelter*.

"I answered a couple of questions," Ham says, wiping nacho cheese dip from his upper lip. He breaks a fry in half and dunks it finger deep. "Miss Sunshine asked me if I knew you on a personal level."

I wait for the guy at the front counter to finish shouting, "Order up," then ask, "What did you say?" I'm fighting to stay focused on why Principal Falsetto's sister is speaking with Mr. George. She said she wanted to chat with me the next time she was in town. But she hasn't. As far as I know, she's only spoken to Ham and Mr. George.

I lift Seung's hand off my knee and swirl his knuckles with my finger.

Seung ignores my hint and massages my knee with both hands.

"Then what?" I ask, getting impatient. "What did you tell her, Ham? Did you ask her why she was so interested in me?"

"Or why she doesn't talk to Linden herself?" Seung says.

Ham huffs. "Look, Linden. It was a while ago. Memory's a little hazy after the wreck. I mean, I could be dead, you know. Should be dead. Yet here I am, ready to share my story with the world."

Now it's Seung's turn to huff. "If she's so interested in Linden, why hasn't she talked to me?" He slides his arm around my back and Ham winces.

"I'm not used to you two, you know, all touchy and shit."

Seung presses his chest against me and says, "You mean this?" He licks my cheek. I repeat, he licks my cheek.

"That's just wrong," Ham says, and I push Seung back onto his side of the booth.

Secretly I adore Seung 2.0 and his physical affection bursting with overconfidence. It's refreshing, really. But I can't stop thinking about the journalist lady. I wonder if her sister, our principal, even knows she's questioning students, midweek and during school hours. Has she even checked in at the office?

I lean over and kiss Seung on the side of his mouth. He reaches for me with both hands, but I slide out of the booth and say, "I'll find out for myself. Pick me up after school."

I bump into Jarrell on my way out the door and race for the crosswalk.

"Hey, Linden. Is Ham inside?" Jarrell shouts.

"He is!" I yell, running across the street. "Go find him! Tell him how you feel!"

When I reach the front office of the school, Principal Falsetto is in a meeting. I say, "I'll wait," and the office manager says, "You'll be waiting awhile."

I wander into the hall, finding my way back to the newsroom. With Principal Falsetto busy, Mr. George is next in line. Besides, he was speaking to the source of my confusion and I need to know why. She said she wanted to share journalism stuff with me the next time she was in town. Well, here

I am, and she hasn't looked me up, just rushed me out the door and asked questions behind my back.

I glance through the window and barge in the door. "Mr. George. We need to talk."

Mr. George looks up, stone-faced, while Principal Falsetto's sister tilts her head and smiles. Mr. George chomps on his cheek and kneads his forehead like he's molding clay.

I extend my arm and Miss Sunshine reaches for my fingers. "We meet again," she says, and squeezes my hand like she's trying to send a message. "You're the one I'd like to speak to, now that I've spoken with everyone else."

Mr. George clears his throat and interrupts before I agree to talk. "I didn't ask," he says, "but have you checked in at the office?"

Miss Sunshine fidgets, fluffs her bangs. She looks nervous, but I suspect her nerves are made of metal. She smiles again, at Mr. George. "Of course."

Mr. George squeezes my shoulder. "Okay then, Linden," he says. "Keep it brief. I need you in class, and to reschedule your test date. We have a lot of work to do."

When Mr. George leaves, Principal Falsetto's sister nestles into his chair and invites me to take a seat. She says, "Call me Helen," and I nod.

She tips her head, signaling that it's my turn to talk.

The only question I don't answer at first is "What's your address?"

She slings information she shouldn't, couldn't, possibly

311

know. She says Principal Falls contacted her a few months ago after becoming suspicious and started poking around. She says, "My sister normally doesn't see the forest for the trees, but sometimes she's full of surprises, especially when her students are involved."

Principal Falls found an old article and sent the link to her journalist sister. She asked if she could get in trouble for not helping, because she never knew. Miss Sunshine, I mean Helen, says, "It's only when people look that they see."

The article said there was a teenage girl found in a closet. The same one who ran away from the morgue.

She asks if I know this person and if I think she needs help.

She asks if I know where this person lives, and I wonder why she's playing this game.

I glance at the window in the door, hopeful I'll find Mr. George's shadow or maybe Seung's face. All I see is blank space.

Miss Sunshine tells me she has connections to move mountains and in my mind I picture anthills. She says she'll find me a place to live, and in my mind I see distance. From my friends, the people I love. She thinks she knows what's best for me. She thinks she's my saving grace.

She tells me they found my mother's killer and that I deserved to know.

She asks if she can quote me. Use my name in an article she's writing for some big-name press. "I want to share your story," she says. "How you hid in plain sight."

She pauses for an answer, a breath. Taps her toe three

times. She's counting on the word *yes*. But it's lodged in the back of my throat, far from the tip of my tongue.

"Is that why you're here? To deliver the news?"

She nods. "Going where the story takes me."

I scoff. "Well, it took you to everyone but me. Journalists go straight to the source, right?"

She opens her mouth to speak, then clamps it closed.

"Was he arrested?" I ask.

She nods again.

"Who is he? Who killed my mom?"

She pushes her hip against the desk and rakes her teeth across her lip. I'm not sure I'm ready to hear the answer I think I already know. For the first time in her career, I don't think Miss Sunshine is ready to deliver the news.

"You sure you want to know?" she asks.

"I think I already do."

She reaches for my hand. I let her take it. "He doesn't know about you, Linden. He doesn't have to, either. He thinks your mother gave you up for adoption when you were born. He knows nothing about you." I stand and stumble. Miss Sunshine grabs my arm.

"Why'd he do it?" I ask. "Why'd he hurt her?" I shake my head but it won't stop the room from whirling.

"We don't know, Linden." She stuffs her hand in her pocket and sighs. "I suppose because he could." She palms my back. Pat. Pat. Pat. Swirls her fingers in circles and squeezes my shoulder.

*Every time I move us forward, he pushes and pulls
us back.*

Who, Mama?

Every time I hide us, he finds us.

Who, Mama?

Every time we vanish, he appears.

Mama? Do I know him?

No, Linden. And he'll never know you.

Miss Sunshine says my name three times and asks if I need
her to find Mr. George. "I want to help you," she claims. She
promises my father doesn't know I'm here. She swears he'll
never know where I am. I have to believe. What else can I do?
I don't want to run again.

I lift my bag over my shoulder, offer a smile that tells her
I'm good, okay, fine enough to go. She steps back and I scoot
toward the door. She says, "So about that story, Linden. I'd
love it if you let me share. I'll do it justice."

I stop. So does the spinning ceiling. "I don't think so. This
isn't your story to tell."

CHAPTER TWENTY-EIGHT

PRINCIPAL FALSETTO CALLS ME OUT of Mr. George's class. I sit, refusing to respond to my name on the intercom. I knew she'd call but didn't expect it would be so soon.

Mr. George says, "Linden. Over here, please."

By the time Mr. George quits talking, I'm panicked and pressured. He hands me a piece of paper from his briefcase: my *curriculum vitae*—course of my life.

- Woman murdered in Portland apartment. Daughter found hiding in closet.
- Daughter of deceased prostitute flees morgue. Social worker unable to locate child.
- Ethel Rose, resident of Just Like Home in central Oregon, dies of complications caused by stroke. No known next of kin.

- Linden Rose—no address on file.
- Honor roll listings for 2018 include . . . Linden Rose. . . .

They don't seal the gaps in between. Their dot-to-dot won't connect. Facts aren't really facts. Truths only partial. But good journalists take their jobs seriously. Wrap research in tight little bows. Miss Sunshine lives by the station's slogan. Pushes Mr. George to the front line when I refuse to let her speak. Maybe she *is* watching out for us, for me.

"Is this you?" Mr. George asks, tapping his notes with his finger and gnawing his cheek like a gristly piece of meat.

"Daughter of deceased prostitute"? No. That's not me. My mother was someone different to me. She read books, started classes, saved money for emergencies. She hid me every time he pounded on the door. She said, "He doesn't know you exist. He won't ever know." She protected me, kept me safe, even after she died.

I draw my breath and stare at Mr. George's face until his features blur behind the tears pooling in my eyes.

"Linden? It's okay. You can tell me the truth."

But the truth, Mr. George, will jeopardize my present, my future. If I tell him I live here, open my arms, and twirl like a princess showing off my room, my charade is over. Done. Kaput. No more Linden Rose, honor roll student, scholarship recipient, school journalist, or best friend. There will only be Linden Rose, runaway. Linden Rose, arrested for squatting in her high school. Linden Rose, prison bound.

"Linden? Where do you live?"

"Here and there," I whisper.

"Do you stay with friends?"

"From time to time."

"You're homeless?"

He wants to hear the word. He wants confirmation. When I say it, everyone will shift into action. Do what they're supposed to do. Send me away from the only family I have. The people who matter most. My stare should be blank, but words bubble and pop and push at my brain.

"I can't leave here," I blurt. "Please don't let them send me away."

Mr. George leans in, breaks the teacher rules of conduct, and places his hand on the top of my wrist. He squeezes and it feels like a promise. I have to believe it's a promise.

"There should be a goddamn homeless shelter in this town," he says.

Mr. George pats my hand, then straightens his tie. "We need to talk more about this, Linden, but Principal Falls is waiting for you."

The room begins to whirl, or is it my ears? Ringing. Maybe my phone? I tap the screen, two hundred times. Mr. George promised. Didn't he? He squeezed my hand as if to say, "You're not alone." Why do I feel so alone?

"Can't you talk to her for me?" I plead. "Tell her I don't want to leave?"

He shakes his head. "Go now, Linden. Don't keep her waiting."

I stuff my phone into my pocket. *Nice knowing you, Mr. George.*

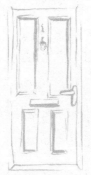

CHAPTER TWENTY-NINE

PRINCIPAL FALSETTO DRUMS HER DESK with the pink eraser capped to her pencil. She's conflicted, confused, but masking it well. Her sister filled her in on important details concerning one of her honor-roll students.

"We want to help your situation, Linden. But you're going to have to help us, too."

I nod to the rhythm of her pencil, bopping and bouncing on her desk. I hear, *Linden. Linden. Linden.*

"Where have you been living?" She looks me in the eye, not to stare me down but to lift me up. She wants to help. Compassion smeared like concealer all over her face.

If I tell her the truth, my future stops as soon as I cough out the word.

I can't stop fixating on the eraser, bumping up and down. Up, down.

"Linden?"

Bounce. Bounce.

"Where do you live?"

Bounce. Bounce.

"Linden?"

Bounce. Bounce. Bounce.

"Are you listening?"

Bounce. Bounce.

"Linden?"

Bounce.

"Here."

CHAPTER THIRTY
ONE WEEK LATER

WHEN I WALK INTO THE newsroom, Mr. George and his husband are the first people I see. They smile. I smile back. Mr. and Mrs. Rhee are sitting in desk chairs with grins spread across their lips. They nod. I nod back. Mrs. Rhee rises and walks toward me with her arms open. I go in for the hug and the squeeze.

Ham's parents are there, too, motioning to an empty chair beside them. The Royses insisted I move in with them, following the big reveal, but after a week of sleeping in a room next to Ham's, I'm ready for some space. We're working through some sibling rivalry, especially where the bathroom's concerned.

The social worker assigned to my case taps at her phone and scribbles notes on a yellow legal pad.

"We're waiting for Principal Falls," Mr. George announces.

"And Seung," I say.

"And Seung." Mr. George smiles, winks.

On cue, Seung enters, followed by Principal Falsetto. Seung tosses his bag into a chair and sits beside me. "Sorry I'm late," he whispers.

Principal Falsetto greets the parents and perches on the edge of Mr. George's desk. "Linden," she says. "Thanks for coming." As if I had a choice.

I nod and mouth, "Thank you," and it flows from my heart.

"The reason for this meeting, as you all know, is that we're concerned about Linden's living arrangements. The Royses have been kind enough to offer their home, but things need to become formalized. At least temporarily. Decisions must be made." Principal Falsetto nibbles the tip of her pen. "Correction," she says, and motions to me. "We need Linden to make some decisions."

I glance at Mrs. Rhee. She's in front of me, and her entire face beams. "Linden," she says, "we thought you could come live with us. We'd really love it if you would move in with our family."

Seung shifts in his chair.

"We have a spare bedroom," she continues. "And, although you'd share a bathroom with Seung, you would have your own space. We'd make sure of it."

I side-eye Seung. His chair shifts have become squirms.

Mrs. Rhee's smile is contagious, though. She tilts her head,

322

eager for my answer, then glances at Seung. I puff my lips and blow air too loud, too much. Seung slips his hand into mine. "You okay?" he asks.

"Yep," I peep out like a chick.

Seung laughs and we both fall back against our chairs. My shoulders relax and I drop my head against Seung's arm.

"Seung," Mrs. Rhee says, "tell Linden how much we want her to live with us."

"Mom," Seung says, his voice serious, "I'm not sure your idea is going to work."

I sit up in my chair.

"I mean, we're together." Seung points at me with all five fingers, then at himself. "Together, Mom."

"Together?" Ham's dad interrupts. "Ham? Is this so? I thought you and Seung—"

Ham groans but a smile spreads from lobe to lobe. He stands and shuffles up to an invisible podium. "Dad. Mom. Seung and I are not together." He pushes at the air with his hands. "We are *so* incredibly not together."

"But I don't understand, Son." Mr. Royse's voice whines, then turns into a whisper. "You're not gay?"

Ham laughs. Oh boy, does he laugh. "Oh no, Dad. I'm gay. As gay as Seung is straight. And he's not my type. I mean, have you seen his chest, those thighs, his arms? They're spaghetti noodles compared to—" Ham whips around to face Seung. "Sorry, dude."

Seung rolls his eyes.

"But you are gay? Right?" Ham's dad scoots to the edge of his desk chair, leans in, and whispers, "Please, Son. Tell me you're—"

"At ease, Dad." Ham pats his father's shoulder. "I'm gay. I'm seeing Jarrell. And the world is ours. Happy now?"

Mr. Royse exhales and Ham plops into his chair, grinning.

"Well, then." Mr. George claps his hands. "I—I mean *we*—want to present an offer as well." Mr. George and his husband walk to my desk. Mr. George squats beside my chair. "You're welcome to live with us," he says, and takes my hand. "We"—he motions to his husband—"want you to live with us."

"Hold up!" Seung blurts, his finger in the air. "I need to talk to Linden, alone." He stands and motions for me to follow to the back of the room. "It will only take a minute. Promise."

We rush to Mr. George's coat closet, and Seung reaches for my hand. When we feel everyone's stares, Seung yanks me inside and slams the door.

"Linden," he says, fumbling in the dark for my other hand, "my parents really want you to move in with us. *I* want you to move in with us. But I don't think you should."

I nod, but Seung can't see me. "I don't, either."

"You don't?"

"I don't." I hear Seung exhale.

"It could get weird."

"Incredibly weird."

"Why mess up a good thing?"

324

"We're just getting started."

Seung traces my arm, wrist to elbow. I slip my hand behind his back and pull him toward me. We bump chins and noses until our lips find each other and lock into place.

"What if we have a fight?" I whisper at his mouth. "Things could get complicated."

"And what if we decide to have sex?" Seung whispers back. "Things could get even more complicated."

I'm not sure how to respond, so I don't. My face does, though, with heat. And my lips, my tongue, never stop responding.

We aren't ready to live together. I'm still learning how to live.

For several minutes, we forget we're making out in Mr. George's coat closet with teachers and parents in the room. When we finally open the closet door, Mr. George and his husband welcome me with open, inviting arms. The perfect helicopter parents I never had.

CHAPTER THIRTY-ONE

THERE'S A LINE IN ONE of Ham's mob movies that defines family as who you are sworn to, not who you were born to. Friends included.

My friends have become family. My family is my friends.

One month glided by since my new family officially formed. The world braked, backed up, opened a door, and begged me to climb in. Unstoppable spinning screeched to a halt. I didn't think it was possible for that spin to stop. But when you quit running and hiding, you can finally slow down, take breaths, and settle into the moment. Your mind quiets, your brain quits buzzing.

Mr. and Mr. George are the perfect parents. Offsetting pastries for breakfast with kale-packed super smoothies. "It's all about balance," Mr. George says. He knows exactly what I need.

I haven't stopped logging what I owe Mr. George, or everyone else in my life for that matter. My journal still hides beneath my pillow, keeping me close to my mother. I think it's something she would have done. Something she'd be proud I'm doing.

When I sit here in Mr. George's home, now my own, on my pillowed platform bed, my body wrapped in one-thousand-thread-count sheets, I think about the heavy curtains in the theater room that kept me warm for over a year, the powdered soap that kept me clean. All those nights I missed security by minutes and slept in the dugout. I was cold, tired, scared, but I was alive and ready to fight for one more day.

Painful memories slip in and out, as they did before, but they're different now. Not as hurtful today as they were yesterday. And tomorrow . . . yeah, tomorrow . . . bursts with promise.

CHAPTER THIRTY-TWO

THREE MONTHS LATER

I TAP THE MICROPHONE THREE times and clear my throat.

The crowd in the gymnasium hushes except for my front-row cheering squad. Folding cha irs lined up in rows are beginning to fill with students as they flood through the doors and into the middle of the gym. Ham's standing at his chair beneath the makeshift stage, waving at me like a parent at a child's preschool graduation. He wears a T-shirt with script words: *#HomelessIsWhen*.

Ham started a nonprofit, said he was trying to "bring awareness" and "shed light on shit." He demanded that I help, since, you know, I'm the spokesperson. I would have volunteered anyway without the arm twist or promise that it was his ticket to college with me.

Ham's hashtag went viral. In our school, that is.

Bea and Beth colored posters spreading awareness and plastered them all over the gym, halls, and classrooms. The posters say things like *#HomelessIsWhen We Don't Look* and *#HomelessIsWhen We Don't See*. Bea's a different person with Reed out of the picture. Well, with Reed being home-schooled, or attending school out of state, or being arrested for hitting another girl. I'm uncertain which rumor is truth.

I smile as Jarrell pretzels his arms around Ham's back. Ham drops his head against Jarrell's chest, which is wrapped in a black custom T-shirt with block letters that reads: **I'm with Him**, only the *i* in *Him* is slashed and a red *a* inserted in its place. Ham's become a beautiful bubble I never want to pop.

Someone shouts, "You've got this!" And in that moment, I think, *Shit, maybe I do.* Beth motions for Bea to sit down, and Bea shoos her away like a bug. Bea nods in my direction and I nod back. She lifts her hands and claps the tips of her fingers together. Minuscule movements, baby steps forward. Small, but I'll take it.

Bea and I aren't best friends. But we're not enemies, either. We're just two girls finding our way in a world that often pushes back against us for reasons that are different, yet the same. We smile in the halls, always say hello. Our support for each other is understated. We don't have to state it for it to exist.

Mr. George petitioned the city for a halfway house so women in abusive relationships can escape. He also asked me to help lead Hinderwood High's donation team, but when Bea stepped up, I stepped aside. Bea leads with ease. It just took her some time to find her stride.

Kristen runs toward the front row waving a banner that reads:

Congrats, Linden!

She trips on a guy's boot blocking the aisle and whips around with her finger aimed. She scolds him for laughing, and for manspreading. Then she squeezes next to Ham and flops the flag against the heads of three students. She hops up and down and cheers.

Toby pushes his way to the front row. His peach-fuzz eyebrows are growing in nicely. The bronzer finally wore off his face but left blotches of orange like a patchwork necklace along his neckline. He decided to leave his hair neon orange, thought it made his eyes pop beneath his football helmet when he defended the line. Fear factor, he said.

Toby inches beside Seung. He nods, giving Toby the go-ahead to grab him like a teddy bear and lift him above ground. Seung pats Toby's back, a signal to put him safely on the floor where he belongs. Toby drops Seung and grins. He now hugs Seung any chance he gets. He tries to hug Ham, too, but Ham stiff-arms and shouts, "I'm already taken!" before Toby can wrap his arms around him. The hugs are Toby's way of apologizing for all his racist bullshit. And it's Seung's way to always forgive. Seung and his amazing heart.

The gym is brimming with students and parents and people from town. Deputy Boggs and his tiny team sit toward the back. Mr. Ryckman, the janitor, stands by the door. Eva, my grandmother's old nurse, scoots toward an empty chair into the middle of the crowd. She waves when she sees me and yells, "Go, girl!"

I fix my eyes on Seung in the front row. He takes a breath, which I know is for my own benefit, and before he exhales, I begin.

"Thank you all for being here today."

The gym hushes.

"Thank you. To all the teachers. To Principal Falls. And the students and parents who took the time to come."

Complete silence.

"Thank you for having me."

You could hear a pin drop.

"Thank you for letting *me* share my story."

When I finish, the crowd claps. Okay, erupts.

Seung is the first to leap to his feet and cheer, then the first to climb on his chair and shout. In my honor. Ham and Jarrell hop onto their folding chairs, too. Ham yells my name, and within seconds, everyone else in the room is chanting, too.

Lin-den.
Lin-den.
Lin-den.

Tears flood my face and I'm too busy smiling at the crowd, standing on their seats and chanting my name, to give a damn.

Toby jumps up, cheering. Mr. Dique holds his hand out and Principal Falls steps onto her seat. Her turbulent claps make Mr. Dique duck his head before scurrying over to a vacant chair and climbing up. Every teacher follows. I even see Coach Jenkins shake open a folding chair and stomp upon the seat while pumping his fist.

I stand at the podium and listen to the rhythm of my name bounce off the rafters and against the matted walls. Principal Falsetto's sister, Helen, smiles in my direction and winks. She shoots me a thumbs-up, then turns to speak into the camera. I gave her permission to share my words after I shared them with my school and the people I love. She promised she'd only report facts. She even put our agreement in writing.

Mrs. Rhee stands on her seat and hops, while Mr. Rhee holds her elbow for balance. Mr. Rhee catches my eye and offers a friendly salute. I salute him back.

I scan the crowd for Mr. George, but he's vanished. I don't remember seeing him during my speech. Probably started wailing and had to run out of the room for tissue. He hasn't stopped blubbering since I filled him in on my plans. After living at Hinderwood High, I figured it was the right thing to do. I needed to share my story here, first, with the people who became family in such a short time. What I didn't figure was how everyone would accept me, with open arms and a standing-on-chairs ovation.

A guy in the back shouts, "Look out!" He points up and half the gym cranes their necks toward the ceiling. A drone dips and darts and dives above heads. It's coming straight for me, now hovering near the podium, aimed at my face.

I duck as Mr. Dique leaps off his chair and lunges toward me like he might tackle or rescue or flatten me onstage. He yells, "No more interruptions!" and swats his hands at the machine. The drone's engine revs. "I said now is not the time!" Mr. Dique shrieks.

The machine buzzes above me, gently lowering itself onto the podium. Mr. Dique steps back as a dozen yellow roses drop from the landing skids and plop into my arms. As I look out into the crowd, someone in the front row gasps. Then a student shouts, "I knew it wasn't one of us! It was one of *them* all along!"

A grin slowly spreads across Mr. Dique's face as he nods at Mr. George, pointing and shouting, "You got me! You got me good!"

Mr. George climbs the steps of the stage and pitches the remote control onto the podium. I grin, thinking, *Mr. George really is the perfect helicopter, I mean drone, parent.* He wraps his arms around me and doesn't stop squeezing until Seung taps his shoulder and says, "Cutting in."

"Homeless Is When"
a speech and article by Linden Rose

winner of the National Scholarship for Journalism
Willamette University, Spring 2018

A complete version of this op-ed piece
was published on KOIN 6's news blog and
in Hinderwood High School's online newspaper.

RESOURCES

THOUGH THIS BOOK IS A work of fiction, I wholeheartedly acknowledge the real-life teens who face homelessness and poverty. Their situations may reflect, in some way, Linden's experience. Unfortunately, poverty and homelessness impact millions of youth.

If you need immediate help and aren't sure where to turn, contact Safe Place at www.nationalsafeplace.org/safe-place-teens or TXT 4 HELP. Text the word SAFE and your location (address/city/state) to 69866 for help in your area. If you are located in a city or town without a Safe Place program, help is available through the National Runaway Switchboard—a national toll-free hotline for runaway, homeless, and other youth in crisis. Call 1-800-RUNAWAY or go to https://www.1800runaway.org.

If you would like to join an advocacy team to take action on ending homelessness in your community, please visit the National Alliance to End Homelessness at www.endhome-lessness.org.

And if you are a victim of abuse, or have a friend or family member or know someone in an unhealthy relationship, visit: Love Is Respect at www.loveisrespect.org or call the hotline: 1-866-331-9474 or text LOVEIS to 22522.

ACKNOWLEDGMENTS

YOU MADE IT TO THE acknowledgments page, and for that I am grateful. It takes a village, as they say, and the amazing team that helped put this book on the map deserves all the gold stars in the sky and my heartfelt thanks.

To Melissa Edwards, for your belief in this story and ability to champion it beyond my dreams. To the hardworking and dedicated people at Aaron Priest Literary Agency and Stonesong Literary Agency, with a special thank-you to Frances Jalet Miller for her early reading and editorial acumen.

My brilliant editor at HarperCollins, Alyson Day, helped make this book immeasurably better and navigated me through the muck with encouragement, insight, and sheer thoughtfulness. Tessa Meischeid made me smile every time we emailed. Abbe Goldberg shared her support. Renée Cafiero, my copyeditor; Joel Tippie, my designer; Bess Braswell, Tyler Breitfeller, and Mitchell Thorpe, the most amazing marketing and publicity folks. Megan Beatie has been a tireless advocate, and I am deeply grateful. And every person at

HarperTeen who helped transform this book from imagination to tangible pages.

I owe a tremendous amount of gratitude to the English department at Whitman College. And, from my childhood, thank you to the librarians at Harney County Library, who never questioned why a parentless kid camped in their aisles from sunup to sundown.

So many thanks also to my fellow writers at the Electric Eighteens, especially Rebecca Sky and Rachel Lynn Solomon, for their willingness to lend eyes and ears at the drop of a hat. To Dana Mele and the struggle bus. We're on this ride together. Thank you to Naomi Hughes for your early reads and Professor Linville for your words of encouragement when I lost my way.

To these authors, many of whom have now become friends, thank you for paving the way for me to tackle hard topics and write from the heart: Kathleen Glasgow, Kerry Kletter, Jennifer Niven, Caleb Roehrig, Amber Smith, Carlie Sorosiak, and Jeff Zentner. I respect you and your art.

Thanks also to my parents for believing in me. To my brother, Scott, for encouraging me to chase my dreams.

To my girls, Madysen and Ava, for love notes and hugs that last all day, and those five little words that kept me going: Mom—You can do it.

To Bryan, my rock, my home, my heart. You'll always be the most amazing thing that ever happened to me. I love you.

Finally, my heartfelt thanks to my grandparents, who left this world a better place. Thank you, Papa, for showing me homelessness was only a start, not the end.

BRENDA RUFENER spent her childhood stomping through the woods of Oregon in search of bat-filled caves and Bigfoot. She successfully located one of the two and spent the rest of her time penciling short stories. A double major in English and biology, Brenda graduated from Whitman College. She lives in North Carolina with her family and is an advocate for homeless youth.

www.brendarufener.com